I0726804

THE TERRAN SUMMIT

An Intergalaxia Novel

By

Anna Zogg

MBI

The Intergalaxia Series

The Paradise Protocol

The Xerxes Factor

The Terran Summit

The Terran Summit
An Intergalaxia Novel
© 2017 by Anna Zogg

Published by Mountain Brook Ink

White Salmon, WA 982

Edited by Sharon Hinck
Copy edited by Ginny Smith
Cover design by Nick Delliskave

Library of Congress Control Number: 2016912027

Print ISBN- 13 978-1943959150

Dedication

To my daughter, Morgan Motsinger,
whose trust in God continually
amazes and humbles me

Acknowledgement

Thank you to the many faithful readers and fellow writers—without you, this book would never be. A special thanks to Virginia Smith for believing in me from the beginning, and to Sharon Hinck who admonished me to never say, "Am I really a writer?" You two are incredibly precious to me.

Chapter 1

There they are!

Exhilaration flooded Eva. She stared hard through her archaic monoscope, focusing on the two people who did not quite blend with the distant crowd. Thoroughly familiar with Xerxians, she waited for the couple to betray their Terran origins. Garbed in the traditional deep blue robes of Xerxes IX, the fugitives traded with the humanoid villagers, apparently confident in their disguises.

Perhaps others might be deceived. Not Eva Hilliard.

While they occupied themselves with bartering in the

town's center, she stashed her scope in her backpack. She scrabbled over the crest of the hill, careful to not stir up orange dust. Once out of sight, she hiked up her long robe and sprinted across an uncultivated field. She ducked behind a low stone fence to catch her breath. Several times she changed locations, drawing closer to the humans. Though the low, adobe-like buildings impeded a clear view of the town square, she dared not risk being spotted by a Xerxian.

With her hood pulled over her head, she could fool from afar. Up close, the Xerxians would assume she was a girl. Eva's short stature—a mere five feet five—would alarm the tall, matriarchal women who fiercely protected children. That would change the moment they saw her pale skin. However, she would end up having to explain who she was and why she was there.

In the confusion, the fugitives would flee.

Eva couldn't chance that. The tentative peace of the known universe depended on successfully apprehending the escapees. Their flight to Xerxes IX had put events into motion that would affect every alien culture with whom Earth had a treaty.

How she knew this, she had no idea.

A large tree stump gave her the perfect place to spy unseen. After settling, she peered again into the village's center.

No doubt, it's them.

The woman filled water skins at the fountain while her male companion stood guard, eyes darting like a hunted animal. They had every reason to be nervous. Intergalaxia pursued them.

After the two had evaded a tribunal on Earth, Eva and three other operatives had taken the first transport to Xerxes IX. The High Council had granted special permission for them to assume a Xerxian disguise if needed—a first in their alliance of twenty-six years. Allowing them ten standard days and only crude weaponry to accomplish their mission, the Xerxians vowed to neither help nor hinder Eva and her colleagues.

While Eva's teammates had begun searching the plateau cities, she beelined for the planet's more rural areas. Her instincts had paid off. Why the fugitives had chosen to hide on Xerxes IX, no one knew. The reason mattered little. She must complete the mission.

USF Special Agents Layne and Song have gone rogue. The directive played again in her mind. *Apprehend them with or without the use of deadly force.*

Eva would prefer to capture them. Irrelevant if the two resisted. She flexed her hand—a nervous habit—as she considered terminating their lives. One way or the other, their journey ended here. The stakes were too high.

Behind the tree trunk, she studied them through her scope. As they bartered with the villagers for supplies, Eva got a good look at them.

The woman—Kelli Layne—looked Xerxian, complete with black hair and pale green skin. Her height of five feet ten was a little short for the average adult female, but passable. With Layne's hood pushed back, Eva could see the sparkle of a Xerxian earring dangling from one lobe. Her mannerisms were nearly flawless as she haggled. The way she talked with head held high and with bold eye contact alerted Eva that this woman had perfected her impersonation.

Her friend—Jayden Song—maintained a subservient posture, hood pulled and head bowed to disguise his Asian features. Hands tucked into his sleeves, he concealed his taupe skin color. Had Layne and Song somehow convinced the simple townsfolk that his presence was no cause for alarm? Eva pushed the speculation from her mind.

She dug through her knapsack and tore open a food packet. A couple bites and a gulp of water were all she needed before she was ready to go. Behind the town lay an open area, the perfect place to set an ambush. She stashed her canteen and rose.

Too late. A herdsman shouted in dismay as a dozen domesticated animals stampeded to a grassy plot not far from her location. Stifling a curse, Eva again crouched. From the sounds, the animals—much like Terran sheep—were gobbling the long blades of beige grass. Their contented grunts warned her they would not be easily shifted.

How long before the herdsman enticed them away? She glanced into the sky. Many hours remained until sunset.

She dared not move. Dared not risk running across the field to the distant hill. Someone would see and give chase. Xerxian women were particularly tenacious.

And Song and Layne would disappear.

I must not let that happen.

Eva flattened herself against the weathered wood and forced herself to be patient. Now that she'd identified the fugitives, they would not elude her.

Through the long night, Eva sought the pair. Twice they had changed course and had picked up their pace. Not until midafternoon did she again spot them. As she paralleled their path, she kept Song and Layne in her sights. When they rested alongside the road, Eva flattened herself in the tall grasses and waited. Too many Xerxians were traveling on the same byway. She couldn't approach the escapees yet.

As she viewed them through her scope, a crackling noise caught her ear. What was that? Tensing, she stared over her shoulder. The rustling ceased. If it was one of her colleagues, they should have alerted her of their approach. Was it an animal then? If so, why did her skin crawl? She got the distinct impression someone watched her. Several minutes passed, but nothing more sounded.

Shaking off her unease, she double-checked the fugitives' location. After consulting a crude map, she calculated that the road they followed led to a sizeable village, an hour away. Would they spend the night there? No doubt they were tired. Kelli Layne's ankle, fractured and mended mere months ago, had to be causing her pain from the miles she'd walked. The town must be their goal.

Got 'em.

Eva exhaled in triumph. This would be easier than she thought. She would camp outside of the village until dark, then make her move. In a burg that size, she would have to check two, maybe three inns. While the pair dozed, she could incapacitate them at her leisure.

The fugitives rose and retrieved their things. After they resumed their course, Eva trailed at a safe distance. Again the sense that she was being watched assailed her. Though she threw several glances over her shoulder, she saw no one.

The landscape rose before her, hiding Song and Layne for many minutes. She slowed. With usual precaution, she approached the summit and peered over the other side. By now they would have reached the town where friendly lights beckoned. Was Layne in the town square, negotiating the best price for accommodations? The innkeeper would provide a generous dinner before the pair settled for the night.

With the road now empty, she pushed through the tall grass and headed down the incline paved with flat, white stones. A glance around assured her she traveled in safety. By the time she reached the bottom of the hill, doubts assailed her. Would the fugitives really let down their guard by sleeping in town? Stupid to assume that. This would be the first time Song and Layne erred. Their course changes and quickened pace proved they'd grown more cautious.

Eva veered off the road and crouched behind a bush. Perhaps they counted on a follower hanging around outside of town until the middle of the night. To buy time so they could slip away?

That's what I would have done.

If they weren't ahead, where were they? Eva studied the direction from which she'd come. They hadn't backtracked. She would have spotted them. So, which way? Open fields spread out to the east. To the other, a dense forest.

In the fields, they would be visible still. If Eva had been on the run, she would have chosen the forest. She rose. A careful check along the road confirmed her suspicions. Broken twigs caught her eye first. A deeper look revealed a partial footprint beyond the border of trees.

This way.

Given the length of their strides, they were running.

The silhouette of branches clawed the gray-splashed dawn by the time Eva paused. She glanced upward, assessing the time and her disappearing advantage. All night she'd tracked Layne and Song. Despite the dark, she'd been able to follow their trail. Until now. Subtle signs—from the occasional footprint on the semi-moist forest floor to disturbed shrubbery—had disappeared.

Had they spent the night above? Taking her time, Eva circled the area, searching for some indication of their passage. Nothing. An abundance of climbable trees in the area provided ample hideouts. With the ever-increasing light, she would soon be visible to them. Eva would not be so foolish as to believe they didn't possess some weapon that could incapacitate her, even from high above.

Weariness dogged her. Four days of little sleep and food eroded her energy. She pushed aside the weakness and forced herself to concentrate.

With as little noise as possible, she slipped off her backpack and outer robe. After pulling out what might appear as harmless plastic tubing, she assembled an air gun and loaded a neurotoxin dart. She pocketed another since the gun could fire only one projectile at a time. After stashing her belongings under a fallen log, she crept forward, confident that her dark clothing would provide adequate camouflage.

She traveled a hundred feet when some sixth sense made her freeze. A faint rustle met her ears. No breeze penetrated the forest. Was that an animal nosing through the fallen leaves? Eva hunkered down, listening. Again the sound came. No, she amended, two distinct noises grated against her senses. One seemed to come from a small rodent, busily searching for its breakfast. She concentrated on the other—a stealthy scraping, as though skin met bark. A subdued inhale. A muted thump. A controlled release of breath. Then nothing.

Someone was waiting. Noiselessly she drew in air, willing her heart to slow. Seconds—minutes?—passed as she remained frozen.

A person exhaled slowly. Confident they were safe? Presuming they didn't know she was nearby, Eva craned her neck to one side to peer around the foliage. Her pulse pounded through her.

Jayden Song crouched at the base of a tree, staring hard in the direction opposite her. The foraging rodent likely distracted him. This might be Eva's only chance. In one smooth motion, she lifted the air gun and squeezed the trigger. Besides the muted pop, it made no other sound. She quickly loaded the second dart.

Jerking, Song swatted at his arm. For a moment, he looked wildly around, then struggled to rise, but the neurotoxin was already taking effect. His legs buckled. Back braced by the tree, he slowly slumped to one side with a whispered grunt.

Where was Layne? Attuned to a possible trap, Eva peered through the shrubbery, but could see no one else. Up above? She studied the tree branches and foliage. Still nothing. Had the pair split up? During the night, she had not been able to verify that.

The brightening sky forced her to make a risky decision. Better to secure one fugitive while she could. Once he was bound, she could concentrate on finding Layne.

Eva laid aside her gun and crept forward, all the while listening. Though Song appeared to be unconscious, she wouldn't assume so. After watching a moment, she reached with a cautious hand. She was about to feel his pulse when foreboding shot through her. In her mind's eye, she saw herself sprawled on the ground. She jerked away from the motionless man.

Out of nowhere, a Xerxian woman flew at her, mouth set in murderous determination. At the last second, Eva deflected an incoming karate chop. Despite the woman's disguise, she recognized Layne. There was something decidedly Terran in the clenched jaw.

Deflecting blow after blow, Eva struggled to overcome the disadvantage of surprise and difference in height. How had Layne moved so noiselessly? Irrelevant now. Eva fought to keep herself from being disabled by a crippling strike.

Stay alive.

The former agent used a street-fighting method unknown to Eva. Layne's hands moved like lightning, hitting her torso with quick thrusts. Eva absorbed the blows that were meant to wear her down. *Assess.* Falling back across the forest floor, she gave way. Though Eva protected her throat, she coughed when Layne's knuckles grazed her windpipe. Her arm stung when Layne chopped down hard, the pain reverberating through her body. The torso beatings resumed.

Block. Feint. Dodge. Nothing sounded but their sharp breath, grunts and muted thumps as blows semi-landed. Almost incapacitated. In a short time, she noted Layne favored one ankle—her sore one. At last, a weakness!

Sorrow swelled as she prepared to kill the former agent. But Layne left her no choice. This had to end here. *I must succeed.*

Now the aggressor, Eva pressed her attack. For a split second, shock flashed across Layne's face. No longer did Eva merely take the blows. She made certain Layne stepped on her sore ankle more often. Soon it would give out.

On a steep incline, it did.

Layne faltered—ever so slightly. On the abundant leaves, she slipped. Hands spread to catch her balance, she left herself wide open. One solid blow to the chest would end her life. *Now.* With all her might, Eva threw a punch.

And hit air.

Equilibrium lost, she pitched forward on the slope. The bottom of a rocky ravine rose with terrifying speed. Unable to break her fall, Eva landed hard. A sickening crack thundered through her before blinding pain snuffed consciousness.

Chapter 2

Undetected by the two Terran women, Zahn ducked behind a tree to get a closer look. A chill ran through him as he watched the humans fight. His people favored friendly matches—and Xerxian women were adept at wrestling—but this encounter was nothing like that.

This was a battle to the death. Determined to vanquish the enemy, the bloodlust of these humans resounded in grunts of pain and labored breathing. Their fierceness betrayed the savagery of their race. Zahn's own blood stirred as they fought their way across the forest floor. The tempo of his pounding heart echoed the cadence of their blows.

Though the tall one looked Xerxian, Zahn knew her to

be human. Kelli-Layne. The smaller of the two—Eva-Hilliard—wore no disguise.

She will be the victor.

What Eva-Hilliard lacked in height, she more than made up in skill and determination. The fluid motion of her body almost resembled a dancer as she absorbed or dodged blows. She seemed unaware of the pain her enemy rained on her as she pressed her attack. It wouldn't be long now.

The next moment proved Zahn wrong when Eva-Hilliard disappeared over the edge of the ravine. A muted thump ended her soundless fall.

He caught his breath. How had she failed? The answer came to him in an instant—the hand of God.

Zahn glanced to the heavens, astounded at the turn of events. This was God's will that Kelli-Layne should be the victor. Would she now kill her enemy?

In a quandary, he pressed his back against the tree. Should he intervene? The Xerxian High Council had tasked him to observe. Nothing more. But what did the Lord God want him to do? In the silence, he sensed he should wait. Let the drama play out before him.

When he again peered around the tree, Kelli-Layne had clambered down into the ravine. Given the distance, he could not hear what she said to her captive. When Eva-Hilliard cried out, he steeled his heart. Did Kelli-Layne hurt her to extract information? Or to punish her?

Again he fought with himself about what to do. The clear answer again came—*wait.*

Not much later, Kelli-Layne dragged the smaller woman up out of the ravine on a makeshift pallet. He followed them to her unconscious companion, the human male named Jayden-Song.

Eva-Hilliard's injury was severe. Though Zahn had little knowledge of Terran medicine, her panting breath and whimpers made that abundantly clear. A broken leg perhaps? So it seemed.

He clenched his fists, battling the urge to interfere. Her agony resounded through him, more than what was appropriate for a Xerxian man. He forced himself to stand rigid behind a large tree. Fought the overwhelming desire to render aid. Digging his fingers into the bark, he closed his eyes.

Lord, God of the heavens, give me strength to obey You.

Though he could not see, he still heard Eva-Hilliard's pain. Sensed something that went beyond the physical. How was that possible? The Creator had given him gifts of the *pneuma*, but never before had Zahn felt such a connection to a human—a stranger. And a woman at that. Because of her suffering? That had to be the reason.

He again studied the Terrans.

Kelli-Layne appeared to debate a course of action. Several times, she looked between her companions—one unconscious, the other bound and racked with pain. Both needed medical attention. Mind apparently made up, she rose. When she lifted Eva-Hilliard to her shoulders, Zahn gaped. Did she plan to abandon Jayden-Song? What was she going to do with her captive?

The puzzle could only be solved if he followed them.

Rigid with pain, Eva sat beside the road. She fought the instinct to lie down. To give up.

How long had she been waiting? No travelers had come along the road as Layne had assured. Torment built and built. As the morning waned, the possibility of a rescue faded. Death in all its stark ugliness loomed ever nearer.

Dust from the nearby field pelted Eva's face, agitated by the ever-present wind. Its lonely whine mocked her. The large daytime star beat down, stealing moisture from her mouth as she panted. Every shallow breath exacerbated the agony of her battered body.

Her mind wandered. Of all the places in the known universe, why did she have to die on Xerxes IX? The irony bit into her soul. How fitting—the planet that had birthed her sorrow would be her final resting place.

A sob tore her throat.

"Stop it." Eva spoke out loud. "Concentrate on your training."

She forced herself to assess her situation.

Status—*stranded.*

Condition—*fractured leg, concussion.*

Equipment—*on the orbiting space station, inaccessible. Missing too was her sub-dermal chip. Its removal had been the prerequisite to accessing the planet's interior.*

Sustenance—*two food packets and a half canteen of water.*

Most likely, she would succumb to dehydration. From where she sat, she could see no body of water. No town. No travelers.

Her death promised to be long and excruciating.

The makeshift splint that Layne had constructed of branches and a torn robe dug into her flesh. Beneath her thigh, a sharp stone embedded. Eva dared not move. The trip through the woods had been agonizing. Ramrod straight for many hours, her back protested. She swallowed the sandpaper in her throat. Agony grew.

How long before the end?

Time crawled. She peered into the distance, but the road remained dismal. Empty. If a passerby would come, she could implore them for help. Xerxes IX and Earth were on friendly terms. The humanoids would give assistance.

As her mind again wandered, memories crept back and lodged in the forefront of her thinking. Yearning slowly ate into her soul. Its twin, regret, devoured her peace.

To die without seeing her mother one last time...

Eva steeled herself. Too late to seek out the one who had deserted her so long ago. Much, much too late.

The giant sun cast the land in a hazy orange as it climbed into the afternoon. The scent of grassy fields intensified in the warmth, causing her eyes to prickle. This place smelled like the Rocky Mountains. The memory of her parents' cabin clutched at her.

The instinct to survive wrestled with her reconciliation to death.

I will not pray. I will not ask God for help.

Eva vowed to welcome her passing. Dying would finally release her from the torment that had held her captive for twenty-six years. After she was gone, let the universe sort out its own future. She would not be there to help.

Ripples of heat danced across her vision. In the distance, a formless mass shimmered as it rose from the ground. A specter of death? Or proof of encroaching madness?

She shifted her weight. Burning flared up her leg and through her core. A primeval cry tore her throat. Back arching, she willed her mind to subdue her body. What was that ancient, alien text?

"Pain can be controlled." She ground out the words once. Twice. The intonation eased her. Again, she panted, "Pain *can* be controlled. I will...will master it."

"And the one who conquers pain will overcome." A man's voice, speaking English, cut through the silence and finished the recitative.

Her head snapped in his direction.

A Xerxian male stood not more than fifteen feet away. How had he appeared without a sound? A sense of unreality seized her.

Eva closed her eyes. A Xerxian, deep in the heart of his homeworld, would likely not understand *Common* as they called English. Even more impossible that he spoke it. Breathing deeply, she opened her eyes.

The road appeared empty once again.

A mental picture of herself raving tore through her mind. Huge racking shudders gripped her.

"Pain…pain can—can be…" She fought to utter the words. No good. The interruption had disrupted the soothing self-sedation.

A whisper of sound met her ears as a shadow fell across the ground. Eva cried out as the phantom materialized beside her. When something brushed her cheek, she batted it away.

This wasn't real. It couldn't be.

"Forgive me my touch." The man's English sounded a little stilted. As he knelt beside her, he placed a gentle palm on her forehead.

Combating sluggishness, Eva stared at him. Where had he come from? Training rescued her from a building hysteria.

Xerxian male. Younger than forty. Skin of the palest green, tinted with teal. Dark cropped hair. Military? No—Xerxes IX did not have armed forces. *One earring with two charms.* What did the symbols signify? Unimportant. *Subtle refinement in manner and expression.* Not a farmer. Laborer? *Clothing crude. Minor cuts on his hands. Familiarity with knives.* Craftsman?

Her suffering eased, cutting short her evaluation. A sigh escaped her.

This was no hallucination.

For a moment, she reveled in the absence of pain. But only a moment. While his palm rested on her forehead, she fixed her gaze on him. "Are you a healer?"

Chastising herself, she clamped her lips together. Why had she betrayed herself by speaking his language?

The man's eyes widened. In the stark sunlight, his black pupils contrasted with the ebony of his irises. "You speak Xer." He reverted to his native tongue. "And very well."

Wave upon wave of relief washed over her. She relinquished her tight self-control to his touch.

"To answer your question, no." He continued in Xer. "However I am versed in the practice." He removed his hand, but her pain remained at bay. The relief would be temporary. She had perhaps minutes to beg for his help.

Without preamble, she invoked the formal Xerxian plea. "I adjure you by the God you worship to grant your assistance."

"I gladly pledge it. Fully. Without reserve."

Astonished by his quick response, she gaped. He hadn't asked why she was there—a Terran on his planet. Hadn't inquired about her injuries or how she ended up on an abandoned road. Nothing. But by his words, he vowed to do everything, including forfeiting his own life, to protect hers.

The Xerxian scrutinized her body as though to ascertain the full extent of her injuries. When he came to her fracture, he placed one hand above the splint. "May I?"

She nodded.

With infinite care, he rested his palm on her injured leg. Throwing back her head, she groaned as a tsunami of torment battered her.

"Your bonds are too tight. This must be corrected. Immediately." With a whispered touch, he unknotted the strips of cloth.

As he worked, she couldn't stifle her cries. Spasms racked her. The more she tried to repress the tremors, the worse they grew.

The Xer grasped her hands and forced them together. "This practice is for Xerxians, but perhaps it will ease your suffering."

Through the haze of agony, she recognized the ancient healing ritual. How would she react? While he murmured the invocation, he pressed his palms against the back of her hands in ever-increasing pressure.

Unwilling to listen, Eva blocked out the words. God had not heeded her prayers as a child. Though she had begged and cried, He had not brought back her mother.

Placing one hand on her head, the Xerxian continued the ritual. Static electricity seemed to snap from the contact. She resisted the uncomfortable sensation. It built until she could scarcely breathe.

Energy, like a lightning bolt, shot through her core.

Eva screamed and blacked out.

Chapter 3

Where am I?

Eva slowly awoke. Training kept her body rigid as she fought the cobwebs of unconsciousness. She recalled the fight with Layne, the agonizing trip to the road, the endless waiting...until the Xerxian male had shown up.

His healing arts had nearly killed her.

That bolt of energy had no lingering aftereffects. Her brain didn't feel fried. The minute twitching of her fingers proved they still had sensation. Pain from her fracture remained at bay, but the slightest tightening of her calf muscle nearly caused her to shriek.

Not a good idea.

Without opening her eyes, she grew aware of her surroundings. She was inside a building of some sort. The crackling of a fire snapped in her hearing. The smell of food—and an herb that reminded her of sweet basil—gave her stomach an excuse to grumble. Movement from nearby told her that one person shared the room with her.

Was it the Xerxian?

He moved almost without sound. Barefooted? She sensed him, even before she opened her eyes. Because he *felt* safe?

She resisted the unfamiliar desire to yield to the emotion.

Don't let down your guard.

She had to maintain her distance. That was the only way she had survived as an Inter-G agent. She always got the job done. Before the fugitives escaped yet again, she had to capture them. But what if Layne really hoped to rescue a kidnapped girl, as she insisted? No matter how compelling the woman's arguments though, Eva couldn't allow herself the luxury of being sidetracked. Only the mission mattered.

The sooner she was on her way, the better.

Zahn watched the young woman as she reclined on the crude cot. Was Eva-Hilliard merely pretending to be unconscious? Despite her relaxed pose, she had been subtly restless for many moments. The movement of her eyes under their lids, twitching fingers, and sighs betrayed her.

He spoke quietly. "Forgive me for hurting you."

Though she did not respond, he was certain she heard him. She grew still. Listening?

In her own good time she would reveal herself.

He allowed himself to study her. Certainly she was not

beautiful, nothing like the women of Xerxes IX with their height averaging over six Terran feet. This human before him was diminutive in comparison. Almost fragile.

Soft brown hair, unbound now, framed her heart-shaped face. Full lips, a tiny chin, and the delicate curve of her eyebrows intrigued him. Though she looked nothing like the strong-jawed females of his world with their black hair, her features still pleased. Her body, however, presented a mystery. Intense training had sculpted her, not the result of the natural-born litheness of Xerxian females. Yet, he sensed she pushed herself with rigorous exercises, evidenced by her thinness.

How could she appear so soft, so vulnerable, yet so strong at the same time? The more he learned of her, the greater his fascination.

An odd feeling, one of strong protectiveness, buffeted him. This was the second time. Xer males did not have protective emotions. Especially toward Terran females. When Kelli-Layne had abandoned her beside the road, he had reluctantly followed the fugitive as she headed back to Jayden-Song. But something had urged him to return to Eva-Hilliard. The Lord God? He alone superseded the orders of the High Council. Zahn had run nearly the whole distance, afraid he might not be in time to save the injured woman.

When he'd seen Eva-Hilliard, panting in pain, he knew he'd done the right thing.

Her eyes fluttered open. Brow wrinkled, body tense, she glanced about like a caged animal. How suspicious these Terrans were, despite the fact that he'd helped her. He'd not only saved her life, but had pledged to safeguard it no matter the cost. Had she forgotten?

He couldn't blame her. As a Terran, she was accustomed to the male-dominated societies of Earth.

She studied everything—his plain outer robe hanging by the door, the hand-braided rug, the rough table and chair, the single shelf laden with food and herbals, his traveling bag. She stared at her shoes beside his, which he'd placed by the door. Not much else occupied the large, one-room dwelling.

Zahn waited until after she'd seen all she wanted. "I am sorry, little one." More comfortable with his native tongue, he bypassed what Terrans called English. Her word choices and inflection indicated a deep knowledge of Xer. Uncommon for a human.

Her gaze finally met his.

"I apologize for my clumsiness which caused you to lose consciousness. I erred in assuming the healing ritual would benefit you. Before today, I have not touched a Terran."

Her deep brown eyes widened, betraying a hint of panic. Why?

"Where are we?" she finally asked.

He kept his voice low, comforting. "My humble abode."

Though this place belonged to the community and therefore open to anyone, Zahn withheld the details. He rose and stirred the fire. The warmth chased away the night's coolness as it crept through the slatted shutters and closed door. He moved the cooking pot away from the flames to keep the soup from boiling. Next to the dark red embers rested a flat loaf of bread, nearly heated. He sat again on the single chair.

"How long was I unconscious?"

"Three standard hours."

"Three? I need to contact..." She bit her lip as though aware she'd said too much.

He pretended he didn't understand what she meant. "As soon as you are able, we will travel to the main city. To Xer Prime. There you can meet up with your friends."

Her eyes narrowed. "Why do you assume I want to go to Xer Prime?"

He made sure to shrug with nonchalance, deception difficult because he had so little practice. "Doesn't everyone?" When she didn't respond, he added, "Besides, you were on the road that leads to our capital city." He did not add it was a long-unused road. If he had not returned to her, she would have died.

"I must go. Now." Groaning, she struggled to sit up.

He merely watched, with both admiration and amusement. Terrans were not known for their strength of will. She would soon give up. Panting in exertion, the woman fought to straighten. Her pain had to be excruciating. Any moment she would relent.

But she did not. With awkward and almost superhuman strength, she swung her uninjured leg over the side and lifted herself with her arms.

Finally intervening, Zahn rose and placed his palms on her shoulders. He pressed her back down onto the bed. "You can go nowhere. If you move now, you would only damage your leg more."

Straining against his touch, she continued to resist him.

Although it went against his nature, he compelled himself to speak with firmness. "I have set and re-splinted the break. You threaten to undo the healing that has begun."

"I cannot stay." She gritted her teeth.

He kept steady pressure on her shoulders. Stubborn female! Zahn lifted her uninjured leg back onto the wide pallet. To keep her prisoner, he sat on the wide cot's edge. "Lie back. You must." Again, he strove to speak with a dominant tone.

Lips parted and eyes wide, she slowly acquiesced.

He placed his palm on her forehead, a calming gesture that Xerxian fathers used with children. After a few moments, it produced the desired effect. She began to relax under his touch. However, her Terran blood would not fully succumb. Gaze fixed on him, her body lost tension but her eyes still rebelled.

Concentrating harder, he willed his serenity to flow to her. Zahn had just begun to utter the prayer of contemplation when her resistance flooded against him—as though an invisible force pushed his hand, rebuffing him. Hissing in astonishment, he pulled back. How had that happened?

Brow pinched, she appeared just as surprised.

Terrans did not practice the healing arts, did they? No. If they did, that would explain how she had repelled his touch. Unless...

He decided in an instant. *The fault lies with me.*

They were so near to each other, her breath brushed the skin of his arm. In the light of the lantern, he detected the slashes of gold in her dark brown eyes. Even in the dimness, the shards seemed to brighten.

Zahn mentally shook himself. "You need time to heal. I beg you to rest until your condition improves. Please allow yourself this."

Her shoulders slumped. He was surprised when tears sprang into her eyes. Why didn't she hide them? She merely gazed at him, betraying a deeper pain...pain that went beyond the physical. A single tear rolled down one thin cheek.

No woman had ever cried before him. The emotion was so sacred that Xerxian men were taught to turn away, to shield their eyes. But Zahn could not. Not when her look invited him. She wanted him to see this. Why? Perhaps she was unaware of that single tear.

Even more shocking.

He caught the drop with his forefinger and lifted it. In the dancing firelight, the liquid bead glimmered with a rainbow of colors. So tiny, yet so powerful. In honor to her, he touched the saltiness to his tongue. Then he rose.

Without a word, he ladled soup into a bowl and broke off a hunk of bread. He set them on the chair and scooted it next to the bed. Then he helped prop her up. Her muffled whimpers betrayed how she suffered. As he retrieved his outer robe to fashion a pillow for her back, she breathed shallowly as though to combat the pain.

How like a child she seemed, accepting his ministrations one moment, fighting the next. Were all Terran females like this? He thought not.

His fascination grew.

As she took her first taste of soup, he murmured a prayer of thanksgiving. She paused only a moment, before continuing as though she'd not heard. Why did she decline to give thanks? If not in Xer, then in Common? He had no doubt she knew the prayer. Like his people, some Terrans worshipped the true God.

He resisted the impulse to ask. "As soon as you are able, I will take you to Xer Prime. The trip will be difficult, but I believe we can make it in one day."

"I would appreciate that."

"But first, I will bring a medic who is acquainted with Terran physiognomy. She will be able to—"

"No. No doctor."

"But your leg...?"

"It'll be fine."

Her refusal confounded him. "The bone may not heal properly. You risk walking with a limp the rest of your life."

Intent on her soup, she shrugged. "I'll wait until I can see my own physician. On Earth."

More and more odd. If she did not get the proper care, the impairment could very well jeopardize her career. As an operative for Intergalaxia, she relied on physical strength and endurance. A lack of specialized care would cripple her.

If she refused to see a doctor, he should not move her for many days. However, in her present state of mind, he hesitated to speak it.

After she finished her meal, he took the bowl and spoon. A bucket of water sufficed to clean the items. She did not thank him, obviously knowing that his vow to help required no expression of gratitude.

Where had she learned so well Xerxian ways?

"I put an analgesic in the soup, to ease your pain." He

spoke with his back turned so she would not detect he withheld the whole truth. Zahn had not perfected the art of deceit, so revered on Earth. He put the dish and utensil on the shelf.

"Thank you. I feel its affect already."

"Good." He sat cross-legged on the rug. This way, his head would be lower than hers, inviting a more relaxed discussion. Xerxian or Terran, she would no doubt respond to the deference he showed. "What is your name?"

"You are not permitted to ask." Her abrupt response revealed she knew of their tradition of not giving names to strangers. They were reserved for only relatives or close friends.

He smiled slowly. "Terrans prefer names. I ask only out of politeness."

"Now you have put me in a quandary." Her head tilted as though she were instructing. "Since you asked for my name, I should give it out of respect. But for me to *not* give it is the more correct response."

How clever she was. He did not hide his admiration. "A designation then, if you prefer."

Already, he could tell the analgesic had begun to work. The woman's defenses were lowering. Her breathing deepened. Shoulders relaxed.

Her eyelids grew heavy as she mulled over his request. "You may call me...Eva."

"Eva...*full of life.*" Though he already knew her name, he pretended to contemplate it. But why had she given her first? Why not Special Agent Hilliard? "The name is beautiful and fitting for the bearer."

She blushed, then asked with boldness, "And yours?"

Was she flirting with him? He tamped down the thought. It was the medication in her body. Nothing more. "You may call me Zahn."

"You're breaking your culture's protocols?"

"Merely bending." A designation would have been more

proper, but for some reason, he felt compelled to provide his given name, not the matronymic.

"Zahn." She spoke almost dreamily. Relaxing against the makeshift pillow, she appeared to grow more comfortable with each passing minute.

It would not be long now.

Though he knew the answers, he asked anyway, curious about how she would respond. "How did you end up alongside an untraveled road in the middle of my homeworld, Eva?"

"I fell. Into a ravine."

He stifled a chuckle at how she dodged the whole truth.

"You fell into a ravine?" He pretended to muse aloud. "I know this place of which you speak. And you crawled from the ravine to the road? An extraordinary feat considering your condition."

One corner of her mouth curled upward. She obviously knew that *he* knew something else had occurred. But she would not elaborate.

He couldn't help but add, "I hope you've forgiven the one who caused your fall."

She shrugged. "I have no one to blame but myself."

Not entirely true. But Zahn liked the camaraderie. Found himself wishing it would go on. "Tell me of yourself, Eva."

Her expression grew alert, something shuttering behind her eyes. "I am Terran. Isn't that enough?"

"You betray your prejudice, not only of me and my people but of you and yours."

That made her think. He saw the struggle in her tightening mouth, jutting jaw.

She was quiet for many moments. "I am bound by an oath to not reveal who I am, beyond the name I just gave you."

"That is not what I was asking."

Her gaze sidled away, a haunted look falling like a

shadow over her countenance. The soul of this child-woman hid under layers of protection. He sensed a great depth and even greater sorrow.

He prayed for insight. Prayed that he could say something that would open her heart to him. He settled his body more comfortably. And waited. *Yes, there.*

Zahn drew in a deep breath and closed his eyes. "I see a young girl, laughing as she dances through a field of flowers. They have multiple white petals, tall stalks, frail green fronds. Hundreds of them sway in the gentle breeze. The girl gathers an armful. Light glints off her brown hair, spilling like sheets of burnished metal under a hot yellow sun. She runs to a large wooden house of logs. Her father opens the door as she calls to him…"

Detecting something behind the man, Zahn sought to focus. The vision passed. He opened his eyes.

Fright etched Eva's features. Her mouth gaped, eyes narrowed to slits. "How did you…?" She clamped her lips together.

He was wrong. This young woman did not know *all* Xerxian ways.

"A gift from our God." Without pride, he spoke the simple truth. Zahn had not meant to show off, but merely to open a door. An invitation. He tilted his head, studying her. "Tell me, why did you drop the flowers when you reached the log house? What was behind your father?"

A spasm of pain flitted across her features. Her expression hardened as she looked away.

He didn't press for more information. God had given him enough for now. This woman had not only a broken leg, but a wounded spirit. She had limped her whole life.

Someday, Zahn vowed, he would discover the truth about Eva.

Chapter 4

While she slumbered, Zahn slipped away. With the amount of herbs he had put in the soup, she should remain unconscious all night. Outside the cabin's door, he paused, securing a water pouch at his waist. He had one vital task before he tracked the two humans who were deep inside the forest.

Kneeling in prayer, he asked God for guidance and wisdom as he sought Kelli-Layne and Jayden-Song. Then Zahn rose and jogged up the path. Eva had been a distraction, but not a deterrent to the task he must finish.

The triple moons of Xerxes had not yet risen, but the

night was no hindrance to him. His black clothing and the darkness would shield him from the limited vision of the Terrans he tracked. They would be heading to Xer Prime, the capital city. The couple had been clever, avoiding the roads when they grew suspicious that they were being followed. Using their original bearing, he cut into the woods.

The trek took time, but he had prepped for the physical exertion, jogging most of the way. If necessary, he could travel all night to intercept them. A deep ravine cut across his path, but he kept looking for signs. The first two moons rose, providing light that was almost as bright as day.

At last.

Bending, he studied the nearly invisible footprints in the dirt. Had they covered their tracks? As the third moon rose, the visual path became more obvious. They came from the place where the two women had fought. Zahn followed the trail. Here the Terrans had clambered down into the ravine. But something was wrong. He backtracked a little, analyzing the prints more closely. The signs were like an open book as he took care to decipher the message.

From the gouging of the soil, he could tell something plagued the man who was called "Asian." Obviously, he had regained consciousness. What now distressed him? The woman had assisted her partner, but he seemed ill. Even with her height and strength, Kelli-Layne could not possibly carry him. Taking care, Zahn slipped down into the ravine. The path told a clear, readable story.

Here the man had fallen. His companion had helped him stand. Urged him forward. The footprints showed he staggered as though intoxicated. The soil's impressions indicated a growing difficulty. Zahn could see where the female had coaxed him on. Something was seriously wrong. But what? Zahn could only speculate. Sensing they were nearby, he stopped.

Then he heard her. Heard *them.*

Listening, he moved closer.

Obviously distraught, the Terran woman was rambling. She projected anger. Helplessness. With caution, Zahn peered over a large fallen tree. Kelli-Layne stood, fists clenched, staring into the sky. Where was her partner?

There. Lying on the ground, Jayden-Song moaned as his body twitched with uncontrollable spasms. Zahn turned his attention back to Kelli-Layne who panted with frustration and fear.

With long black hair and green skin, she appeared Xerxian. Her height was nearly perfect and her build similar to the females of his world. Not only that, she was exceedingly intelligent. Jayden-Song had not adopted a disguise since his height, skin color and almond-shaped eyes marked him as Terran. Posing as her official Companion, complete with the proper earring that identified him as an indentured servant, he too had blended in just enough.

The High Council would be very interested in these details.

Kelli-Layne slumped to the ground, distress overcoming her. Zahn watched, having no prodding from God to help. No, he must merely observe.

Had Eva been responsible for Jayden-Song's condition? That seemed the best explanation. Though Zahn had witnessed the fight between the two women, he had missed seeing how Eva had injured this man. From the sounds the Asian made, his situation grew critical in mere minutes. As spasms racked his frame, he cried out in torment.

Jayden-Song would not live through the night.

Is it Your will, my God, that he should die? Should I but watch and give no assistance?

Zahn sensed he should merely watch, as though a strong hand pressed against his chest. The Lord of the heavens would act.

Loud enough for Zahn to hear, Kelli-Layne began speaking again. "Since you're real, God, prove it and heal Jayd."

He rocked on his heels. Not only because she had called upon the Lord, but had addressed Him in such a demanding tone. Zahn held breath. How would God answer?

With difficulty, the woman rose to her feet, turning as she looked up at the sky. She seemed to search for the Prayer Star.

Astounding! Of all the celestial bodies, why had she picked Xerxes's most sacred?

Zahn again turned his attention to her as she spoke.

"I don't know how to ask You. I know You see what's going on here. You must see how desperately Jayd needs You." She spread her hands, voice shaking. "I can't help him. So I ask. Please, God. I beg You to heal Jayd. Don't let him die, God. I couldn't bear it." She paused, then knelt. "I surrender all to You. My life. My will. No matter what happens. Only please, *please* save Jayd."

Zahn felt he should shield his eyes from the beauty and fervency of her petition. From the humility and soul-stripping honesty. How had she gone from a petulant, demanding child to a humble worshipper in mere seconds?

The Lord God. He revealed Himself to her and wrought a change in her spirit that only He could accomplish.

Kelli-Layne wept, meekness and vulnerability entwined, forming a soul-song that floated to the heavens. A river of tears ran down her cheeks as she remained looking up at the star. A sob tore through the night air, piercing Zahn's soul. Transfixed, he could not move. Waiting. *Waiting.*

After many moments, she turned to her companion who had grown quiet. Not because of death. Because of healing?

O God of the universe, You heard her cry. You heeded her prayer.

Zahn fell on his face and worshipped.

"How can they know of you, O God?" he murmured. "How can she call upon You in such a manner?" He had heard of Terran believers, but had never met one. "We are not the only ones who know of You."

Prostrate for many minutes, Zahn prayed for the humans. Prayed for safety and success in their journey. Finally he arose to see how the heavenly answer would play out.

Kelli-Layne lay beside her ill companion and covered him with a blanket. Her demeanor spoke of trust in her God. She had pleaded. Now she waited for Him to answer as He chose.

What faith!

Zahn watched a little longer, then headed back the direction he'd come. He had seen enough. His task here was finished. He turned his face toward the other human, the one who lay sleeping in his cabin.

"You *must* take me to Xer Prime. Today." Eva raged against the Xerxian man who continued to hold her prisoner in his home. For ten minutes she had cajoled and begged. This was her third day of isolation. She *had* to get out of here. Had to get off this planet.

Why wouldn't he listen? The fate of the universe was being decided even now. His refusal could destroy her world. His as well.

With the analgesic flowing through her body, she felt out of control. Frustration built until a scream threatened to burst from her. "I *demand* you do as I say." The force of her tone surprised her.

As he prepared the noonday meal, Zahn turned calm eyes toward her. "And I tell you, for the last time—*I will not.*"

She played her only trump card. "You gave me your word. A Xerxian vow is sacrosanct."

There! He couldn't excuse himself from that.

Zahn didn't answer. Nothing could be heard but the

muted chirp of a bird outside and the hiss of the water as it heated in the pot.

"I gave my word that I would help you." He remained implacable in his calmness. "Helping you would best be accomplished by your remaining in bed so that your leg will heal."

"I *cannot* stay another moment."

Zahn rose from beside the fireplace, knife in hand.

Gasping, she shrank back against the cot. Would he harm her?

Without a word, he gripped the hem of her pants and slit the material from ankle to thigh, leaving only the bandaging around the splint intact. He laid open the cloth and revealed her swollen, purple leg. Only the powerful painkiller kept her from screaming in agony.

"If you knew anything of our ways, Eva, you would realize that helping sometimes means we cannot do what the requester asks. Rather, we must follow our conscience."

Her chest heaved, not with suppressed tears, but with dread. If only Zahn had left her to die, she would not see the terrible consequences of Layne and Song's escape. A vague and dark future lodged in her mind—one that couldn't be explained and couldn't be banished.

"Calm yourself, little one." For once, Zahn's voice failed to soothe.

She sank into the bed. An ominous clanging in her head warned that the window of opportunity to apprehend the fugitives had passed. A mental picture of herself rose in her mind—a tiny figure with arms spread, standing before a tsunami of events she was powerless to stop.

Zahn sat beside her and pressed his palm to her forehead as he had done several times before. "Your health is more important than whatever, or whoever, awaits you."

No, it wasn't.

However, his touch worked its magic. Fears ebbed, morphing into a deep apprehension.

"That's better." His low voice comforted. "Tomorrow, I will take a message for you to the nearest town while I restock our supplies. From there, it can be sent to wherever you want. Will that be acceptable?"

"I suppose." Hope flamed and, with it, a renewal of plans. Perhaps the capture of Layne and Song was still possible if she could get word to one of her colleagues. Were they still on Xerxes IX? Better yet, Eva determined to travel to the nearest road. Where did Zahn store his herbs? If she took double the pain meds, she might be able to travel with a crude crutch.

Her gaze flickered to the shelf in the room. However, from her position, she could see nothing. Then the absurdity of the plan struck her. She'd be unable to move much less fashion a crutch.

His fingertips lingered on her skin. "Let your mind be at ease as well."

Could he read her thoughts? She pushed her schemes away.

"Good." Zahn rose to bring her food. "Eat. And may you be strengthened."

She did as he bade, again ignoring his whispered prayer of thanksgiving for the meal. As he sat nearby, she realized that he ate nothing. He hadn't consumed anything since her arrival at the cabin. Not even that morning. "What are you having?"

He merely shook his head, a small smile touching his lips. "I hunger not."

Gulping, she grew aware that he had gone without because he'd given her all his food. How could she be so selfish? However, to protest would not only insult him, but dishonor herself. After all, she had exacted a vow for his help. That meant he had laid aside all his needs in her favor.

Mortification ate into her soul. With more meekness, she finished the simple meal.

He brought in a bucket of water to fill the pot. As it

heated on the fireplace, he crushed some leaves into the warming water. A wonderful fragrance filled the cabin, of a lavender-like scent and the sweet grasses of the plains. He set a bowl next to her bed and knelt. Astonished, she watched him dip in a clean cloth.

Realization slammed into her. He intended to bathe her?

"No." She blocked his hand.

A heartbreaking memory flashed through Eva's mind of her mother giving her a bath. They had traveled to their mountain cabin. An ancient claw-foot tub, filled with warm water, awaited. Her mother used some of her own, exotic bath salts. Smelling of roses mixed with the faintest touch of gardenias.

That had been the night before her mother disappeared from her life. Forever.

Frowning, Zahn opened his mouth to say something, then shut it. After putting the cloth aside, he pursed his lips. "You know much of my people, yet you lack some basic information. Allow me to instruct." He sat back on his heels. "The males in our society care for their children. God has equipped us to nurture. At our children's youngest ages, we clean and dress them."

"I am not a child."

"Yet you sometimes act as one." His rueful expression softened the harsh truth. "Regardless, you must take into consideration your injury. Will you not be more comfortable bathed? Will you not permit me to serve you in this manner?" His black eyes met hers steadily.

She struggled with his request, knowing that to refuse would shame him. But she could not let him play nurse for her.

He must not look on my abdominal deformity.

"I understand Terran modesty," he said in a low voice. "And I will respect your privacy. But please allow me to honor you in a small way."

Despite the trepidation that gripped her, she nodded.

His face relaxed. Grasping the cloth again, he dipped it in the water, then wrung out the excess. Gently, he smoothed it over her face, taking extra care around her eyes. As he washed the back of her neck and behind her ears, he lifted her head, easing her hair out of the way.

With self-consciousness entangling her, she could not relax her muscles. But soon, his touch and the scent soothed her. A deep sigh escaped her as he washed her arms. Intent on his task, Zahn merely smiled. He gently dabbed the scrapes on her knuckles and the bruises on her arms, the ones she'd gotten when she had fought Layne. Not once did he ask how she'd gotten them. He spent time on a deep purple blotch on her forearm, soaking the cloth and holding it on the discolored skin. Then he removed her socks and rolled up the pants on her uninjured leg. With meticulous care, he washed her feet. Shivers traveled from her heels to her spine.

Slowly her focus shifted from herself to him. The source of her sighs shifted from pleasure to curiosity. What would it be like if they had an understanding?

Such a shocking thought. For more than twenty years, she had never allowed herself to become involved in a relationship. Was she now wishing for this man's attention? The walls of protection that had served her well eluded her. Anger and aloofness, her best defenses, could not be manufactured in this situation. She could not escape him that easily.

Zahn was handsome. His strong square jaw, impossibly long black lashes and wide, calm forehead pleased her. But it was the deep contentment emanating from him that intrigued her most. He understood himself and knew his place in the universe. The smile lines creasing his eyes and mouth showed he could laugh at life. The certainty of his soul called to her. Promised her a peaceful haven where she could run.

His hands—soft, certain, gentle, strong—mesmerized

her. She had no fear of him taking advantage. Peace and selflessness flowed from his capable fingertips.

When he finished washing her feet, he turned his attention to her injured leg. After carefully loosening the splint and bandaging, he dabbed her skin with the cloth. Even the lightest touch made her hiss in discomfort. Yet she sensed the herb-laden water hastened the healing. With great tenderness, he again bound her leg.

"Let me reheat the water. Then I will step outside while you complete your bath." After a few minutes, he brought her a fresh bowl, pleasantly warmed, with additional ground leaves. He set it on the chair next to the bed. "Call me when you are finished." He left the cabin.

Anxious, Eva washed herself without removing her clothing. In her haste, she sloshed water on the chair and floor. Though she longed to be thorough, she wouldn't chance his coming back into the one-roomed cabin.

She called out. "I'm done." Exhausted, she reclined on the bed, breathing as though she'd run a mile.

Pausing at the doorway, Zahn assessed the mess. Without a word, he opened the shutters and allowed sunlight to spill into the room. As he cleaned the floor, she found herself growing sleepy. Not only the pain meds and floral scent, but the warming sun tranquilized her.

After he restored order, he again filled a bucket with water from the well outside. She could hear the squeak of the pulley as he lifted the pail from the depths. Comforting sounds. When he reentered the cabin, he moved quietly. Turning to face one window, he stripped off his tunic and washed his torso. He moved the wet cloth over his shoulders. Barrel-chested, his muscles bunched and released. Water trickled down his back, the beads glistening in the sun.

He was a beautiful man. Except for the pale green skin and black irises, the physique of a Xer male was nearly identical to a human. However, Eva reminded herself, she had no time or interest in a relationship—human or Xerxian. Any man who knew the truth about her would scorn and reject her. With deliberation, she turned her face away.

She must have dozed because later, her twitching body awakened her. Keeping her eyes closed, she listened for Zahn's movements in the room. Nothing. With caution, she looked for him. He sat across the room, reading a red-bound book. As he frowned over the pages, his lips moved as though he were committing a passage to memory. The charms on his earring reflected light, spraying the cabin walls with tiny, dancing stars. The effect added to her sense of unreality. He surprised her when he slid to the floor and knelt, his profile to her as he lifted his countenance to the open window. Sunlight streamed over him.

If she were not so entranced with the vision, she would have covered her eyes. Never had she seen such worship on anyone's face. His features were rapt. With love for God? Yes, she heard him as he prayed. Zahn whispered the Lord's most holy name.

How could anyone feel that way? How could a Xerxian man be so enthralled with his Creator?

The beauty of the scene held her captive.

The next moment, Zahn turned his head. His gaze locked with hers. Obviously he had been aware that she watched him. Yet, his features did not contain annoyance or recrimination, rather an understanding. Or was that an assent of some kind?

He rose and moved into the shadows. For a moment, as the bright sunbeam pooled on the floor, she lost sight of him. Seconds later, he reappeared by her bedside.

She bit her lip. *Don't apologize.* Even though she should not have stared, she could not now mention the incident. He knelt beside the bed. As her gaze fixed on his still-damp hair, her cheeks grew hot from the reminder of his bath.

Oh, the absurdity of considering a relationship with him.

"It is no accident that you are here," he spoke with care.

"I believe in the sovereignty of our God. You were meant to be at this cabin." He paused, gaze searching her face.

Eva could not imagine how she should reply. Something momentous was about to happen. A mental picture of herself, sitting atop a snow-packed hill, flashed through her mind. The sled teetered. Any second it would slip down the steep embankment.

"All my life, I have devoted myself to study and prayer, certain that God prepared my path. For many years, I have ministered to my people. I have obeyed with single-minded devotion, convinced I was doing His will. Or so I believed. I see now that I erred." Zahn paused as though gathering his thoughts. He bowed his head. "However, I submit to Him. No matter the cost."

Why was he telling her this? His deep voice revealed the absence of doubts. He had no lack of faith.

The illusory sled tipped, seesawing on the edge.

He took a deep breath. "I asked my God, while you slept, to give me guidance." He stopped speaking Xer and switched to English. "And He has."

Her sense of expectation heightened.

His head tilted. "If you were watching me as I finished my prayers, I would know how to proceed."

The sled slid over the edge. She opened her mouth to protest, to tell Zahn to speak no further, yet the words stuck in her throat. A silent shriek remained locked away in the exhilaration and terror of the downward plummet.

"Know that once I utter this, I will not rescind it. Ever." He took her limp hand. "I desire, Eva, for you to accept me. Allow me the privilege of becoming your husband."

Chapter 5

In the chambers of the High Council, First Chancellor Ileya beckoned to her attendant. In patience, the man had waited across the room while several members pontificated. At last, the meeting was drawing to a close. Soon Ileya would learn what had become of their missing envoy. During the gathering, no one had brought up his absence so it was up to her to find out the reason for his continued silence. She stifled her impatience while various clan leaders murmured their obeisance to Xerxes IX in the closing ritual. Would they never finish? Her assistant made his way toward her, moving with care so as not to disturb.

The Speaker's Ball, striking the wooden base, signaled that another member wished to eulogize.

Ileya squelched her groan.

The one Terrans called "ambassadress" struck a pose in the center of the circular room. "My sisters, other esteemed members and guests, I beg your consideration."

The members, sitting in tiers around her, hushed in deference.

Ileya stifled any irritability. "Speak. You have our attention." Her long-time opponent and prominent daughter of another clan liked to hear herself talk. After she had accepted a position as ambassadress to Earth, Ileya had hoped her long-winded speeches would end.

Apparently not.

Ambassadress Aeliana made a point to look at the clan leaders, slowly turning in a circle. "Hear the plea from my heart. Our world is in danger, more now than ever."

This was new. Ileya shushed one of her aides who leaned in to whisper something.

"I have a report that a Terran fugitive, one Kelli-Layne, disguised herself as a Xerxian and infiltrated our world."

"Old news, Aeliana," someone across the room retorted. "Intergalaxia requested we take her into custody."

"And we refused," another added. "They dispatched their own agents, as we permitted."

"Right up to the point where we had to escort two off," someone said under their breath. The room filled with tittering.

An unfortunate event, but the woman and man had embarrassed themselves in a village. It was one thing to allow the Terran operatives onto their world, another for them to insult an esteemed member of the community. Ileya herself had ordered their removal from Xerxes. They were no longer welcome.

"My liege," whispered her attendant.

Without looking at him, Ileya held up her hand to

silence him. "Wait," she mouthed. She fixed her eyes on the woman who refused to move from the center of the room.

"There is more." Aeliana waited until the room quieted. "This fugitive, Kelli-Layne has taken a girl from Xer Prime and fled."

"A Xerxian child?" Distress rang through the voice of a councilwoman.

"No. A human." The ambassadress lifted her chin. "But a child nevertheless."

Ileya watched as the pronouncement had the desired effect. Any time someone mentioned children in danger, outrage would surely follow—regardless of their race. The ambassadress knew well how to stoke the passions of their people.

Aeliana turned to her. "Have you nothing to say, First Chancellor?"

Before speaking, Ileya weighed her words. "We are aware of Kelli-Layne. The High Council gave permission for Terran agents to disguise themselves as Xerxians to track her and her comrade. You were, unfortunately, on Earth at the time and missed the vote."

"Yes, yes. Those facts I know. The events about which I speak are more recent."

Ileya remained silent. How to get information without appearing anxious? "When did you receive this report?"

"Only this morning."

"And your couriers are reliable?"

"Without question." Chin rising, the woman's eyes glinted with provocation.

"I would like to see the full report and launch my own investigation." She made a decision in an instant. "Every member here, I'm sure, would like to know more."

Perhaps the meeting would not be as long as she feared.

"I have them here now." When Aeliana motioned, an assistant entered with a stack of papers, which he handed to every member of the council.

Clever.

"I recommend we retire as we study these notes." Ileya bridled her tone to reflect only serenity. "We will reconvene later this afternoon." She rose in dismissal.

"I beg for a mere moment longer." The ambassadress fixed her with a gaze, the mute challenge unmistakable.

Oh, Aeliana, you never change. War burns within your blood. What was she planning? In which skirmish did she yearn to engage?

The woman's lips twitched slightly. "The crimes outlined in my report are not as important as what they represent."

Ileya sank back onto her chair.

"A missing child not important?" challenged Second Chancellor.

Good for her. Ileya stifled a grim smile.

"You mishear me." The ambassadress bowed, three fingers to her chest in a sign of humility.

"Excuse me, but I need clarification." Ileya waited until she had everyone's attention. "Was this girl Kelli-Layne took the same one kidnapped from the outpost some months past?"

The woman's eyes hooded.

As I thought. That changed the tone of the so-called abduction from Xer Prime. Was Aeliana skewing Kelli-Layne's actions so that she appeared as a kidnapper rather than a rescuer?

"Irrelevant," the ambassadress finally answered, "when you consider that these crimes are but a foretaste of greater ones on our horizon. How many more Terrans or other races will come to our world without our suspecting, and take whatever or whomever they please? We have no way of knowing who is truly Xer and who merely poses as one."

Alarm spread through the council, evidenced by stiffening shoulders and hardened faces. Aeliana had been successful in deflecting attention from the facts of the so-called abduction.

"You speak as though that is an everyday occurrence," Ileya chided. "This incident with Kelli-Layne is an isolated event. The first in our twenty-six year history with Earth."

"Not the first crime against us," the ambassadress dared counter. "And that you know."

Ileya caught her breath as panic gripped her soul. Did she know about…? Impossible. That secret was safe, buried for nearly three standard decades. She inhaled slowly. "I mean, my friend, we need facts. If Kelli-Layne did indeed rescue the Terran child, then she deserves our thanks."

"You're missing the point."

"No, *you* are. Let's go back to the inciting event. That was the first time a kidnapping has occurred. And don't forget—the child was human and on the Terran outpost. Not on Xerxes."

"Irrelevant." The woman drew closer and gripped the railing between them. "Can you not see? Though the outpost is disputed territory, it is the gateway to our world. If we let this incident pass, it will set a precedent. I remind you of our maxim—*a precedent becomes a habit, a habit becomes law.*"

Many council members murmured in agreement.

"Then clearly," Ileya spoke with a slightly raised tone, "it is time to settle the status of this disputed territory. Will you take up our cause with the Terrans? With Intergalaxia?"

"Gladly." Aeliana's eyes flamed. "But more than that, we must be ever vigilant on our own world. This is why we must take action now to prevent this sort of thing happening *here*. Ever."

The ambassadress clearly would get out of hand if Ileya didn't do something. She rose. "I will hear more of this later. Better yet, record your ideas and recommendations, then submit your report."

Without giving Aeliana another chance to further agitate the council, she rose. Her departure signaled the adjournment of the meeting. Babbling voices broke out before she exited the room. Without waiting, she passed through her private door.

Ileya was halfway down the corridor when a voice called. "First Chancellor."

Aeliana.

Taking a slow breath, Ileya turned. "I was about to have repast. Would you care to join me?"

A subtle reminder, she hoped, that the ambassadress now imposed. These corridors led to Ileya's personal chambers—usually off-limits without her express permission.

"Food can wait." Demeanor implacable, the woman drew closer. "You *must* listen to reason."

"I hope I am ever open to logic." Ileya folded her hands into the sleeves of her robe. "I am at your disposal."

"How can you *not* see the danger? By withholding safeguards, we risk the peace and security of our world."

Ileya pressed her lips together. "What would you have me do, my friend?"

"Investigate ways to screen those who come to our planet. Institute stricter laws that would guarantee punishment for everyone who disguises themselves as Xer. For starters."

For starters. Instinctively Ileya knew this woman would not be content with just those actions. They would lead to more and harsher measures.

Aeliana drew closer. "Do you not care about our future? For the future of our children?"

"Of course I do. You have no need to—"

"Then *do* something. Don't sit idle while our very way of life is perishing."

Ileya drew a slow breath. What did this woman know? Or believe she knew? With care, she chose her words. "The Terran Summit begins in the near future. What other items will you bring before the conference besides the disputed space station?"

A mask of stoicism fell across her features. "That is all. And of the utmost importance right now."

A lie. Ileya read clearly something else was on her mind. What was the woman planning? She forced a smile. "That is a good first step. To decide once and for all who has control of the outpost." She bowed. "And now, I take my leave of you."

Ileya had already turned when the ambassadress stopped her with, "What guarantees do I have that you will consider my other requests?"

She gritted her teeth at the blatant disrespect imbedded in the words. Could the fact that the illness of Aeliana's mother—leader of her clan—be the source of her more than usual fractiousness? Only that morning Ileya had learned the graveness of the elderly woman's affliction.

Before she could answer, the ambassadress drew closer. "I would consider your word a token of goodwill."

Tamping down indignation, Ileya made a decision. "You may approach Intergalaxia about installing scanners at our port. However, I remind you, no further action can be taken without the approval of the High Council."

"Of course. But can I count on your support?" The ambassadress' mouth tightened, eyes hooded.

A trap? Ileya knew her long-time opponent would use her word against her given the right circumstances.

"You always have my support," Ileya answered with manufactured calm. "But what gesture of goodwill do you extend in return?"

Aeliana drew back, ever so slightly. Because she hadn't expected Ileya to take the offensive? "I'm sure you will think of something when the time comes."

Ileya allowed herself a slow smile. "Since our youngest years, I am glad we still understand each other." She extended her hands.

A hint of disdain flashed across the woman's face before she touched her forehead to Ileya's palms in honor. Without another word, she stalked away.

Ileya had no moment to contemplate the exchange as her attendant appeared from behind a closed door and bowed. "Forgive my persistence."

"There is no need. Speak." In her haste to escape Aeliana, she had forgotten the attendant might have news.

"About the envoy you dispatched..." He drew closer and lowered his voice. "We've had no word from him. The one sent to bring news of the two humans."

Ileya sucked in a slow breath. "Do you suspect he's been harmed?"

The man's countenance darkened. "It is possible. The Terrans he tracked departed two nights ago from Xer Prime. My sources say they are already on their way to Earth, even as we speak."

"Yet no word from Zahn?"

The man shook his head.

"How many days since we've had contact?"

"Too many. We have no explanation for his silence."

For the first time since Ileya had heard the news of the humans on Xerxes, anger gripped her. While Kelli-Layne and Jayden-Song had traipsed over her homeworld, she had listened to reports of their exploits with amusement. The stories were almost unbelievable, how these two had pulled off a charade of incredible magnitude. They had fooled everyone they met.

But now they had departed Xerxes IX? Had they harmed Zahn? The tales lost all humor if he were indeed in jeopardy.

"You will send word immediately if you hear from him?"

"Yes, my sovereign."

"Thank you." Ileya clenched her fist as she strode toward her private chambers. Perhaps the ambassadress was right. Perhaps the time had come for more stringent restraints when it came to their world. She was surprised at the fury that grew exponentially at the news—an emotion

which she thought was long dead.
     Crimes against Xerxes IX would no longer be tolerated.

Chapter 6

Eva wept for me. She gave me the priceless gift of her tears.

As Zahn pulled a squeaking handcart along the dusty path, he reflected on the events. Had it ever left his thoughts? Regardless of his activity, the picture rose up before him. Even now, as Eva rode in the small cart behind him, the memory had not faded in the three days since he had proposed marriage.

He grunted as he struggled up a deeply rutted incline, the ground hardened from recent rains followed by hot days. With every bump of the cart, she endured suffering, evidenced in her stifled gasps. He was torn between traveling slowly for her comfort and hurrying so that they would reach the city before nightfall. Despite the herbs she had ingested and the bundles he had placed around her, she soon gave up hiding her pain.

As the sun warmed his back, Zahn again reflected on his petition to the fragile woman behind him. When he had first asked her to be his wife, he'd seen shock, followed by disbelief and deep reflection. Eva had opened her mouth to reply but unexpectedly, she broke down and wept. Every time she rallied herself and tried to speak, emotion again overwhelmed her. For many minutes she'd been unable to answer.

While he knelt before her, he sensed the sacredness of the moment. More amazing was that while he watched her struggle, his own lashes grew wet. Xerxian men did not cry. Yet, he'd fought the burning in his own eyes.

Exhausted, she had finally calmed. After reclining, she had begged him in a broken voice to allow her to rest. Allow her time to think.

But she had not refused him. Not then or in the days since.

Her weeping had been a confirmation from God. In obedience, Zahn had offered her marriage. When the time was right, Eva would answer. He vowed to be patient. For a lifetime if need be.

When the cart's wheel bumped over a rock, she cried out. Stopping, he berated himself for not watching the road more closely.

"Perhaps a brief rest would be in order." From the back of the cart, he retrieved her canteen.

Lips white, she accepted the water.

As she drank, he sampled his own water pouch. "We are not far from the paved road." He hoped the news would encourage. "Travel will be easier then."

She nodded. After splitting a fruit pod, he gave her half.

"Thank you." Her eyelids fluttered, as though she still

could not fathom why he had petitioned her to be his wife. He, too, had trouble believing God had directed him to seek her hand. But the prompting had been unmistakable. And her response had confirmed the rightness of his actions.

She had wept. The treasured and hallowed beauty of that moment burned into his memory.

Sighing, Eva leaned back against the soft bundles. Sunlight danced in her hair, creating a glow about her head. Zahn could not help but stare. Every day, she grew more beautiful. Even her pale skin no longer looked odd. He thought he began to understand the emotions she betrayed when her dark brown eyes sparked shards of gold.

She shifted as she adjusted her tunic.

"Is that causing you discomfort?" He had purchased a Xerxian outfit for her when he had made the trek into a nearby town, along with new bandages and thin slats of wood that were better suited for a splint.

"It's fine." She smoothed the hem. "Just a little big."

"I am sorry I misjudged the size."

Her lips pulled into a crooked grin. "I suppose you're not used to buying women's clothing."

He hoped that was a compliment. But in truth, the garments he had purchased were crafted for a child.

"I appreciate the clean clothing, Zahn. Thank you again."

"Is your leg comfortable?" He both feared and longed for an affirmative answer because he recognized his ulterior motive. Rearranging the bundles would give him an excuse to touch her. A shocking thought. Again, so un-Xerxian. Zahn felt as though a part of him that had long slept was now awakening. It both disturbed and thrilled.

"Yes." Yet a small pinched line persisted beside her mouth.

He struggled with himself...and lost.

"Let me check your splint." He tested the new bandages to make certain they were not too tight. Then he felt the temperature of her ankle. The warmth indicated an adequate blood supply reached her foot. His breath caught.

Her skin is so soft. Like a newborn's.

He shook himself to concentrate on the task. The new bandages appeared to be doing a better job keeping her leg immobile without cutting off circulation. "How does it feel?"

"Good." Her gaze followed him. Did she guess why he tarried?

Unable to help himself, he let his fingertips linger. Soon they would reach the capital city. Afterwards she would fly away to Earth.

Once that happened he would need to exercise exceeding patience.

The cost of waiting would be great. But he would do as the Lord of the heavens had directed. Since He had set His plan into motion, Zahn must trust Him to see it through.

Again, he shifted the bundles to provide maximum comfort while she rode on the borrowed cart. Without a word, she accepted his ministrations. Finally, he pulled his hands back. "Ready to go on?"

"Yes." But before he could move away, she pressed his arm. "Thank you for everything."

It mattered not what she was thankful for. Her voicing appreciation was enough. While her fingers rested on his skin, his heart quickened. Blood coursed through his veins.

The seedling of love, planted and nourished, promised to flourish for a lifetime.

He would guard it. No matter the cost.

Again he resumed his place at the front and pulled the cart. Despite his deliberate pace over the uneven path, they made good time. Finally they reached the Great Lift and were on their way up to the cliff towns below the plateaued city of Xer Prime. Zahn allowed himself to enjoy the dizzying view as the platform rose well over a thousand standard feet. The sight always filled him with awe, yet also with sadness because it meant he must return to his hectic life.

The trek up the steep streets grew difficult, especially with the crowds of people who also traveled to the capital. However, others helped push the cart from behind, relieving the burden of the task. It was early evening by the time they reached the main city.

Zahn stopped to rest. "Where is it you would like to go?"

"To the shuttle." She didn't have to think before answering.

"But your friends?"

"I'm sure they are gone by now."

That would make sense considering what had occurred a few days before. When he had offered to dispatch a message from town, Eva had changed her mind about contacting her colleagues. Was it normal for her organization to abandon their operatives after so many days of silence?

"Do you need funds?" he asked. The shuttle from the capital city to the space station could be arranged with just his word. However, the passage from the Xer Outpost to Earth would require money. After one stop, he could secure enough to cover that expense.

"I have a ticket waiting." She looked at him squarely. "You've done more than enough."

"As long as you are in my care, I will continue to provide what I can."

She chewed her lower lip. "I have provisions waiting for me at the space station. I will be fine once I reach there."

"Then I will see you to the outpost. The peoples there may be less helpful."

She opened her mouth as though to protest, then shut it. To travel in her condition would be difficult, especially alone on the space station.

Once they reached Xer Prime's terminal, he left her on a bench so that he could find someone to return the borrowed cart to the plains. Interest showed on Eva's face as he negotiated the task with a laborer. Anxious to please, the man bowed several times after Zahn gave his designation.

"Come to me for payment once you return to Xer Prime." He clasped the man's shoulder in thanks.

"No payment needed. I do this out of honor."

Zahn bowed. "Many thanks, friend." He returned to Eva. "Now let me arrange passage." Before she could say anything, he strode to the ticket counter. The cost was quickly negotiated with promise of remittance.

"Did you give them money?" A frown creased her brow.

"No. My word is sufficient."

Though puzzlement still marked her expression, she didn't ask anything more.

"The next shuttle leaves in fifteen minutes. We must hurry." With care, Zahn lifted her. She was small. Easy to carry. She felt so right in his arms.

Clenching her teeth, she gripped his robe.

"I'm sorry to cause you pain."

"It can't be helped." She spoke with difficulty.

He waited until she released the breath she held. "Ready?"

"Yes." She pointed to the bundles he'd brought from the cabin, sitting on the bench. "What about your things?"

"They will be here when I return."

She frowned. "Are you sure?"

He merely smiled. Those of Earth trusted so little. Someday, Zahn hoped to be able to show her the *better* way.

With little time to spare, they reached the shuttle. He made certain she settled comfortably, even securing the opposite seat that faced their row so she could prop up her leg. As the flight prepared to depart, Zahn bowed his head to those who recognized him. Eva merely watched the exchanges.

By the time they arrived at the outpost, her pinched frown and tight mouth betrayed her exhaustion and pain. The crowds at the space station were much denser. Peoples of many planets carelessly jostled them. With difficulty Zahn found an ancient hover chair. Its controls were nonfunctional, so he manually guided the vehicle.

Because of the noise, he had to lean down and speak in her ear. "Where to?" He smiled at her hesitation to answer.

"The Hotel Genévre. I can make it from there."

"We shall see." He steered the chair onto the sub-rail and finally located the largest hotel at the center of the Xer Outpost. Once they reached their destination, he detected her reluctance for him to accompany her. After he parked her by the welcome desk, he sauntered across the lobby to wait. The clerk greeted her, apparently recognizing her. Keeping his face impassive at the inquisitive glances the clerk sent in his direction, Zahn merely watched. Eva soon indicated for him to return to her. On her lap sat an electronic key.

She looked past him, as though she found meeting his gaze difficult. Was she nervous? Zahn waited for her to speak.

"The next ship to Earth leaves in a few hours. I already have a ticket."

"And a room here, I see."

"Yes." Pink blotched her cheeks. "They held one for me. My things are being moved upstairs right now." Her eyes darted about. "They are making arrangements for a hover chair for me. The latest model so I can operate it myself."

"Then it is time I bid you farewell."

Her eyes widened.

How easily I can read you, Eva. You are fearful. In turmoil.

Her fingers tightened and loosened around the key. "Thank you again for all—"

"You have already expressed your thanks. However, I appreciate it." He took her free hand and held it while he spoke. "Until we meet again, Eva Hilliard." He pressed his forehead to her wrist, an intimate Xerxian farewell. Without looking back, he strode away.

Chapter 7

With water streaming through her hair and over her body, Eva sighed with pleasure. She luxuriated in the multitude of floral-scented bubbles as she lathered herself. It was good to be back on Earth and in her own apartment. At last.

After her arrival the night before, she'd caught up on the news—especially about the status of the kidnapped child. As Eva showered, the latest info blared from her comm-panel. A reporter, who was interviewing one of Kelli's acquaintances, expressed his outrage that she had been incarcerated. Apparently her arrest had occurred shortly after she had reunited the child with her mother.

Eva turned off the noise. So the fugitives really had been on a rescue mission, just as the Kelli Layne had said. Though Eva had no idea how this turn of events would affect the future, relief swept over her once again. Could her mission's failure be good in the long run?

Except for the pattering of the shower, silence closed in around her. She considered the report she had prepared and sent the night before, which detailed everything that had happened to her on Xerxes IX. Well, almost everything.

She refused to reveal the details of her encounter with Zahn. The personal aspects about him and his desire for a relationship were not pertinent to the mission. No one needed to know. She outlined her injury, her rescue by a Xerxian commoner and her recuperation in his cabin.

As she stood in the shower booth, she tested her leg. Pain radiated upward, but not enough to prevent walking on it. While she'd been at the space station and as she'd traveled to Earth, she'd applied her personal mender. However, Zahn was right. The delay in using the equipment had not been wise. One of the hazards of fieldwork. She limped and probably always would, as Zahn had predicted.

As she thought of him, she braced her hand against the glass wall of the shower booth. Water cascaded over her shoulders. Why couldn't she get him out of her mind?

He was merely a love-smitten peasant. Likely he had never seen a Terran woman before and had grown infatuated with the idea of having a human wife. That was all.

Even as she reexamined the events, she couldn't convince herself. Yet again.

What was so different about Zahn?

Then there was that incident as he had said goodbye to her on the outpost. Hard to believe it was already five days ago. He had used her full name. How did he know? Had she blurted it out while under the influence of the pain meds? Unlikely. She had been trained to resist drugs. It must have been when she checked in at the Hotel Genévre. Zahn had to have overheard the clerk use her name. Right?

Straightening, Eva toggled off the water jets and turned on the blowers. Since Inter-G insisted she take a mandatory day off, she decided to make one small trip. USF had incarcerated Kelli Layne in a maximum-security facility outside New Washington. Why had she surrendered to authorities after returning the kidnapped girl? Layne and Song could have holed up for years.

Eva needed answers. Something nagged at her core. Like the ripples caused by a pebble dropped into a still pond, the effects continued to push outward. But instead of fading, the ramifications swelled.

Over an hour later, Eva waited while sitting on a hardback chair positioned behind a blue force field. Not that she worried about her protection. From down the hall, two voices met her ears. She tuned out the guard's and focused on the other.

"So is this what you do all day?" Kelli spoke to someone out of sight. "Escort prisoners?"

"I wouldn't complain if I were you." The guard's tone held a note of teasing.

"Oh, I'm not, believe me."

As Kelli rounded the corner, the smile on her face blinked out of sight. "Eva." She spoke with breathless tension.

Rising, Eva allowed her one-time enemy to take in her appearance. And Kelli did just that, studying her from the crown of her head to her low-heeled shoes. Next, she glanced at the force field between them. To make certain it functioned? Like she feared Eva had come to kill her?

"You do me honor." Eva spoke in Xerxian as she bowed.

"You honor me as well." As Kelli mimicked the posture, she stiffened, apparently startled that she had slipped so effortlessly into Xerxian customs and speech.

Eva smirked. "Some things you never forget."

Kelli's eyes narrowed as she perched tentatively on the edge of her chair. "So, I'm guessing you're not here to finish the job?"

"Not today."

Looking her over, Eva noted the agent's thinness. A restless pallor lined her face. Kelli looked nothing like the last time she'd seen her. Blue eyes and blonde hair had replaced the Xerxian black while her robes had transformed into the unforgiving orange of detention wear. At least the prison had not degraded her by making her wear a halo necklace.

"I must admit, I didn't recognize you at first," Eva said.

"Oh, yeah." Kelli fingered the natural-colored tresses that fell to just below her shoulders. "I'm still shocked when I look in the mirror."

"I'll bet." Eva tilted her head to one side. "So how are you doing?"

"Great." Her cheerful tone contrasted with the tightness of her mouth. "This place is awesome. Food is passable. And I love their workout program. Every day, I get to beat up as many guards as I like."

"I'm sure."

"Want to join the club? I could put in a good word. I'm certain we could find you a spot."

This time Eva laughed. "No, thanks. I like it out here."

Kelli sobered. "I would too." She gripped the edge of her chair, tension radiating from every muscle of her body.

"Scared?" The word surprised Eva when she said it.

The prisoner waved her hand to indicate the room. "They call this 'administrative detention.' Nice, huh? Since I haven't been formally charged with a crime."

"Call it what you want. It's still prison."

Her jaw tightened.

"Listen, the reason I came is…" Eva paused and looked away. Why had she come exactly? She pushed away the secondary, more obscure, reason. "I wanted to thank you for saving my life."

"After I tried to take it."

"Yeah, well." Eva shrugged. "It's a toss-up about who started the fight."

"How's the leg?"

"Good enough." Eva raised her chin a notch.

Kelli's eyes narrowed. "I hope you didn't have to wait too long after I left you. Someone come along soon?"

"Nah. I crawled to the nearest town. It takes more than a broken leg to keep an Inter-G agent down."

Kelli laughed. "Liar."

Smiling, she shrugged. "Makes a good story."

"If anyone asks, I'll give 'em that version." Then Kelli cleared her throat. "I'm glad you're all right. No hard feelings?"

"None." Eva studied her a moment. "I wouldn't be as forgiving, though, if you had killed me."

"I'll bet not."

"How's your friend?"

"Jayd? Doing well."

"He obviously recovered from the neurotoxin?"

Something in Kelli's countenance changed. She looked down at her clenched hands, visibly hesitating to answer. "It was touch and go for a bit."

"Well, I hope *he* doesn't hold a grudge."

"Nope." She looked up. "He got a pardon, if you didn't know already. Restored to full status with USF."

"Congrats to him. I only got back to Earth yesterday."

"Welcome home."

"And I hear you successfully rescued Ella Reese?"

"Yes." Kelli nodded for emphasis. "Hearing Ella call to her mother when they saw each other was..." Her voice caught with emotion. "I've never felt such a rush from anything I've done before. When Aric and Ella embraced, it...it was incredible."

For a moment, Eva had trouble breathing, like

something expanded her chest, stealing precious room from her lungs. "Reuniting the girl with her mother was vital."

The USF agent spoke slowly. "Best thing I ever did."

They both fell silent.

Eva spoke first. "Well, I need to run some errands."

"I appreciate your coming." Kelli pressed her lips together. "It means a lot."

She nodded. "You'd do the same for me."

But would she? Without a doubt, Eva knew this would not be the end of Kelli's story. The sense of an impending event, hovering on the horizon, hit her so hard she clenched her fists. Somehow Kelli's and her futures were inexplicably tied. How was yet to be revealed.

Eva grinned. "Don't tell anyone, but I heard Inter-G has taken up your cause."

"Really?"

"I just want to reassure you that we'll do everything we can to help you."

Tears welled in Kelli's eyes. "Thanks. Appreciate it."

"Not only that, but someone leaked your story to the press. Already there's a hubbub about your incarceration."

"I hope that's a good thing."

Eva grinned. "The guy's pretty vocal. You have some faithful followers already."

"Who is it?"

"Some instructor in a local gym. Jorge?"

"Oh, him." Kelli rolled her eyes. "A personal trainer I used to work with."

Eva's handheld comm-unit beeped. After glancing at the incoming message, she rose. "I've got to go." She nodded farewell. "Keep the faith."

Why had she said that? Eva didn't believe in faith. No matter how much she once believed, God hadn't answered. Her mother hadn't returned.

Finally, Eva had stopped pleading.

After she stepped into the bright sunshine, she called her

team leader. "What's up? I thought I had the day off."

"Change of plans." His voice grew terse. "Get here ASAP."

Chapter 8

"What's going on?" Out of breath, Eva met her sup on the conference floor level of Intergalaxia's headquarters. She pressed her hair into place. Her "go bag" had little more than cosmetics since she'd not had time to repack it. Though she wore business casual, she regretted not having her uniform ready.

Her supervisor grabbed her arm to hustle her down the echoing corridor. "The Xerxian Ambassador arrived with her retinue. The director asked for you personally."

When her leg twinged, Eva hissed inwardly. "For what reason?"

He released her. "She's threatening to call a general conference session."

"Now? The summit's a couple weeks away. She can't wait?"

"Are you kidding? She isn't exactly the waiting type."

"Okay." Eva tried to absorb the implications. Her head still spun from all the details with which she'd been bombarded since her arrival back home.

"This is her second visit, by the way. You missed her first a few days ago. While you were still traveling from the Xerxian outpost."

"And what was the outcome of that meeting?"

"She was really on her high horse. Demanded that Earth quit 'corrupting her world.' Or something. Even threatened to expel every non-Xerxian from the planet, including their capital city. Immediately."

Ignoring the shooting pain in her leg, Eva increased her pace. "That sounds serious."

Her supervisor pushed ahead. "At first we believed she was just freaking out about one of their missing operatives. Since he was found, we thought she'd cool off. But apparently not."

"So why does the director want me?"

"Because you're fluent in Xer. And you're female." He threw a look over his shoulder. "Besides, did you know you're the only one who didn't mess up the Xerxes mission?"

"What?" This was news. She stopped. "What happened?"

Smirking, he retraced his steps. "One team nearly caused an intergalactic incident at one of the remote villages. Apparently *he* allegedly assaulted a Xerxian female. That was bad enough, but then *she* blabbed to save their skins. The High Council had been explicit when they agreed to let Intergalaxia pursue the fugitives. We were to maintain a low profile, remember? The director had to scramble to soothe more than one ruffled feather."

Not good.

One thing the Xerxians hated was to have their peaceful lives disturbed. They had made a huge concession in allowing Inter-G agents to disguise themselves as Xerxian. That didn't include running roughshod over their planet and offending their people.

"They both got reassigned offworld." His chin puckered. "Let's just say he's uncomfortably hot where he is and she is excessively damp."

A number of locations popped into Eva's head. None of them pleasant. She was still dwelling on that when her sup glanced around, then stepped closer.

"If you ask me, I think something was going on between those two." He spoke under his breath. "Rumor has it they had a thing for each other. Of course, where they are, all they have now are memories. But you didn't hear any of this from me."

Based on Eva's own observations, it made sense. "Relationships between colleagues are always a bad idea."

"Especially if it involves the director." One of his eyebrows rose.

She spread her hands. "What's he got to do with this?"

"Seems he's wanted a relationship for himself. A long time." When Eva didn't reply, he added, "I've always wondered why he favored you."

She glared at him. This was not the first time he'd made a remark about Director Rosborough and herself. "Then I'd better not keep him waiting any longer." She moved away, walking stiffly down the corridor toward the conference room. Whatever her sup had implied, the director was not interested in her. Not in that way.

She found the room. An aide leaped up from his seat, knocked on the door and announced her arrival.

The group waited in a medium-sized chamber, not too small, not too large. Eva admired anew the director's understanding of the different races he dealt with. Too small of a room and the Xerxians would be put off by the forced intimacy. Too large and they would become more demanding as they associated the space with their importance.

As Eva stepped in, pain shot up her leg. She winced. In her rush down the corridor, she had pushed it too hard.

"Ms. Hilliard." The director came toward her and held out his hand to direct her to a seat. "Madame Ambassador, this is the special agent I was telling you about."

The imposing woman did not rise to welcome her.

After stationing herself beside her chair, Eva made certain to meet the gaze of each Xerxian. "I bid you greetings." Speaking in Xer, she used an old but formal salutation. She addressed the three aides as well. All were female.

Eva fixed her gaze on the seated woman. Dyn'Perzsi Aeliana had accepted the ambassadress title seven years before. Not only did she belong to one of the leading clans, but she was one of Xerxes IX's most powerful women.

Following protocol, Eva bowed. "You honor us with your presence."

"You honor us as well." She too spoke in Xer, inclining her head a little. Then she continued in English. "Thank you for accommodating us."

Eva bowed again, choosing the common Earth gesture, not the more formal Xerxian with the three fingers to the chest. Given Aeliana's mental state, she might see it as an insult.

"You may sit in our presence," the ambassadress said.

Eva schooled her expression to remain impassive, aware that the woman overstepped her rank. Only the First Chancellor of Xerxes IX had the right to keep someone standing in her presence.

This meeting promised to be interesting.

After sliding onto a chair, she noticed the director

waited until all the women sat before he did. The ambassadress would have been affronted otherwise.

Eva waited until everyone settled. "How may we be of assistance to you today?"

"We demand the human known as Kelli-Layne." Aeliana did not waste time stating her objective.

The director cleared his throat. "As I've stated before, Madame Ambassador, Ms. Layne is being detained. Once we have finished—"

"How long must you continue to interrogate her?"

"She is to be questioned before a formal tribunal."

The woman's mouth flattened. "And when will she stand trial on Xerxes IX for the crimes she committed there?"

Eva folded her hands on the table, drawing attention back to herself. "And what crimes would those be, Madame?"

The ambassadress turned dark eyes to her. Without a word, she held out her hand. One of her aides placed a parchment in her palm. "They are outlined here." She slid it across the conference table.

After shooting a glance at the director, she pulled the sheaf closer. To verbally ask his permission would offend the matriarchal Xerxians. He nodded ever so slightly. Glancing through the list written in Xer, Eva noted that Kelli's primary crime was disguising herself as Xerxian. Other offenses were the desecration of several temples, the improper use of sacred symbols, and a false accusation against a man whom she claimed violated her.

Was this the incident that involved Eva's colleague? Now was not the time to ask, nor was it pertinent to this meeting.

The list, of course, didn't include the things Special Agent Layne had done right. No mention was made of her successful rescue of Ella Reese. Layne had not harmed any Xerxians during the girl's liberation from the kidnappers. She had not involved any of the indigenous population in any of these alleged crimes.

Kelli Layne didn't kill me.

Not only that, she saved Eva's life when she planned to take Kelli's.

She pushed those thoughts away. Her personal life would mean nothing to the ambassadress. Even less in light of the woman's growing prejudice against Terrans.

Debating how to ask, Eva licked her lower lip. "Should Special Agent Layne be found guilty in your court, may we ask what the usual punishment is for such crimes on Xerxes IX?"

"These are not usual crimes. Therefore, the punishment will not be usual either."

Fearing what that meant, she sucked in a slow breath. No use debating the point now. Without first seeking Director Rosborough's approval, she stood. "We will have to take these serious matters under consideration. I realize that Xerxes IX is beautiful in its simplicity regarding legal matters, but Special Agent Layne has broken the laws of Earth as well. It will take time to process her crimes here before we surrender her to you. We recognize and appreciate your patience in this matter."

The ambassadress shot to her feet. Her mouth hardened. "I will expect Kelli-Layne to be handed over to us no later than at the end of the summit."

"That should be sufficient time for our formal tribunal. Again, we are supremely grateful for your understanding." Eva bowed and remained in that position while the Xerxians took their leave and exited the room.

Once they'd gone, she blew out her breath. The aide who'd shown her in immediately stuck his head into the room. "Sir?"

The director looked at her. "Coffee, Eva?"

"That'd be great. Black is fine." She again took her seat. Apparently the meeting wasn't over.

"Two cups," he said to the young man who disappeared

behind the shutting door. Tension melting from his shoulders, he turned to her. Rosborough leaned against the shiny conference table a couple feet from her. "Good to see you, Eva. I was relieved to hear you were well."

"Thank you, sir."

"Call me Jordan. Please. At least, behind closed doors. I tire of formality."

She managed a small smile and nod. This was not the first time he'd asked. Her team leader's insinuation flashed through her mind. She was aware that Rosborough was close. Too close. While seated in her chair, she could think of no graceful way to back away from him.

Her gaze flickered from his wavy salt-and-pepper hair to his manicured fingernails. The director took care of himself and it showed. His lean body and graceful form belied his age of forty-three.

"I read your report last night, Eva. Surprised you sent it so soon."

"I thought it important to record details while they were fresh in my mind." She studied the room's wood grain walls, reflected on the table's smooth surface.

"How's the leg?"

"Improving."

"You still limp. Why not visit my physical therapist? She's great."

"Because of the delay in getting medical attention, I've been advised that nothing may help at this point. Unless I want a doctor to re-break my leg." Eva had consulted a specialist via tele-comm on the space station, sending him scans of her leg. When he concurred with her suspicions, she decided to refuse any further treatment. Two opinions, hers and the doctor's, were all she needed. "There's no guarantee it'd heal correctly afterwards."

"That's a shame." Rosborough's tone revealed nothing but sincerity as he rested his elbow on his thigh. The action created even more intimacy. "I'd hate to lose an excellent field agent. Although I wouldn't mind your being out of harm's way."

Warning bells clanged in her head.

"Are you suggesting it's time for me to find another line of work?" That didn't sound right. "Like a grocery clerk? Maybe a tour guide?"

"No." He smiled. "How about a desk job? Here at Inter-G, of course."

"I guess I'll find out when my review comes up." She managed to keep her tone light.

The director straightened when coffee arrived. Releasing her breath, she concentrated on the delicious aroma from the cup the aide put before her. This was not the break-room stuff, but something exotic. Laotiacian?

After the aide again departed, Rosborough pointed to the parchment the ambassadress had left. "Explain this."

She scooted the sheaf toward him, even though he couldn't read it. "According to the Xerxians, Layne hasn't done one thing right while she was on their planet. These would be considered pretty inconsequential 'crimes' to us—"

"But not to them," he finished for her.

"I'm afraid not."

"Give me a run down."

"The biggest crime is her passing herself as Xerxian."

"Yet they allowed our agents to."

"Correct, but with their permission. They also didn't like Special Agent Layne using their symbols. For both her and Song."

"Which means what?"

"Notice the earring each Xerxian wore? Everyone in their society – that is, those with a good reputation – wears charms on their earring. Each charm bears specific symbols that reveal their marital status, standing in the community as well as other social clues."

"And Layne's part?"

"Apparently, she tricked someone into giving her an earring. Or perhaps she stole one. I caught a glimpse of it when I saw her." Eva glanced at the parchment again, but it gave no clue what crime she had committed with their symbols. "It doesn't say here, but her even having an earring offended the Xerxians."

"Hmm." Rosborough frowned. "What else?"

"They didn't like her visiting their temples. Xerxians are fanatic about safeguarding their religion. They are so protective that no one is allowed to catalog their beliefs."

"Even after almost twenty-seven years?"

"Correct. That's clearly delineated in our treaty with them. Our libraries and every other institution on Earth have next to no information. If we violate that..." She left the sentence unfinished.

Though Eva was versed in Xerxian beliefs, she'd never shared any information. Because it would feel like a betrayal?

After Rosborough sipped his coffee, he cradled the cup for a few moments. "Translate this into English. Add your own thoughts as to what they're not saying between the lines. I'm setting up a meeting with SARC to find out how to proceed."

"Yes, sir."

He was pulling in the Synecological and Astrobiological Research Center? Of course, SARC would have been the first to make contact with Xerxes IX. It made sense. However, Eva squirmed in her seat. Before her father had retired many years ago, he had worked with SARC.

The director continued. "I toyed with the idea of your overseeing that group, but you'll be more useful in another area."

Relieved that she wouldn't be assigned to the SARC team, she waited.

He tilted his head as he looked at her. "What do you think of Aric Reese joining that team?"

The mother of the kidnapped child? As a synecologist, her expertise on alien cultures would be invaluable. This whole mess had started because of her daughter.

But did the director really want to know Eva's opinion? He usually had his mind made up.

She spoke slowly. "I think Mrs. Reese would be a great asset. And the PR wouldn't hurt either."

The director nodded, apparently pleased by her answer. "I want you to be available to the ambassadress and party. Keep them happy. You have some rapport with them."

Eva nodded.

"Oh, another thing. A contingency of Xerxian delegates will attend the summit. You'll be the liaison between them and Inter-G. Keep an eye and ear on them. Report to me directly if you learn anything about the Layne case."

Apparently, he was serious about her not going out into the field again. What other changes did this imply?

The director rose and leaned a hand on the table. "You're capable, Eva. And it'll be a huge help. Although Layne bent rules, she successfully rescued Ella Reese. The press is hailing her as a hero."

"She deserves it." Eva spoke sincerely.

"What will they do if we turn her over to them?" Rosborough asked.

"The Xerxians?"

He nodded.

The desire to reassure him poised on her tongue. She couldn't downplay this situation. In her mind's eye, she saw events looming on the horizon. Moving closer. Eva hesitated to speculate, but couldn't forget the look on the ambassadress' face. Cold. Hard. Determined. "Taking into consideration their present state of mind..."

A premonition chilled her.

Rosborough's brow lowered. "Go on."

She met the director's gaze. "If they find Kelli guilty, they'll demand her execution."

Chapter 9

"I am glad you are well, my son."

In submission and love, Zahn knelt before his mother on one knee and took her hand to kiss it. His Birthing One deserved his deepest affection and respect. "I am sorry for the anxiety I caused you."

"It is forgotten."

"You got my message?"

"Yes, by courier bird. Thank you."

"I came as soon as I was freed from my other obligations to the High Council." He would tell her about them later.

"Please sit. Let me hear how you have fared since your

last visit." With the ceremonial tea dishes already prepared, she set about steeping the delicate leaves.

With a graceful wave of her hand, she indicated where he should sit. Not for the first time, Zahn found himself admiring her beauty—a loveliness that transcended years and sorrow. He was amazed that in God's goodness, He had chosen her to give him life. His mother moved with elegance, her face still youthful though it should be lined with the years of weighty obligations. Her faith sustained her. The small streak of silver in her hair lent her an air of authority, yet compassion.

He looked around the room, so comforting, so like her. Preferring a simple life, she kept her rooms sparse. Some would say austere, but Zahn saw it as orderly, like her. She remained focused on what was most important and did away with the extraneous frippery that enthralled so many. Her bound consort, Zahn's stepfather, had known what type of home and furnishings to prepare for her. Uncomplicated. Elegant.

How right her mate had been.

His mother's plain, cream-colored robe was one Zahn had crafted for her. He had taken care to weave in strands of blue and gold, her favorite colors. She wore the loose gown over an unembellished blue tunic and pants with plain slippers.

As she prepared the brew, he waited until she handed him a delicate demitasse. Together they lifted the teacup on fingertips, but in honor to her, he delayed tasting his drink until she took the first sip.

He cleared his throat. "I wrote my report about the two Terrans and submitted it to the High Council as they requested. So my obligations for this evening are finished."

"That is good to know." She touched his arm, always supportive of his responsibilities.

"But that is not the only reason I asked to see you tonight."

"I wondered." Serenity filled the smile she cast his way. "You seem different."

He ducked his head to consider his tea. "I could never hide anything from you."

"A mother's extra sense."

He smiled. "First though, I wanted to talk to you about this Kelli-Layne."

His mother set down her drink. "I've heard reports about her."

"I sense a growing hostility toward her among our people. Can you explain?"

"Dyn'Perzsi Aeliana is very verbal about this woman's crimes against Xerxes. She has been stirring up passions that are antihuman. Anti-Terran."

"To what end?"

"I believe she intends to launch Xerxes into a period of greater isolation. From all alien races, but most particularly those of Earth."

Zahn bowed his head in thought. "And how do you feel about this, *Emaa?*"

"I reserve judgment."

"Yes, but how do you *feel?*"

She glanced away, sighing deeply. "I cannot deny that ill feelings have been stirred up because of this Kelli-Layne incident. However, my personal views cannot color what is best for our world."

"Kelli-Layne has broken our laws. It's true. However, based on the reports I have read, she is not the criminal she has been made out to be."

His mother nodded.

"There is something more you must know. Something I didn't include in my report. Not until I spoke to you."

"Oh?" Her head tilted to one side.

"She is a true worshipper."

Her face betrayed surprise. "You are certain?"

He hesitated to speak, still captivated by the vision of

Kelli-Layne as she called out to God. "I saw her. Heard her worship. She pleaded for the life of her comrade and our Lord answered." Zahn paused a moment, reliving the beauty of the scene. "It does not excuse her crime of impersonating a Xerxian. However, it changes the tone of the other accusations against her, specifically the desecration of our temples. I believe, without doubt, she was offering true worship." He paused. "That is no crime."

Brow pinched, she pondered his words.

Zahn acquiesced to the silence, knowing she would speak when ready.

Her gaze finally met his. "Would you be open to a suggestion, my son?"

"Yes. Anything."

"The Terran Summit is in a few weeks. Would you be willing to be part of the contingency attached to the ambassadress? It may require that you be on Earth for two or more standard months."

He could not hide his smile. *You are putting everything into place, my God.* Zahn's mother was His unwitting tool to accomplish His will.

"I see it does not displease you, my son."

"On the contrary, I would be happy to be at the disposal of the High Council."

"I will put forth your name and ask that you be included. However, Aeliana will make the final decision."

"Of course."

"If she agrees, I adjure you to use your own judgment when it comes to influencing her and her party."

"I am pleased to do your bidding." He fell silent, waiting for the moment to talk of other, more personal matters.

His mother finished her tea. "What else did you wish to speak of this evening?"

Briefly, Zahn squeezed shut his eyes, both excited and fearful of what he would share. "I have found my life-mate."

Face alight with joy, she sucked in a slow breath. "Oh, my son, I have long desired—"

"She may not be what you have wished for." He dared to interrupt, but knew the importance of quickly correcting misconceptions.

Her expression tightened as her dark gaze searched his face. "What do you mean?"

"She is human."

Recoiling, she bumped the table. The delicate glassware clattered before settling. Shock rippled across her features as she backed away from him.

If he had not been so certain that God had directed him, Zahn would have quaked to disappoint her. He read fear—even revulsion—in her features.

Kneeling before her, he spoke in a low voice. "Please listen as I tell you the tale, *Emaa*. I beg you to lay aside your prejudices."

Out of deference, he kept his face lowered. He sensed her emotions in the deep breaths she took, the hesitancy to speak, the rigidness of her body, her clenched fist. It was imperative that he wait. He must have her permission before he could proceed.

"Speak." The word came out in a strangled tone.

"This woman was injured and asked for my help. She implored me, using our sacred Xerxian imperative. I vowed to do all I could for her. While under this inviolable obligation, I gave her all my food. I went without for many days until I could restock my supplies." He sought to downplay the implications, not wishing to brag, but to set the stage for the facts. "During that time of fasting and prayer, our God spoke to me." He paused, again overcome by the truth.

"I know you have ever desired a life-partner, as well as children. And that you put aside those longings, certain God had redirected your life."

"True. But believe me, this particular day that thought

had not entered my mind as I made my devotions." He paused, giving his mother time to absorb his vehement statement. While he lingered, he shifted his weight on his knees. "I know—without a doubt—the Lord God directed me to ask her to be my bride."

"And did you?"

"Yes. I laid before her all that was in my heart."

His mother was silent for many moments. "What was her reply?"

Zahn hesitated to share, Eva's response too sacred to voice. With care, he spoke. "She gave me a holy sign—without knowing she did. I am convinced I did right by asking." The truth compelled him to add, "You must know that she has not yet agreed, however she did not refuse." He grew quiet, waiting with bated breath. His mother had the authority to break the vow he'd made to Eva.

Sensing the struggle in her soul, he remained kneeling, head bowed. She took a long time responding. He could not blame her, yet she of all people must understand how this woman would perfectly suit him.

Her answer finally came with a soft hand laid upon his head. "God's blessing on you, my beloved child. Godspeed as you pursue your mate."

"So, Sean, what do you think about this request?" As Aric Reese spoke to her husband, she leaned against the doorjamb. The one-inch by one-inch communications chip rested in her palm. She tapped it to emphasize the urgency. For two days her husband had avoided discussing the contents of the message. "I really need to answer. And soon. I can't keep ignoring it."

Now desperate, she had resorted to trapping him in their bathroom while he shaved. Since he wore his work pants already, she had at least ten minutes to verbally harangue him before he slipped on a dress shirt and ran off to work. Then she'd have to come up with a new way to entrap him.

Blade hovering over his foamy face, he paused to look at her. Funny how he'd maintained the primitive ritual, still using shaving cream and a razor. It was a holdover from their days on the planet Empusa III where they had lived without modern conveniences. And, as usual, Aric loved watching him.

"Like I've already said, it is totally up to you." He went back to his morning routine.

She gazed at him, unintentionally lifting her chin as he moved the blade carefully up his neck. Whenever she watched him shave, she ended up mimicking his facial expressions. "No, it's not up to me. It's up to *us*. And I'm still waiting for your input."

He rinsed the razor under hot water. "It could be a great opportunity for you to step back into the science community, since we live so far from SARC headquarters."

"Yes, yes I know all that." Aric dismissed the facts with a wave of her hand. "I want to know how you *feel* about it."

He shrugged. "No feelings one way or the other."

She thumped the doorframe with her palm. "I know you do. You're just not telling me."

Ducking his head, her husband was unsuccessful at hiding his grin as he set down his razor and wiped his face with a towel. He surprised her by grabbing her about the waist. "The only feelings I have are for you."

Was he trying to distract her? Again? She squirmed in his hold.

"Oh, I wouldn't do that if I were you." A mischievous glint lit his eyes. "Gives me ideas."

"Yeah, well, *ideas* will make you late for work."

"I'll call in sick."

"*Right.* That'd happen maybe in a million years."

A mock serious expression flitted across his face. "Then I've gotten too predictable. This might be the day I change all that." He nibbled her neck.

"Sean!" Shrieking, Aric braced her hands against his bare chest to escape. He was much too strong. Using his eight-inch advantage in height, he lifted her so he could get at her neck more easily.

Giggling, she suddenly became aware of a small figure standing quietly at the bedroom's doorway. She stiffened.

Mouth gaping, their eight-year-old observed them.

"Hi, Ella." Sean didn't seem fazed by their watcher. He let Aric slip from his grasp.

Ella's brown eyes were huge. "Were you biting Mama?"

"Nope. Tickling her. Like this." When Sean grabbed their daughter and nuzzled her neck, she squealed.

Heart swelling, Aric smiled. It was good to see her little girl relax around her stepfather again, even allowing him to tease and play with her. For many weeks, Aric had been afraid the trauma of the kidnapping might make Ella fearful of men, especially Sean.

What a wonderful father he had become.

"I think you like it too." Sean lifted his adopted daughter, holding her high in his arms. "Want me to do it some more?"

"No!" Grinning, Ella covered her neck with both hands, shoulders scrunched to further protect herself.

"Okay, I was just checking." He swayed a little as he held her. "Are you ready for school?"

Eyes fastened on him in love, she nodded.

"Then how about I drive you?" He cast a sidelong glance at Aric. "Since I'm already going to be late for work."

"Okay."

"I'll let Frick and Frack know." Aric used the code names for Ella's bodyguards. Since the kidnapping, Universal Security Forces insisted their daughter have a pair. For now anyway. After making the call from another room,

Aric returned to the bedroom.

Legs dangling, Ella sat on the bed as she watched Sean slip on shoes. Aric sucked in a breath, marveling at how handsome her husband looked in his business ensemble. But then again, he looked great no matter what he wore. Or didn't.

"You think it's a good idea?" He brushed lint off his pants.

"Yep." Eyes bright, their daughter nodded.

"What's this all about?" Aric planted fists on her hips, looking between them.

"Daddy says I'm going to have a baby brother or sister."

Her cheeks burned. "Oh he did, did he?"

"But he says we have to wait a long time." Ella appeared crestfallen.

"That's so your mom can get ready." Sean rose, smoothing down his tie.

Aric frowned at him. "Well, we're going to have to talk about it first."

"Please?" Ella jumped off the bed and tugged her hand. "Please, Mama, *please?*"

She looked at her daughter, then her husband, at a loss how to answer. *It's too soon.* She and Sean been married for a little over seven months. They needed more time together first. She wanted to learn how to be Ella's mother again. While Aric had been offworld, she'd missed out on years of her daughter's life.

Her husband intervened. "Ella, why don't you grab your school things? I'll be right down."

"Okay." Their daughter reluctantly released Aric's hand before heading out of the room.

She turned to him. "That was...a surprise."

"A good one, I hope." He tilted his head down so he could study her face. "How do you feel about having another child?"

Crossing her arms, she glared at him. "Oh? You're

allowed to ask me how *I* feel, but not tell me how *you* feel?"

He pulled her close. "I thought it might put me in the mood to talk about emotions."

Stiffening, she turned her head away.

"C'mon. Don't be upset with me." He caressed her back. "Tell me again what that message says? I promise I'll listen."

She relented. A little. "Inter-G invited me to head up a team."

"Um-hmm." Sean ran his hands across her shoulders.

"To address the 'Xerxian problem' as they put it. I've been asked since synecology is my area of expertise. They are pulling others from SARC and anyone else that has experience with Xerxes IX."

"Sounds good to me." He began nuzzling her temple.

"Are you paying attention?"

Pulling back, his eyebrows rose. "Of course. Why would you think I'm not?"

"Because you're getting distracted again." She shook her head. "And you're not very attentive."

"I am to the things I want to be." He kissed the spot near her ear that always made her melt.

She sighed. "So...? Should I agree to Intergalaxia's request?"

"If I say yes, will you say yes to Ella's and my idea?" His voice sounded low. Husky.

She wanted to fuss. Wanted to tell her husband she needed more time to think. Wanted to tell him he was a low-down, sneaking man. But while she was in his arms, *thinking* had pretty much fled. Especially while he continued to nestle his lips against her ear. And he knew it. As usual.

Okay, fight fire with fire.

Aric wrapped her arms about his neck. "Tell you what. You take Ella to school, then come home so we can *talk* about it some more."

Sean's grin nearly split his face. "It's a deal, Mrs. Reese."

Chapter 10

Eva stifled her yawn. It was well past seven and the meeting's end was nowhere in sight. She, along with the other liaisons and assorted Inter-G personnel, were being prepped with the proper protocols when it came to dealing with the delegates for the upcoming summit. She'd been through the training before and really didn't need to be instructed about the correct way to address the Xerxians or to bow. However, since she was part of Intergalaxia, she had to at least feign interest in the orientation. She just didn't like being treated as if she didn't know anything.

Her electronic packet included photos and vitals on all

the members of the Xerxes IX contingent. Because Xerxians didn't use names, all of them had Terran designations—Ambassador, First Aide to the Ambassador, Third Official to the First Aide. The assignments could be a little confusing. To others, perhaps, but not to her. Several people on the team had lamented that they would have preferred names, but the tutors had repeatedly instructed everyone that those were reserved only for friends and family members. Even if a liaison knew the name, it would be considered a breach of protocol to call them that until given permission.

Eva scrolled through the faces, recognizing many of them. A couple slots on the Ambassador's team had not yet been filled. And Eva herself did not yet have an assigned aide to help with the delegates. That meant she would be relying more heavily on her personal assistant who was swamped as well. This wasn't the first time she felt Inter-G could have been a little better prepared.

Across the room, she noticed an assistant speaking to the director. His gaze met Eva's, then he rose and followed the woman out of the room. Eva again focused on the instructor, wondering when the next break would be. Or if they would soon be dismissed. Her stomach grumbled.

"Ms. Hilliard?" An aide stood at her elbow.

For a moment, the absence of her "Special Agent" designation threw her. Then she recalled she's been reassigned as a liaison. Her title, sub-dermal chip and uniform had been shelved for now.

The assistant continued. "The director asked that you meet him immediately. Bring your things, please."

What was this all about? After Eva gathered her information packet and personal belongings, she followed the woman to another conference room.

"You can leave those with me." The aide indicated Eva should set them at the station outside the room.

More and more strange.

Without further instruction, the woman knocked and

opened the door for Eva.

"Ah, here she is." The director stood.

A Xerxian male had his back to her, but turned as she entered.

Eva gasped as she heard the director say, "This is the liaison I was telling you about, Your Excellency, Ms. —"

"Pardon the interruption, but I am already acquainted with Eva Hilliard." Speaking in English, Zahn bowed before her.

In the seconds it took her to recover, she felt the director's gaze pierce her. Snapping her jaw shut, she bowed. Without thinking, she spoke in Xerxian. "I am honored."

Why was he there? To pursue the marriage proposal? At Inter-G?

Thoughts in an uproar, she remained bowing.

"Eva Hilliard may not be familiar with my complete designation." His soothing tone sent a shiver through her. She noticed that he didn't run her names together as most Xerxians did. Why not?

Director Rosborough explained. "Eva, this is his Excellency, First to the High Council. He is one of the last-minute delegates assigned to the Ambassadress. As liaison, you will work primarily with him."

When she straightened, she could not maintain eye contact with Zahn. Time and again, her gaze sidled away from his as she focused on his colorful robe and clasped hands. He wore the same earring as before, now loaded with charms. The symbols indicated status and power. She also suddenly realized that he was tall for a Xerxian male. Unusually so. While she had been on Xerxes, she had not noticed.

How well I remember his voice. His strong arms. His touch.

Rosborough continued. "His Excellency arrived only this morning. He came to pay his respects."

"Although I am not yet adjusted to Terran time," Zahn

added. "Please forgive my late entry and interruption of your meeting."

Glancing between the two men, Eva fought being tongue-tied. A deep gash forming between his eyebrows, Director Rosborough looked slightly irritated whereas Zahn's face retained a serene calm. As usual.

"However, I felt it important to pay my respects." The Xerxian folded his hands into his colorful robe. "Also, I wish to inform you that all the delegates have been assigned from my planet."

"And we at Intergalaxia appreciate that." The director sounded like he had difficulty maintaining his pleasant tone.

"For now, I will bid you a good evening." Zahn bowed and headed for the door, but turned before opening it. "I am, of course, staying at the embassy. Perhaps we can renew our acquaintance tomorrow, Eva Hilliard?"

"Yes. Absolutely." She rasped out the words. "I am at your disposal."

Zahn bowed again, then departed.

The door barely closed before the director said, "You didn't tell me you knew him."

"I...." Eva fought to sort the implications. Fought to not defend herself. She gulped and found her voice. "I had no idea who he was when I met him."

"Xerxians preferred designations. How could you *not* know?"

Slumping into the nearest chair, she passed a hand over her forehead. "It's...it's complicated." Then her hand dropped. "Are you suggesting I deliberately withheld that information?"

Rosborough moved closer. "I'm still deciding that. I don't like being blindsided."

"I don't either." She raced through her memories, trying to recall exactly why Zahn had given his name instead of his designation. Then she remembered. It was buried under a haze of pain meds.

"I'm waiting for your explanation."

She bristled at Rosborough's bullying tone. "He...I...you read my report, sir. He was the one who found me alongside the road. He gave me some herbal pain meds. And somehow he ended up telling me only his first name." She stared into the memory, trying to piece it together. "I think because I gave him only my first." Yet at the space station, he'd used her first and last.

He knew. All along, he had known who she was. He was First to the High Council? Had they sent him?

"Okay." Frown deepening, the director spread his hands. Because he waited for a further explanation?

"I thought he was a farmer. Or a peasant. He dressed like one. And I met him out in the middle of the plains, not in Xer Prime."

Rosborough's mouth tightened. His irritation had abated not the slightest.

She flung out a defensive hand. "So he's attached to the High Council? What's the big deal?" She still didn't understand the director's vexation. "Aren't there eighty members on the council? And he's male, so his standing isn't as influential as a female's would be."

Rosborough tilted his head to one side. Studying her. "You really don't know." He didn't ask, but rather stated his conclusion. "Don't you recognize him?"

"Not really." Eva shoved her back against the chair. "After his stepfather, El-Abiri Zahn is the second most powerful man on Xerxes IX. He is the only child of the First Chancellor, the current *ruler* of that planet."

Chapter 11

She would never again be able to look Zahn in the eye.

As Eva prepared for the day, she stared at herself in the bathroom mirror. Bright blotches marred her cheeks. Lack of sleep had smudged shadows under her eyes. Cosmetics couldn't hide her agitation as she thought of meeting him in just over an hour.

What must he think of me?

"How can I face him? What will we talk about?" Stomach clenching, she ran a hand across her feverish forehead.

What arrogance to have thought him a laborer. A

nobody. She couldn't have been more wrong.

After the meeting with the director, Eva had gone through every file she could find, searching for information about Zahn. In her defense, she found no mention of his name, as per Xerxian tradition, only his title—His Excellency, First to the High Council. Inter-G had very few images of him. Those she found had been taken at a distance, the quality poor. As though he'd deliberately avoided the limelight.

She had a good excuse for not recognizing him.

According to his bio, he was approximately thirty standard years of age. Never married. The only child of the First Chancellor, adopted stepson to her life-bound consort. Biological father not named. Zahn's education and accomplishments were quite impressive. He was a gifted artisan. A weaver by choice, he also had a strong talent for carving. El-Abiri Zahn was beloved of the people, an ardent servant of Xerxes IX.

It all made sense now. His serenity. The inborn mastery with which he handled power. The greetings strangers gave him. His ease of arranging transport from Xerxes to the outpost.

What would they discuss? Would he bring up his proposal again?

Eva spoke to her reflection as she smoothed her hair into a tight bun. "I'll talk about the summit. What he can expect in the upcoming weeks." She yanked down the collar of her suit. "If he brings up Xerxes, I'll change the topic."

He proposed to me.

She gripped the edges of the porcelain sink, memories battering her.

"Allow me the privilege of becoming your husband."

Never would she forget the look on his face while he uttered the words, nor the clasp of his hand. And what about her own response? She had been about to give him a polite "Thank you for your interest but…" when an explosion of emotion had erupted from her. Uncontrollable sobbing had consumed her for countless minutes. Like an earthquake exposing a long-buried crypt, his proposal had decimated the layers under which she hid.

"I settled this. Years ago." She spoke with brutal harshness. "I can't marry. I can't be involved in a relationship. End of story."

In the past, her speech had worked to center her heart. Why not now?

Because Zahn had gotten closer than any other man. A need to laugh gripped her. *And I thought he was love-smitten because he'd never before seen a Terran.*

When her doorbell chimed, she jumped. The limo? According to the plan, she was to pick Zahn up at the embassy. From there they would head to Inter-G headquarters where she would acquaint him with the protocols for the summit.

She blew out a breath. And another.

Focus on work. Forget what had happened on Xerxes IX.

Eva forced calm through her frazzled nerves. If she stuck to the plan, she would make it through the next several weeks. Review their itinerary. Remain professional. Detached. Maintain a cool demeanor.

In moments, she had regained her composure. She grabbed her things. As she climbed into the limo, she felt in possession of herself.

More or less.

For some reason, Intergalaxia had sent a ground vehicle. Because they wanted to show off New Washington? Or had Zahn specifically requested this? Not all delegates liked to travel by aero-car.

After the limo passed through the huge gates and pulled up to the embassy's doors, a female acolyte stepped closer to speak to the driver. He surprised Eva by exiting the limo and opening her door.

"First to the High Council requests that you join him for

a light repast before going to headquarters." The driver held out his hand to help Eva exit. "I have a tight schedule this morning with other appointments, but will return when you signal you are finished here."

With awkwardness, Eva climbed out. The acolyte, a friendly looking Xer, bowed and motioned for Eva to follow.

How could she refuse? This was not her show. Eva was only the liaison. Her job was to keep the ambassadress and party happy, doing whatever they wished.

Gulping, she followed the tall woman into the imposing embassy. The architecture reflected what the Xerxians preferred—adobe-like interiors, colorful cloths draped over walls, the accents of simple, natural wood. She lost count of the doorways and halls through which she traveled until finally they exited into a small, secluded park.

"Please wait there for His Excellency." After pointing to a large gazebo, the aide bowed and departed.

A cobblestone path wended its way through lush grass. As Eva drew closer, she could see a man waiting. Zahn? With a pounding heart, she walked toward him. He was dressed in a cream-colored tunic and pants with no outer robe. Much more casual than his formal and colorful attire of the night before. Feet bare, he stood with his chin lifted, as though enjoying the cool morning air. Or was he listening to the persistent chirp of a robin? His single earring, loaded with charms that announced his high Xerxian standing and multiple honors, flashed in the sunlight.

She felt overdressed in her taupe body suit with teal accents—necessary attire for Inter-G liaisons since a uniform would be unacceptable. Her jewelry, though simple, was over the top. She had chosen a heavy platinum choker and earrings.

So why did she feel plain? Drab? Like Earth's gray moon when compared to the colorful brilliance of Xerxes's three orbiting satellites.

Compared to him, who was she?

Turning as she approached, he smiled in genuine pleasure. "I bid you welcome, Eva Hilliard." Though he spoke in Xer, he again didn't run her names together like others of his world.

"Please, just Eva." She sounded as though she couldn't catch her breath as she blurted out the first maladroit phrase that came to her head.

He bowed, indicating she should take her place at the small table. Exquisite porcelain dishes of a bygone era waited for an intimate breakfast. Following Xerxian custom, he did not hold her chair. However in deference to her, he poured her a cup of tea after she slid onto the seat. He filled his own cup.

All the while, Eva's tongue remained locked. So much for professional detachment. But was it the man or she herself who was the source of consternation?

After sitting, Zahn held up his cup and waited. Fingers trembling, she lifted hers, striving to keep from spilling the contents. The beauty and simplicity of the ceremony, on fingertips of both hands, struck her. It had been a long time since she'd participated in such a ritual.

He raised his face. "Thank You for Your provision, O God of the heavens. We give You the honor and glory."

"For all things come from You." Eva slammed shut her eyes, aghast that she'd voiced the remainder of the prayer. Though it was custom, she'd spoken out of habit.

I haven't forgotten. Even though once upon a time she had vowed to never again recite the words.

She kept her eyes closed a moment longer, berating herself for not taking more care. When she opened them, she saw that Zahn studied her. A small smile curved in one corner of his mouth. His lips looked soft. Inviting.

Reining in her imagination, she sipped her tea. What was wrong with her? When she was with him, she too easily forgot she was a trained operative for Intergalaxia. An agent who never had trouble keeping everyone at a distance.

Except Zahn.

How did he so successfully remind her she was flesh and blood?

"You appear as though you didn't sleep well last night." He served her fresh fruit and a delicate croissant. "I am sorry I disturbed your calm."

How did he know?

"Why didn't you tell me who you were?" The question bolted from her before she could contain the words.

His smile broadened as he overlooked her rudeness. "I did tell you."

"Only your name. Your first name." But even as she said it, she knew that he'd bypassed convention the first day they'd met. And every day since. He'd allowed her the most intimate standing. Unheard of between strangers, even more so for Xerxians and Terrans.

Scandalous for a man with a woman.

"True." He tasted his drink. "You knew that providing given names is contrary to my society."

"Yes, but since you did, you should have told me your full name."

"You gave me only your first. I responded in kind."

"But it wasn't the whole truth."

He pressed his hands to the table's surface as though to calm her rising tension. "Because of your injury, and other reasons, you would not have been able to accept more."

"So my injury was not the *only* reason you withheld your designation." If her tone contained a hint of accusation, she didn't care. Anger might be her only ally to insulate her from his charm.

Zahn did not reply. Did not offer an explanation.

What had he seen in her those first few moments after meeting her along the road? What had he discerned in the days that followed? A dozen questions burned in her heart, yet she lacked the courage to ask even one.

A light breeze blew through the open gazebo, stirring

the scent of the flowers that climbed the lattice. The fragrance of the transplanted Xerxian blooms stirred memories—deep, long-forgotten images that breeched her calm. She fought the overwhelming urge to cry. Or fight. An urgent need to head to the gym buffeted her. There she could pound a holographic opponent senseless—and her turbulent emotions in the process.

How did he do this to her? When she was with Zahn, the years of carefully placed masks fell away. Her real self could no longer be hidden. Fear and relief enveloped her, warring with each other.

"You do not eat?" he asked.

"I'm not…" Sensing that he would know she lied about a lack of hunger, she broke off what she was going to say. She had bypassed breakfast because nerves had made her feel like she rode a freefalling anti-grav ride. Since her arrival at the embassy, trepidation had been replaced by something much more disturbing.

Almost defiantly, she nibbled the peach slices. They did taste good. And, yes, she was starving.

"I am glad to see you are well, Eva. However, your leg…"

"It is healed enough."

"But you still walk with a slight limp."

She shrugged. "It was time for me to give up fieldwork. My director has promised me a desk job. I think I'll be happier there."

His gaze bore into her. "Your director has a claim on you?"

"What?"

"I saw in his eyes that he wishes to share a relationship with you."

"No." She shook her head. "That's not true."

"Then you don't return his feelings?" Zahn pressed.

"Certainly not." Eva had never encouraged the director. Had never wanted to. Though he'd been widowed for almost two years, she had kept busy and stayed out of his way. Despite being seventeen years her senior, he maintained his excellent shape and health. However she had avoided his interest just as every other man's.

"I am pleased." Zahn poured himself another cup of tea.

She suddenly realized what her protests revealed. Would he think she was open to a relationship with him? Her cheeks grew hot as she picked at her croissant. Would he bring up his proposal of marriage again? What would she say? She would have to refuse him, of course.

The cultural hurdles were unfathomable. How could he, a Xerxian of preeminent standing, seek to bind himself to her? Did he comprehend the political ramifications? The High Council would protest. How would his mother, the First Chancellor, respond? Obviously she would be highly offended by such an alliance.

The list of difficulties grew exponentially.

"Be at peace, Eva." Zahn's quiet voice breached her agitation. "I adjure you to calm your mind. You have nothing to fear from me."

The tranquility of his voice enveloped her. Regardless of his reasons, he had not harassed her. He'd not embarrassed her in front of the director the night before. Zahn had not brought up his proposal again.

He would never pressure me.

But even as she reassured herself, she knew he would never rescind his vow. Ever present, his offer of marriage hung in the space between them.

"More?" He held a spoonful of peaches out to her.

"No. But thank you."

"I find this particular fruit delicious. It reminds me of two or three Xerxian varieties."

"I'm surprised you don't prefer produce from your homeworld." She indicated the transplanted flowers. "I thought the embassy had a greenhouse with fruiting plants."

"It is always pleasant to try something new."

"You will be bombarded by 'new' over the next several weeks." Eva thought of the countless receptions and banquets, not to mention the people of many worlds he would meet.

"With you by my side, I look forward to sharing them."

Her cheeks flamed at the double meaning of his words. "In my official capacity, I will help you navigate through the formalities."

"That pleases me."

She pushed aside her plate. As she waited for him to complete his meal, the quiet morning washed over her. A sham, of course. She seethed despite the implacable calm that cocooned her.

The hurry of the day could wait while she was with him. Everything that pressed her when she was alone evaporated when they were together. The muted roar of traffic sounded in the distance, but the sweet chirp of a robin overpowered the sound. The distant stench of technology faded before the delicate fragrance of nearby blooms. They reminded her of roses with a touch of gardenia.

Zahn appeared to enjoy every bite of the peaches, every sip of tea, every taste of the Terran-baked pastry. His dark eyes glittered when he observed her watching him. Again. However, he said nothing. And strangely, she felt no embarrassment getting caught.

Just like in the cabin. When he saw me staring. As though my perusal pleased him.

Now, just as then, she could not take her eyes off him. He was handsome, but it was more than that. Something of his soul called to her. What would it be like to feel that kind of peace? For years, turmoil had been her faithful companion. Since the mission to Xerxes IX, a new anxiety came alongside—the two flanking her night and day. What impending disaster hovered on the horizon, waiting to engulf the universe? And why could she neither identify the danger nor shake the feeling?

Zahn set his folded napkin on his dish. "That was wonderful. Did you not find it so?"

Was he talking about the meal or their quiet companionship?

"Yes. Of course. Thank you." She rose, anxious to concentrate on her job again.

"Before we depart, I have a gift for you." With an uplifted hand, he signaled someone.

A young Xerxian male approached, carrying a carved wooden box that was at least twelve by eighteen inches. After bowing, he handed it to Zahn and departed.

"I would be pleased if you accepted this." As he inclined his head, he raised the container. "I understand it is permitted to give the liaison an offering of thanks."

He was correct, of course. Still holding the box, he waited while Eva lifted the weighty lid. Inside, a beautiful woven robe nestled in the velvet-like gold lining. She fingered the soft fabric of royal purple interwoven with white and gold thread. Perfect for her coloring. Terrans coveted Xerxian textiles and paid a hefty sum for plain fabrics when they could acquire them. This gift appeared priceless.

"Did you weave this?" When he didn't answer right away, she looked up.

He bent his head in modest acquiescence. "I would be honored if you wore it to the official reception, the first night of the summit."

Again, a reasonable request. Zahn had done his homework. Even if she wanted to, she could not gracefully refuse. Eva gently lowered the lid. The carved wood box alone was of immeasurable value. Without circumspection, she ran her hands over the intricate scrollwork. Had he also carved the box?

"Thank you. I am honored. Indeed." She bowed.

His slow smile spoke volumes. Zahn set aside the box. "With your permission, I will see that my steward delivers it to your home. And now, if you will excuse me, I will take a moment to dress more appropriately for our day."

He left her to enjoy the awakening morning. Feeling as though her knees were about to buckle, she sank down into her chair. Her heart fluttered like the wings of the bird that landed on the grass nearby.

One of the most powerful men on Xerxes had asked her to marry him. He was second only to the bound consort of the First Chancellor. Eva was not immune to the raw power he exuded or of his natural charm. How could she have imagined for one moment he was a commoner? Yet, his quiet spirit had drawn her in. His unassuming demeanor. She had not missed how he treated everyone with deference. It had to be more than his upbringing as a Xer male in a female dominated society.

Then reality, painful and inescapable, reminded her of who—and what—she was.

I'm a fool. How stupid to entertain these ridiculous thoughts.

When he found out the truth about her, he would scorn and reject her. She needed to harden herself to his allure. It would be better for her. Better for him. In the future, his pain and disappointment would be greatly diminished.

With grim determination, Eva slammed shut the door of her heart. She locked it and mentally pressed her hand against the panel.

That door must remain sealed. Forever.

Chapter 12

"Is Dr. Marshall here yet?" Aric Reese peered through the open door of her Inter-G office.

At the desk outside her drab room, Aric's assistant tapped out a quick check on his virtual screen. His frown said all she wanted to know before he gave her a small shake of the head.

Sighing, she shut the door and resumed pacing.

Thomas Marshall *said* he would be there that morning, but still had not made an appearance.

After two no-shows earlier this week, Aric had dispensed with the team meetings and decided to connect with him one-on-one. Didn't he understand how vital this project was? No matter what his personal feelings were toward Intergalaxia or anyone else, he should at least keep his word. Or flat-out tell her "no" rather than leaving her in limbo.

Inter-G had given her a temporary office space at their headquarters while she worked on the Xerxes problem. Other associates had already presented themselves. As team leader, Aric had her work cut out for her. However, everyone in the group was professional, enthusiastic and eager to be of service. All of them promised to strive for a positive outcome.

Except Marshall. He had delayed his flight twice and refused to answer calls from her assistant. Until that morning. He had agreed to meet with her at Inter-G headquarters. Something had finally convinced him to come aboard. What could it be?

But if he didn't keep his promise, she might never find out.

She slumped in her chair. Despite the four gray walls in the basement of Inter-G, they'd equipped her with all the technology she might need, as well as a slew of experts in galactic law. But she needed Dr. Marshall. This task could fail without him. She rose to pace some more.

After another half hour of twiddling her thumbs, Aric jumped when her door chime sounded.

Her assistant popped in his head. "He's here."

Finally! She squelched any residual irritation and forced a smile as he entered, her assistant on his heels.

"Thomas Marshall. It's a great pleasure to meet you." Aric shook the hand of the renowned scientist. He was exactly how she'd imagined—wavy gray hair, prominent nose, and twinkling brown eyes. In many ways, he reminded her of her own father who had passed away a number of years before. This man was a little taller, though, and a bit stockier. For some reason, his mouth looked sad, as though he'd seen more sorrow than joy in his lifetime. His rough hand scraped against hers. Because of the hobbies he'd taken up during retirement?

"Aric Lindquist Reese." Though he smiled, the gesture appeared lukewarm. "I knew Dr. Lindquist, your father."

"I remember him speaking of you, sir." She paused and added, "With fondness."

"Can we dispense with these tiresome titles and formalities? Please, use my first name." He turned to her assistant. "And that would be T-h-o-m for your records, young man."

Her wise assistant said nothing as he took notes.

Aric waved to a chair and sat in one across from the scientist. If she had not been used to hobnobbing with the elite science world, she would have been intimidated by Thomas Marshall's multiple degrees. However, her father had taught her to be more impressed with character qualities. What would she learn about Thom in the next few weeks?

He wore a plain, open-necked shirt and jeans, a statement that he was comfortable with himself and didn't need to impress anyone.

Again, he glanced at her assistant, and back at Aric. "I can't say I'm thrilled to have been called out of retirement, but I am grateful that I can work with someone of your reputation."

"You are too kind." She thrust out her jaw, determined not to be sidetracked by charm. Her dear friend, Kelli, faced a dire future without this man's help.

Aric pointed to the carafe on the sideboard. "Coffee?"

"I'd love some."

Before she could nod to her assistant, the young man leaped up to pour the steaming brew into two cups. Thom's repeated glances indicated his discomfort having their conversation overheard. Best start out on a pleasant note.

"I won't need anything else this morning," she

dismissed the young man. "I'll call you if that changes."

"Yes, ma'am." The assistant left the room. One thing about Inter-G, they had an abundance of eager apprentices who would do anything to get in on the ground floor.

Visibly relaxing, Thom sipped his coffee and sighed in pleasure. "Good stuff." He took another taste. "I was given just a vague idea of what's going on, so I'm not terribly certain why I'm here."

"Intergalaxia's kind invitation." Aric smiled ruefully. "Same with me."

"You didn't specifically request my presence?"

"Correct. The team members were already chosen before I arrived."

"Interesting." Thom mulled over the information.

Was that good or not? Hard to tell. "Did you read the brief?"

He shook his head. "No. I didn't want to be biased before I arrived."

She studied the man before her, a legend in his time when it came to alien contacts. How much should she share? She decided to take the plunge and tell him everything. "If you don't mind, I'll fill you in."

"Let's hear it."

"Kelli Layne was an agent for USF—Universal Security Forces. About three months ago, she was assigned to protect a young girl on the Xerxian Outpost during a formal reception. Kelli was attacked and the girl taken. Because of jurisdiction squabbles and circumstantial evidence, Kelli was blamed for the kidnapping. While suspended from USF and acting independently from any agency, she got a lead on the kidnappers. She tracked them and the girl to Xerxes IX and rescued her."

"Hmm." Thom pursed his lips. "She stepped on toes, I take it?"

"More than that. To gain access to the planet's interior, she assumed a Xerxian disguise. Her masquerade was so successful that she infiltrated the deepest levels of their society. Specialists in intergalactic and Xerxian law are working on this, but our task is to understand the Xerxians. And find a way to diffuse tempers. Ultimately to free Kelli."

He shook his head. "I was merely one of their first human contacts. My expertise is in genetics and biology, not anthropology or—"

"But you *know* them. You know how they think. You were there in the beginning."

Brow wrinkled, he remained silent.

From what she'd read, Thom had developed alliances, even friendships with the heads of major clans. Even though he was male in a matriarchal society, he had smoothed the way for diplomatic situations, even helping draft the first treaty with Earth.

If he would commit to helping them in their current situation, they would gain a valuable ally.

And perhaps a chance to save Kelli.

Leaning forward, Aric pressed her hands on the desk. "Thom, we need to understand why this has become such a personal vendetta for some of the Xerxians. The child was human, the kidnappers human, but everything has gotten muddled since the crimes were committed not just on their homeworld but also disputed territory, that is, the space station orbiting their planet. The Xerxian ambassador wants Kelli Layne handed over to the Xer authorities by the end of the summit. Which—as you may or may not know—begins in less than ten days."

He lifted one hand. "Again, I'm puzzled why I'm here. What information or expertise can I provide that you don't already have?"

Aric took a deep breath. "What has changed in the twenty-six years since we signed the treaty? Why would this incident set them off?"

Nursing his coffee, Thom shook his head. "I haven't kept up with recent news. I thought Xerxes IX was our best, most loyal ally."

"Many thought so as well."

The scientist took another sip of his drink. "Who or what group is the instigator in this breech?"

"Hard to say. I've been monitoring several Xerxian clans but have been unable to pinpoint who started the movement. A couple team members have put forth names, but we're merely speculating." She tilted her head. As she had been speaking, his brow lowered and jaw jutted. "Do you suspect someone?"

He shrugged, face neutral. "Couldn't say."

"But you have an idea?" When he didn't answer, she added, "We are fairly certain the First Chancellor isn't on board with this. Yet. Although we surmise she is sympathetic."

His thumb rubbed the mug's handle as he spoke with forced nonchalance. "What is the name of the current ambassador?"

Aric searched through her notes on her comm-unit to make sure she had the name correct. "Dyn'Perzsi Aeliana. Are you familiar with her?"

She didn't need to ask. The answer was obvious in Thom's stiffening shoulders and pinched mouth.

He ducked his head to look into the depths of his black coffee. "I'm acquainted with her. But it's been—"

"What can you tell me about her?" Aric sensed he was hiding something.

He shrugged. "Not much. A hard woman. Determined. If she's decided to take this course, she will hang on like a *venrislith* with a bone."

Aric grinned at the archaic Zanzilar expression with the even more obscure reference to the extinct predator. For a moment, she studied him. "Why would she suddenly develop a dislike for humans? And why now after all these years?"

For a moment, the scientist wouldn't answer. "I...I don't

know." He sounded tired all of a sudden.

She let it slide. For now. There was more to the story. What it was, she determined to find out.

After finishing her coffee, she pushed away her cup. "As an interesting aside, I received a request for a meeting from one of the Xerxian delegates."

"For what purpose?"

"I am not certain." The elaborate, handwritten note had been signed *Personal Assistant to His Excellency, First to the High Council*. Still unfamiliar with the Xerxian designations and overwhelmed with time constraints, she'd not yet looked up who *First to the High Council* was. "We are to meet in a couple days. By then, I hope to be able to make some headway in this case."

Thom met and held her gaze. "Why are you so passionate for Ms. Layne's cause? What's in it for you?"

He was good. Despite his protestations, this man knew people.

Sitting back, she licked dry lips. "Kelli Layne is my friend."

His eyes narrowed. "And the little girl? The one who was kidnapped?"

"Ella's my daughter."

"Ah. I see." He fixed watery brown eyes on her, studying her. Making up his mind about something.

Aric leaned forward. "What about you? You could have turned down Inter-G's invitation. Why did *you* come?"

He smiled as he fingered his mug. "I too have an agenda. I was hoping to see my daughter."

"She lives in New Washington?" Aric assessed his response. "Or does she work for Inter-G?"

"Both." His mouth pulled to one side, as though he were debating something. Finally, he set down his cup. "You remind me of her a little. Same strength of character."

"I take it she doesn't know you're here?"

"No." He stared down at the palms of his hands, open

on his lap.

Her father used to assume that posture when he was confounded by a puzzle. Like opening an antique, bound book and resting it on his hands helped him think.

I miss him. Terribly.

She took a deep breath. If she helped Thom then perhaps he would tell her what he knew about the ambassadress. Or at least, reveal what he appeared to be hiding. "I can arrange a meeting. If you don't mind my interfering."

His head shot up. After a moment, he answered. "I'd like that. Although, I'd recommend you don't alert her of my presence ahead of time."

She nodded in understanding. "What's her name?"

"Eva Hilliard. She's an agent here."

The name didn't sound familiar.

"Just one moment." Aric summoned her assistant and asked him to check Special Agent Hilliard's current location.

The young man pulled up a virtual map of the complex, but seemed to have trouble pinpointing her. After accessing the personnel list, his face lit up. "Ah, she's the liaison for the Xerxian delegation. I can locate her by the chip in her badge."

Apparently, that difference showed in the color of the small blip on the screen. In the three-D imaging, Aric could see her moving through the building.

Her assistant explained, "It appears she is escorting one of the delegates to the entrance." He pointed to the second dot. "This identifies her companion as Xerxian."

"Can you intercept her before they leave? Ask her to meet me in an open conference room?" Because her office was tucked in the back corner of the basement, a meeting there would be awkward.

The assistant tapped his screen. "Looks like conference room three is open."

"Good. Tell her I wish to speak with her a moment." She turned to Thom. "Would fifteen minutes be enough time? Or thirty?"

"Ten should work." His lips tightened into a semblance of a smile.

Aric nodded to the assistant. After he left, she again turned to the scientist. "Anything else I can do for you?"

Shoulders hunched, he visibly struggled with himself. "I wouldn't mind your presence during this meeting. It might make things go more smoothly."

Smoothly? She shot up a quick prayer for wisdom. "I'd be glad to help in any way I can."

It would be a small price to pay for his assistance with the Xerxians.

Chapter 13

As the tour of Inter-G's building ended, Eva sighed with relief. She had shown Zahn everything he wanted to see, which was almost the entire complex. Several times he commented that in the future he wanted to revisit some parts of the structure. Had he sensed her impatience as they'd breezed through the austere general assembly room and the countless, cluttered offices? Though he expressed his awe at the holographic models in the gym and the floating gardens, she suspected he was more interested in spending time with her than looking over the edifice.

The massive arched windows, simulated white marble,

and echoing great rooms could be breathtaking to a newcomer. To her, they were nothing but concrete, glass and steel. Why had they built headquarters to look like a replicated gothic building with indoor flying buttresses? In order to keep from honoring one particular race of peoples, the huge edifice lacked any personality. Eva found it harsh. Unforgiving.

"Ms. Hilliard?" A female aide intercepted her and Zahn as they headed toward the exit. "Your presence is requested in conference room three."

"By whom?"

The aide checked her comm-unit. "Aric Reese."

The mother of the kidnapped girl? Eva had heard Inter-G invited her to spearhead the *Xerxian Problem* as the rumor mill now called it. But why did the woman want to see her?

She turned to Zahn. "I'm sorry, but—"

"I was hoping you would join me for…" He paused as though searching for the right words. "A light luncheon?"

"I'm not sure how long the meeting will last."

"I will wait."

No use arguing.

"Then follow me." She led him toward the conference room, mind churning how to get out of the shared meal. After she met up with Mrs. Reese, Eva would beg off lunch with the excuse that the meeting might last too long for him to wait.

As they approached the conference room, a young man jumped up from a chair outside the door. Aric Reese's assistant? "They're already waiting inside."

They?

"I'm sure you wouldn't be comfortable out here, Zahn." Eva indicated the hardback chairs nearby. "Please allow this aide to escort you to one of our lounges."

"These seats look perfectly fine." Zahn smiled.

The assistant opened the door to the conference room.

Eva looked past the young man to the opening door. "If

this meeting goes long, then I'd…"

As the occupants inside stood, she felt the space narrow, squeezing her. She couldn't breathe. Couldn't think.

The man who walked toward her was someone she had not seen in nine years. And he was the last person she ever wanted to see.

"Daddy." Her tone was as devoid of emotion as her heart. She clenched her teeth. Years before, she had vowed to never call him that again. Not even "father."

He didn't deserve that honor.

"Eva Daviana." Marshall embraced her.

Why add her middle name? To imply she was to blame for the rift between them? Unable to manufacture any answer, she remained unresponsive as his arms enfolded her. Eva's heart froze into a block of ice, growing more frigid by the moment. Finally, he released her and stepped back.

"Why are you here?" If the question sounded accusatory, she didn't care.

"Intergalaxia asked for my assistance with an issue." His gaze flickered to the man behind her.

Zahn. He's watching.

She bit her lip. He'd seen everything. Heard everything—would somehow garner the intimate details about her and Marshall's relationship without her saying a word.

Zahn would quietly pry until she revealed all.

Pushing anxiety from her mind, she snapped the professional mask into place as she addressed the man who was once her father. "May I present His Excellency, First to the High Council of Xerxes IX." She took a deep breath, waving in Zahn's direction. "Excellency, this is…this is Dr. Thomas Marshall." Because they were on Earth, she named the man—the *scientist*—responsible for her existence. Still, she stumbled as she spoke it.

Zahn held out his hand—a very Terran gesture.

Marshall's eyes narrowed as he shook his hand. "I think

we've already met."

The Xerxian nodded. "I believe so as well. I was a child. Of perhaps eight standard years." He spoke in English.

"Correct." Marshall smiled. "Would you please give my regards to your mother, Excellency. I think of her with great fondness."

"Please, call me Zahn. I know names are preferred here."

"And this is Aric Reese." Marshall indicated the quiet woman behind him. "Also invited by Intergalaxia."

"I am honored." Zahn inclined his head. "Aric Reese? Ah, the mother of the child who was taken."

"Yes." She opened her mouth to say something more, then apparently changed her mind.

"I rejoice with you that your daughter was safely returned."

"Thank you. My husband and I are overwhelmed with gratitude."

Eva's world shrank, crushing her with the weight of so many coincidences. Her father and Zahn knew each other? And Aric Reese—how had she and Thomas Marshall become acquainted with each other?

Of course Aric would know Kelli Layne. Obviously she would throw herself into a project to help rescue the woman who had saved her daughter's life. These three females were the whole reason Inter-G was in turmoil.

And the known universe.

Because of them, would peace unravel? The terrifying possibility consumed her.

"Eva?" Marshall cleared his throat. "I asked if I would be able to visit you when you weren't occupied. I am in town for a couple weeks."

"Yes." She berated herself for momentarily blanking out. "Yes, of course." With mounting dread, she added, "Please check with my assistant or aide for my itinerary."

Why did she tell him that? Under no circumstances would she meet with him.

"I know you are busy, so we won't take up any more of your time." The man who was once her father studied her, the sadness in his eyes almost unbearable.

Please, please *just leave.*

"Eva?" Zahn gestured toward the exit. "We have a lunch appointment?"

"Of course." She managed to nod a goodbye.

She had no idea where Zahn was taking her, nor did she care. She had to get away. Get away from there. Escape *that man.* What selfishness had gripped him when he had decided to create her almost three decades ago?

I should never have been born. Now more than ever, that protest surged from her soul.

She didn't object when Zahn escorted her to a waiting limo. After she climbed in, he scooted next to her.

The driver's voice came over the comm. "By ground or air?"

What? Eva fought to focus.

Before she could respond, Zahn said, "Ground, please. I would like to see the city."

The driver's eyes met her on the computer screen. Blinking, Eva nodded.

Why was Marshall there? Long ago they had decided to never see each other again. Why had he changed his mind? And why not meet somewhere more private than at Inter-G?

Because she would have spurned the invitation and he knew it.

The car pulled away from the curb. The further they got from the building, the more she could begin to handle the bombardment of questions. Her thoughts slowed, chaos quieted.

Zahn had said nothing as he looked out the window. Because he was sightseeing? Doubtful.

He's waiting for me to speak.

She would not talk about *that man.* Not to Zahn. Not to anyone.

"Wh—where are we going?" She finally managed to grind out the words, unable to recall what she'd agreed to.

"Around your great city."

"You'd mentioned lunch. Aren't you hungry?"

"I can wait."

Knowing Zahn, he could go many days without food.

The silence pressed on her, crushing until she could no longer breathe. If she didn't speak, she would rupture.

She punched the limo's secure mode for privacy. "My parents separated when I was six. The vision you had about me? That was the day. I was picking flowers. Daisies. For my mother. She loved daisies. When I reached the cabin, my—my *father* told me she was gone." She paused to suck in a lifeline of air. "Remember asking what was behind him? I'll tell you. Pain. Emptiness."

Betrayal. But she kept the addendum to herself.

"Years later," she continued, voice shaking, "Marshall admitted that he demanded she go. He made her leave."

She tried to swallow the tightness in her throat. But the sorrow stuck. "I never even got to say goodbye." Her voice sounded so small, so broken. Eva stared at her clenched hands.

The agony still burned, despite the decades that had passed.

Silence reverberated in the car, pounding against her soul.

Zahn shifted in his seat. "And you have not seen your mother since?"

"No."

"Have you tried contacting her?"

"I haven't been able to find her. Even with all of Inter-G's resources. Marshall said he doesn't know where she is either." The painful truth pierced her anew. "For all I know, she could be dead."

Air whistled into her lungs, then back out. *There*. The words had escaped. She was free of them. For twenty years they had shackled her heart. This was the first time she'd said them. To anyone.

She started when Zahn gently took her hand.

"A mother-daughter relationship is very important. And not just to those on Xerxes."

She nodded. Would the betrayal never stop aching?

For many minutes, they rode in silence. She could not deny that his hand, holding hers, comforted her greatly. The pain, shared by him, lightened a fraction because she no longer carried it alone.

His sigh drew her attention to him again. He sat with eyes closed, brow drawn—the exact expression he'd worn when they had been together in the cabin. Was he having another vision? Her body tensed as she waited for the earth-shaking news. Would God reveal where her mother was?

Zahn's eyes opened.

She gulped. "What did you see? What do you know?" When he didn't answer quickly enough, she tightened her grip around his fingers. "Tell me."

His mouth quivered. In sorrow? "Perhaps your father told you what you needed to hear."

"What do you mean?"

"That your mother may have chosen to leave. And he would rather you be angry at him than her?"

She shook her head. Not possible!

He clung stubbornly to her hand. "Could it not be so?"

"It—I...no." But what if it were true? Zahn's other vision had been accurate from the color of Eva's hair to the flowers she picked.

What if her mother had left of her own volition? The implications rocked Eva's preconceived notions. She yanked her hand away, unable to deal with her mother rejecting her. Willfully leaving. Abandoning them both.

She squeezed her eyes shut, failing to block the memories she had suppressed for years. Now they made sense.

Snippets of conversations came back to her. The numerous calls, many made in secret. Eva was not supposed to know about the communication between her parents after her mother's departure. The imploring tone in her father's voice. His divesting himself of the cabin soon after their separation, for much less than it was worth. His grief-stricken face as he roamed their apartment in town. The photo he kept in his desk drawer. The one he always locked, except for one day when she was seventeen and found it. He'd destroyed it as he'd shouted for her to forget her mother...pretend she didn't exist. He maintained they'd never see her again.

That was the day Eva and her father had argued so bitterly that she told him he was forever dead to her.

Zahn again looked out the window. "Your mother must have had overpowering reasons to leave. Why else would a mother abandon her daughter? Perhaps she even believed her departure was best for your father." He looked at Eva, his expression wiser than his thirty years. "And what was ultimately best for you."

"We will banish the Terrans from our world and send their corruption back to Earth where it belongs."

The words from the High Council meeting rang in Ileya's mind all day, stealing her appetite and pounding her mind. She was never so glad to retire early to her chambers where she could be alone with her thoughts.

Dyn'Perzsi Aeliana had traveled back to Xerxes to seek support for the upcoming Terran Summit—to oust the humans not only from their planet, but the space station orbiting their world. Though she didn't get the votes for that issue, she did get support for demanding Kelli-Layne's presence on Xerxes IX to stand trial.

Several clan leaders had abstained, including Ileya. It did no good. At the Terran Summit, Aeliana was going to call for a vote to extradite Kelli-Layne from Earth.

But to what end?

Setting down her brush, Ileya sighed. She was First Chancellor of Xerxes IX and wise ruler of all.

Lately she didn't feel very sagacious.

With one hand, she propped up her chin as she straightened the knick-knacks on her vanity. The muted light in her bedroom gave her the illusion that she was alone. The weight of the universe pressed down on her.

I feel so inadequate, Lord God.

What was best for her people? What was best for her? She rose and came face to face with Betzalel. Strange that she had not even heard her consort enter their bedroom.

"You are troubled. And have been since the meeting this morning." He took her hand and flattened it to his chest, then pressed his own on top of it.

No use denying it. She studied her bond-mate of nearly twenty-eight years. How well he knew her.

Betzalel smiled. "What could possibly weigh down the First Chancellor of Xerxes IX?"

He meant no sarcasm. His reminder of her position had always worked to chase away the dark mood that sometimes harassed her.

Not tonight, though. His comment struck too close to her heart.

She pulled away and wandered to the balcony that overlooked the vast plains below. Dusk blanketed the land, shrouding any details that might still have been visible from over a thousand standard feet. No moon had yet risen. However, she welcomed the night.

"What is it, my love?" His tender voice caressed her.

Shoulders tight, Ileya gripped the railing. "Do you regret having no offspring?"

As he stood behind her, she sensed he chose his answer

with care. As always.

"Zahn is the son of my heart, if not of my flesh. I have no need for another child since our God wills this."

A good answer. She had no doubt that he meant every word. However, she again sighed.

"Ah. I understand." Betzalel's voice was as soft as the fingers that trailed across her shoulders. "Even now you long for a daughter. One that could succeed your rulership."

Gritting her teeth, she swept past him and plopped down at her vanity. With more vigor than necessary, she brushed her hair in preparation for bed. He was right. Time and again, that longing had risen in her soul. And each time she'd been able to soothe the emotion. Lately though, she'd been unable to suppress the fear that partnered it.

Without a female successor, her clan could lose the rulership of Xerxes IX. What would happen then?

Betzalel stayed her hand, then gently pried the brush from tight fingers. "Allow me."

In the mirror she watched as he took care to remove the tangles, then smooth her hair from the crown to the tips. The ritual worked its magic. Tension eased from her shoulders and neck. Sighs of pleasure replaced the earlier ones of angst.

The activity also accomplished what he no doubt hoped. Made her more open to sharing what troubled her. She met her consort's gaze in the mirror. "I received word today that the health of the Dyn'Perzsi clan leader is failing."

"We have known for some time that she is not long for this world." He spoke slowly, still brushing her hair. "Just this morning, I dispatched our healer to her home. And to discover if we could do anything to ease her discomfort."

"You are always so kind." Ileya waited a moment, then added, "You realize that when she passes, Aeliana will be the new clan leader."

A frown gathered on his brow as he continued to smooth her hair. "Her older sister has abdicated then?"

"Not officially. But…" She shrugged.

"As ambassadress to Earth *and* as the clan leader, Aeliana will possess enormous power."

Ileya nodded, gaze holding his. His thought process was easy to follow because hers had traveled the same route. Many times.

Her consort moved the mass of her hair to one side. "What if Zahn weds one from another clan?"

"That won't happen." She took a breath. Out of deference to her son, she had not shared what he'd told her. "He is pursuing a mate. Yet not such a woman as we…" She bit her lip and amended her words. "Not someone from a powerful clan." She stumbled over her explanation. "His choice will not sustain our line, but ensure its break."

Betzalel did not ask whom Zahn intended to marry. Did not need to. After setting down the brush, he slid his fingers over hers. "My love, consider. Without a blood-daughter, your successor was never guaranteed. Regardless of whom Zahn chooses."

She lowered her head. How true he spoke. But over her lifetime, she had pushed that fear from her mind. For many years she had held onto the dream that Zahn's wife, a woman from a powerful tribe, would keep the line intact. If the new daughter-in-law renounced her heritage, Ileya could adopt the new bride into hers.

With that no longer viable, she predicted Aeliana's growing power would wrench rulership from her dynasty.

"I fear…" She hesitated to voice her thoughts aloud. But the dam broke, emotion spilling into her words as moisture stung her eyes. "I fear that if Aeliana gains rulership, she will destroy our world. Not intentionally, but from her misguided beliefs. Her isolationist policies may insulate us from corruption, but will ultimately weaken us. And open us up to piracy and greater harm."

Her mate's grip tightened. Slowly, he lowered himself onto the vanity's long bench. For many moments, he said nothing.

Ileya waited for the wise counsel that would come. Many times in nearly three decades of marriage, he had guided her to the right path.

He caressed her cheek. "Isn't this out of our hands? Truly something we cannot control?"

Eyelashes wet with tears, she met his gaze. And slowly nodded.

"And do you not think, my love, that the God of heaven sees all and knows? Do you doubt His care for our world and our people?"

As she lowered her face, a tear splashed on her hand. How right her mate was. Such a man of wisdom. She was truly blessed to have him by her side.

"Then let your heart be at peace, my beloved." He lifted her hand and kissed where the tear had fallen, then her cheek where another slipped. "We will be more diligent in our petitions and prayers. And trust Him regardless of how He chooses to answer. When the time is right, our God will show the way."

Chapter 14

"I don't like it." As Eva glanced around the large public park, every fiber in her body tensed. Why did Aric Reese need to meet Zahn here? From a security standpoint, Eva could not possibly cover all the contingencies at New Washington's Memorial Gardens. Not without a dozen or more special agents.

"What don't you like?" Aric turned to her.

"This location."

Naiveté blanketed her face. "What danger could there be here?"

Plenty. Biting off the retort, Eva continued to scan the

area. Despite the late morning, the place seemed filled with people. Didn't anyone work anymore?

An unwelcomed thought barged into her mind. If Director Rosborough found out about this meeting, her career could be over.

"Besides," Aric added, sounding a bit defensive, "His Excellency specifically requested this park. Despite my recommendation that we meet at Inter-G."

"You should have been more insistent." If that sounded harsh, Eva couldn't help it. The only thought that brought an iota of comfort was that she had a margin of fifteen minutes to scope out the area before Zahn arrived from the Embassy.

Aric spread her hands. "I tried to change his mind, believe me. But His Excellency was not to be dissuaded."

How well Eva knew. Her attitude softened a little. "So why the meeting?" After all, Zahn and Aric had already been introduced at HQ. What did they need to discuss?

Aric's eyes widened. "I didn't initiate this. His Excellency did."

What? Not only had Zahn not told Eva about his desire to meet with the scientist, but he had insisted it take place at a park?

Turning to hide her surprise, Eva studied the area again. In the distance, a camera crew gathered around a recently erected statue. A woman conducted an interview while a curious crowd watched. Some documentary about war heroes? She hoped they remained focused on the exchange, allowing Zahn and Aric privacy.

Her gaze settled again on Aric. "Mind my asking why you agreed to this meeting?"

"I was hoping to plead his help for Kelli." Before Eva could remind her Xerxes was a matriarchal society, the scientist went on. "I know his viewpoint may have little bearing with the High Council, but Kelli would appreciate any support."

"Considering she sacrificed herself for your daughter,

you must now be the best of friends." Eva bit her lip. A stupid comment.

"I'd do anything for Kelli." Aric's eyes burned with green brilliance in the noonday sun. "If you only knew what she..." Her mouth trembled, but she didn't finish her sentence.

How would it be to have won such fierce loyalty from another person? Ever the loner, Eva had no idea.

A car pulled up to the park's entrance. Not Zahn. Then who?

Ella Reese emerged, wearing a white blouse and a pleated, violet skirt. A school uniform? Eva gritted her teeth at this new development. No one had told her about the eight-year-old being part of the gathering. What other surprises awaited?

When two bodyguards emerged from the car, Eva instinctively tensed. As she assessed them, her hand flexed.

Both USF trained, though now working in the private sector. The men hadn't completely shed their military-like stance, but their garb and relaxed grooming betrayed their new employment. If they changed their allegiance once, what would prevent them from doing that again? Eva wouldn't be so foolish as to believe they would remain faithful to the Reeses should the situation grow ugly.

Eva's gaze darted between the men. The shorter, stockier of the two looked like he wouldn't surrender easily. However, the taller, bearded one would give her more trouble. He had to outweigh her by seventy pounds or more. But it was the way he carried himself with taut readiness that let her know he took his job seriously. He'd die before he'd let anyone harm the little girl.

His gaze openly evaluated Eva, eyes narrowing a fraction.

Her hand spasmed again as her jaw flexed. *Yes, you would hurt me, but I could take you both out.*

Almost as if he read her mind—and agreed—the

bearded one inclined his head ever so slightly in grudging assent.

Before Ella reached them, Aric leaned over and whispered, "That's just Frick and Frack. Our names for the bodyguards, of course. Pay them no mind."

Eva couldn't help her grin. Ignore them? Not for one second. If something went sideways, she needed to know if they would run or fight.

Ella skipped toward them. "Guess what, Mama? I got out of school before anyone else."

"It's a special day." Aric hugged her daughter.

Knowing their role, the bodyguards stationed themselves nearby, stance ready.

Eva caught sight of Inter-G's limo as it reached the park's entrance. "Ah, there's Zahn now."

When Aric's eyebrows rose, Eva bit her lip at her careless slip of the tongue. She squelched the urge to correct herself by adding "His Excellency."

While she moved forward to welcome him, Aric and her daughter hung back.

The driver leaped out and opened the door for the Xerxian before Eva could reach them.

"Eva Daviana." Zahn's tone caressed her name, inviting a deeper intimacy.

Placing her hands behind her back, she inclined her head a fraction. "Excellency."

His gaze flicked toward Aric and her daughter who stared their way. Did he guess the source of Eva's discomfort?

"This way please." She cleared her throat, trying to dislodge whatever made her voice rasp.

"Good afternoon, your Excellency." Aric bowed as he approached.

Ella's eyes widened and her lips parted as she visibly shrunk against her mother. Because Zahn looked like her kidnapper? The man who had abducted the little girl had posed as a Xerxian. Only that morning Eva learned he had been condemned to death by the High Council. His one listed crime—disguising himself as a Xerxian.

Would they hand down a similar sentence to Kelli Layne?

The masterminds behind the plot—including Aric's ex-husband—were exempt from Xerxian courts since they had not assumed a disguise. They both were currently serving Terran prison sentences. Both incarcerated at the Dzardian penal colony for life.

Stopping before the mother and daughter, Zahn inclined his head. Ella's hand gripped her mother's so tightly, her fingers turned white.

"Ella." Aric lowered her voice. "This is the man I told you about. The one I said we would meet today. Would you please say hello?"

The girl's mouth tensed into a thin slit. "Hello." The word squeaked out.

Zahn knelt before her on one knee. "I have long wanted to make your acquaintance. May I call you Ella?" Though his English was a little stilted, his soft tone invited trust.

Shoulders relaxing a fraction, she nodded.

"I would be honored if you called me Zahn." He paused, head tilting to one side. "Do you know that Xerxians in my capital city speak of your bravery? I have heard that many prayers were offered while you were on my planet. All rejoiced when we heard you were safely returned to your family."

They had? A shiver slid down Eva's spine.

"In celebration, I brought you a present." From the depths of his robes, he retrieved a small box and held it toward the child.

When Ella glanced at her mother, Aric nodded in encouragement. The girl took the gift and examined it.

Zahn merely watched, not appearing impatient as she fingered the carved wood, turning it over several times.

"Oh. It opens." Ella removed the snug lid. Inside, jewelry sparkled.

"May I be of assistance?" He held out his hand and waited. After removing the delicate silver, he held it up. "The ruler of Xerxes IX herself agreed you deserve this honorary token. It is given only to the most courageous."

Eva sucked in a deep breath at the privilege bestowed to not only a child, but a Terran one. Meeting Aric's gaze for a moment, she resisted the urge to blurt that fact.

Making a sound of wonder, the girl touched the flashing silver with a tentative finger.

Again, Zahn waited.

Growing braver, Ella fingered the chain. "Is it a bracelet?"

"No, an earring with charms. Like mine." He turned his head so she could see. "All Xerxians of good standing wear one."

The girl peered at it. "You have lots of them."

"Yes." He chuckled. "And now you have two charms—a good start. This one," he paused to point, "symbolizes that all Xerxians should honor you as an adopted child of my people. It bears the seal of the First Chancellor. And this one means you have faced danger with exemplary courage."

Ella again touched the earring.

"Would you like me to help you put it on?" he asked.

This time, she didn't look for her mother's approval. Eyes gleaming, the girl nodded.

Zahn fastened the clip on her lobe, then the other on the helix. Eva's breath caught when he placed his palm on the girl's forehead and uttered an invocation in Xer.

A prayer that Eva's mother used to recite. Resisting the beauty of the words, she clenched her jaw.

When he removed his hand, Ella smiled at him.

"It fits you perfectly." Zahn's black eyes softened as his gaze fixed on the little girl.

Eva blinked rapidly when Ella put her arms about his

neck and hugged him. "Thank you." Then she looked up. "Look what Zahn gave me, Mama. Isn't it pretty?"

"It is indeed." Aric's voice cracked. It seemed to take her a moment to continue. "I need to speak with Zahn for a few moments. Why don't you show your escorts?" She pointed to the bodyguards.

"Okay." Ella gave her the carved box. Before turning away, she said, "By the way, their names aren't Frick and Frack. I asked. They're Leo and Bradley."

Her mother chuckled. "Thanks for letting me know." While the girl skipped toward the bodyguards, Aric smoothed her fingers over the delicate wood. Then she spoke to Zahn as he rose. "Thank you. Very much. For your kindness."

He merely inclined his head.

"Would you care to walk?" She indicated a direction that led more deeply into the park.

"Gladly." He turned and waited for Eva to join them.

Shaking off her preoccupation, she stepped beside him. She didn't miss the speculative look on Aric's face.

Though her cheeks grew hot, she managed to speak in a cool voice. "I need to remind you both that His Excellency has a meeting in an hour. That gives us about twenty more minutes here."

"That would be perfect." Because of the soft smile Zahn cast her direction, he might as well have shouted, "I love spending every day with you, Eva."

Clasping her hands behind her back, she marshaled her emotions. Like Frick and Frack, she was merely a bodyguard. She let out a quiet breath of relief when Aric quit staring at them as though ferreting out secrets between her and Zahn.

With him in the middle, they sauntered down the wide gravel path.

Aric spoke first. "Thank you for your invitation to meet here. Although, I didn't expect you to bring a gift for my daughter."

A brief smile touched his lips. "I wanted to meet her. And banish any lingering fear she may have about my people."

The girl's mother spoke in a tight voice. "Thank you."

Eva cast a sideways glance at her. *I know how you feel.*

Only Zahn appeared imperturbable as they walked. Lifting his chin, he inhaled the scents. Most notably was the fragrance from the flowering rosebushes that lined the path. His gaze seemed to take in everything—the preschool children playing in the lush grass, the bicyclists on a nearby trail, the lovers perched on strategically placed benches.

Aric's daughter and her two bodyguards trailed behind them, maintaining a respectful distance.

More than once, Eva caught the curious looks from others in the park. Everyone kept their distance as they walked or jogged by, but a few gawkers stopped and outright stared.

Zahn did not seem to notice or care. "Is there something else about which you wanted to speak, Mrs. Reese?"

She flashed Eva a look as though to ask *how did he know?*

Squelching a smile, Eva ducked her head. Zahn always knew.

"Yes," Aric finally answered. "I did as a matter of fact."

The three of them stopped.

After licking dry lips, Aric went on. "I would like you to help save the life of my friend. Kelli Layne."

He kept his gaze pointed straight ahead as he pursed his lips. "I was not aware that she was in danger."

"Perhaps not now. But you must know the sentiments of your people. Of your High Council."

The cold-blooded pronouncement of death for the kidnapper again rippled through Eva. Yes, he deserved to be punished, but why such a drastic measure? Despite the kidnapping, she had mixed feelings about the impending and drastic penalty. Execution?

It was almost as if the puzzle pieces locked into place—one whose ultimate picture had yet to be fully revealed.

"I would hope that the decisions made by our High Council would be based on truth rather than sentiments." Zahn clasped his hands behind his back.

"But truth—without love, without forgiveness—is too harsh." Aric paused. "As a synecologist, I am familiar with the laws of your people. And I believe in the law. However, in this situation, I ask that you consider the extenuating circumstances surrounding Kelli."

Rocking on his feet, Zahn seemed to consider her words. He looked up at the large trees as their leaves rustled in the breeze. "Love? Forgiveness? Interesting word choices for a scientist."

"I am, first and foremost, a follower of God." Her jaw tightened.

"So when it is convenient, you ignore law and call upon mercy?"

"No, I seek to uphold the law, but with the hand of mercy."

A faint smile flickered across his lips. "As a synecologist, you must know the delicate balances of my society. Let me remind you that it is matriarchal. Though my mother is First Chancellor, my opinions have little weight in the High Council's decision-making process."

"Little would be better than none."

Again, a smile passed over his lips. "What would you have me do, Aric-Reese?"

She took a slow breath, gaze flickering to Eva who drew closer. "Plead for mercy, Excellency. Remember the life—no, *lives*—of the children that Kelli saved. Not only my daughter's, but that of a Xerxian child. Does that count for nothing? I'm not asking for her crimes to be dismissed, but that her punishment be tempered. That it not be...not be so extreme. That she not be..." Aric clamped her mouth shut as though suddenly realizing how elevated her voice had become. She clenched her hands. "Forgive my outburst."

Face impassive, Zahn inclined his head. "There is no need for an apology."

She again glanced at Eva who turned away so that the scientist would not see the burning in her eyes.

I'm sorry, Aric. Eva fought to keep the sorrow from her face. In her heart, she knew the High Council would condemn Kelli Layne as they had the kidnapper. Was Zahn being merciful by not telling Aric the truth?

Eva glanced at his serene face.

No, he really didn't appear aware.

But why do I? How can I know with such certainty?

Zahn turned toward her. "Is it time to depart, Eva? I don't want to disrupt Intergalaxia's delicate timetable."

"Yes." She blinked. "Yes, I believe it is. We should go."

Zahn nodded as he again fixed his attention on Aric. "Thank you for giving me your perspective on the Kelli-Layne case. I promise to ponder what you have said."

Disappointment washed over Aric's features. Ever the professional, she merely bowed. "Thank you for hearing me."

They turned to walk back toward the park's entrance. Ahead of them, a happy Ella skipped, her new earring bobbing and sparkling in the sunlight. Frick and Frack—no, Eva edited—Leo and Bradley kept within an acceptable range.

"Mama, can I smell the flowers?" Ella called as she pointed. "Please?"

"Yes, but just for a minute."

Her daughter stepped off the path and bent her head toward a well-manicured rose bush. The park had an abundance of them, planted in memory of loved ones who'd lost their lives defending their world.

Eva glanced around as though seeing them for the first time, dread settling into the deepest recesses of her soul. Her imagination conjured up hundreds of thousands, covering every grassy inch until there was no longer any space to walk. She squeezed her eyes shut.

Please, God, no.

"I like the yellow best." Ella's nose sampled the bloom on the shrub again.

The image passed.

Aric turned to her and Zahn. "Go on ahead. Ella and I will catch up."

But the Xerxian appeared reluctant to leave. A small smile played on his lips as he watched the little girl. Ella clutched her knees as she bent forward, careful to avoid the thorns.

"Oh, my." Aric chuckled. "I just noticed Ella's mismatched socks. I think I have my husband to blame since he got her ready for school this morning."

Indeed, one pink sock was slightly darker than the other.

His smile broadened. "I am pleased that Terran fathers are involved in their children's care."

"In our home, Sean definitely is." As Aric continued to speak about their lives, Eva moved away to signal the limo driver that they would soon be ready to depart. After he gave his nod, she turned back to the group in the park.

One moment, a relaxed Aric chatted with Zahn, but the next she stopped midsentence, gaze fixed across the park.

What alarmed her?

From where Eva stood, she saw no one beyond the shrubbery.

Aric's mouth gaped, panic flooding her features.

"Ella. *Ella!*" She rushed toward her daughter while the bodyguards instantly hemmed in the little girl.

Brow wrinkled in bewilderment, the Xerxian remained alone on the path.

"Zahn." Eva called, still unclear where the danger came from. Or what it was. Assessing the nearby people, she moved forward.

Zahn turned as a man dressed as a jogger broke through

the shrubbery. Even from the distance, she could see his gaze fix on Zahn. The man's face twisted in hatred.

Eva broke into a run. Dread pounded her.

I won't reach them in time.

One moment the jogger came abreast of Zahn and the next passed him to disappear through a wall of foliage. Eva's ears burned at the profanity he yelled along with, "Go home, freak."

Zahn stared after him.

"Are you all right?" Eva panted the words when she reached him. Her leg throbbed from the sudden physical demand.

"Yes."

She allowed only a second before chasing after the jogger, but her delay had given him too great of a head start. By the time she reached the shrubbery, he had disappeared. She doubted she could catch up. Because she no longer had a sub-dermal chip, she tapped her badge and instantly connected to Inter-G. "Alert level three."

They would zero in on her signal and descend on the park in minutes.

Aric, her daughter and the two bodyguards clustered around Zahn. Since Eva's first priority was to protect the Xerxian, she limped back to his side. "Get to the limo. Now."

They moved *en masse* toward the vehicles.

The crowd that had been lingering near the new statue now surged toward them. More alarming, the camera crew rushed in their direction.

"Take Ella home," Aric spoke to the bodyguards. "Go."

Eva grabbed her arm. "We'll need you at Inter-G." When the woman nodded, Eva told the men, "Get Ella out of here. *Now.*"

The bearded man scooped the girl into his arms while the other guarded their flank. In moments, they leaped into their waiting car. Instead of driving away, the vehicle shot up to a hover position as they prepared to merge into the air traffic pattern above.

Eva's eyes met Aric's. They both sighed in relief at the same time.

"Let's go." Eva directed them to the limo while she shielded both Zahn and the scientist with her body.

A bright light from a camera blinded her as a reporter fired questions in their direction. Ignoring him, Eva backed into the limo. A force field snapped into place to prevent any unlawful entry.

After a warning blast, the car also lifted into the sky while the door slid shut.

Only after the vehicle locked into the traffic pattern of the aerial highway did she relax. Monitors showed their airspace was secure. On the monitor, Eva stared at the group that gathered below. The interviewer still pointed the camera at the limo. The clustering crowds looked up as they ascended. Most faces reflected curiosity, but some...

Eva squinted and leaned closer to a side monitor. Anger marred the faces of at least six people. Because of the incident? Or—the question had to be considered—because a Xerxian had dared invade a Terran park? The horde began to disperse as Inter-G and police ground units descended and cordoned off the park.

She sniffed as an odd smell permeated the inside of the limo. Turning, she saw Zahn brush something off his robe. Across from her, Aric's eyes widened as she stared at the excrement that marred his beautiful clothing. Their eyes met, Aric's face mirroring the horror she felt.

Zahn caught her gaze, expression wry. "It seems I came away with my own gift."

Mouth gaping, Aric flushed. "I'm so sorry, your Excellency. This is unforgiveable."

Eva sucked in her breath at the woman's choice of words. Hadn't they just been speaking about forgiveness?

"Let the blame fall on me." Eva spoke in Xer despite the fact that Aric would not understand.

"This isn't your fault," he replied in English.

Eva darted a look of apology at the woman across from them and continued in Xer. "Please don't let this incident affect how you feel about Terrans."

His dark gaze bore into her. "Never," he whispered in his native tongue.

Was he talking about Kelli Layne or...?

Understanding dawning, Eva turned away. Her face singed with heat. That's not what she had meant. Impossible to explain that to him with Aric Reese in the limo, watching them closely. Eva pressed her lips together to keep silent.

"I think that gentleman has a strong attachment to Kelli Layne," Zahn announced, again in English.

Eva studied him. "Why do you say that?"

"Then you didn't hear?"

She had heard enough. Was he talking about something else?

A sardonic grin pulled his mouth to one side. "Although I am glad I did not grasp his epithets, I did understand one thing."

"What was that?"

"Before he graced me with this," Zahn pointed to the dark stain on his clothing, "he said, 'This is for Kelli Layne.'"

Chapter 15

"Excellency, the transmission from First Chancellor should be coming in soon."

The moment Zahn stepped through the embassy doors, a technician came alongside him. Together they hurried through the shadowy halls.

"I will take it in my room. Please." Zahn sought to squelch his annoyance. The communication from his mother could not have come at a worse time. He had been on his way to Intergalaxia when he had received word to immediately return to the embassy. Because of the park incident, his afternoon meeting had been canceled. The limo driver had dropped him off before continuing to headquarters.

I should be with Eva.

Together they would face the director with the truth about what had happened. Though it was not her fault, Rosborough would no doubt spill his wrath on her. Knowing Eva, she would accept all responsibility. Would it cost her the position of liaison?

He had just reached his room and stripped off his soiled outer robe when the transmission came through. Dabbing perspiration from his forehead, he stationed himself in front of the comm-panel on his desk and tilted up the screen. In the moments before they connected, he opened a window to let in a late afternoon breeze.

The image of his mother flickered, then solidified on the display.

After their customary greeting and a few minutes of chatting, she said, "And how is your stay on Earth, my son?"

Had she really interrupted his afternoon to ask such a banal question? Or was she asking about his pursuit of Eva in a not-so-subtle way? His earlier annoyance nipped at him once again.

He took care to temper his tone. "I am overwhelmed with all the newness I have experienced since my arrival."

"No doubt you are enjoying it."

Despite his irritation, he managed a tight smile. "You know me well."

"And how are things progressing?"

Again, the vague question piqued his impatience. *I need to be with Eva. Right now.* He gripped the edge of the desk. Even if he begged off from his mother, it would be too late to call for a limo and go to Intergalaxia. By now Eva was in Rosborough's office. Or perhaps she was gathering her belongings because she'd been dismissed?

He pushed the distraction from his mind.

Pretending his mother's question aimed at his duties as

a delegate, he finally answered, "Suitably. I am learning so much about humans that I never before knew."

He was discovering a great deal about Eva. So much explained. Yet, until he could prove his loyalty and love, she would continue to keep him at arm's length. Though she'd not refused his proposal, in subtle ways she continued to reject him.

And today he'd abandoned her when she needed him most.

His mother nodded. "It is good to know your allies."

Zahn tried to focus on what she was saying. As they talked for several moments, catching up on news, he drew up a chair. The moment his mother signed off, he planned to send Eva a message. The most appropriate kind would be a handwritten note of apology about the park and...

"Something is troubling you, Zahn?"

As he stared at the screen, he realized that his mother leaned forward. What had he missed?

Though distracted with Eva, he owed his mother his full attention.

"Yes." He straightened in his chair. "I am concerned about Kelli-Layne."

"Tell me more."

"The Terrans become more restless every day."

The incident in the park was further proof. Since his mother would not have received word of the occurrence yet, he decided not to volunteer it. However, if the reporters identified him, he would have to explain—but at a later date.

"I have seen news accounts." Her brow furrowed.

He chose his words with care. "The number of demonstrators in front of the embassy grows every day. Especially as the summit draws closer."

"They are hostile?"

"I sense they are. With a brooding anger." Exceedingly dangerous.

His mother pressed one finger to her lower lip. "Take

care, my son, as you travel among them."

"Intergalaxia provides security. My personal liaison is well trained in fighting techniques." Zahn withheld the information that Eva was his intended.

"That gives me comfort."

He adjusted the screen again since he was now sitting. "I finally met the child who was kidnapped. And her mother."

"Did you give them the earring?"

"Yes. Both were pleased."

"I'm glad you insisted on presenting that gift." His mother smiled. "What can you tell me about them?"

He held up a hand. "One moment, please."

After rising, he shut the window and accessed the room's control panels. In moments, he activated the eavesdrop-prevention field. He should have done that upon his arrival, but blamed his preoccupation on what had happened at the park.

"Secure." Again, he sat.

"You were about to say, Zahn?"

"I sense the mother and child both have a strong attachment to Kelli-Layne."

"Understandable."

"Yet, it goes beyond that." Zahn sought to explain what he'd sensed during the meeting with Aric-Reese. "She pleaded, quite passionately, for her friend. As though..." Again he paused. "As though Kelli-Layne was her sister."

His mother pressed her hands together. "That would be consistent with what she told the Fourth Chancellor. Kelli-Layne saved her daughter. Did you know?"

"Ah. I see the connection now."

"Kelli-Layne is a most disturbing human. In a good way." She paused a moment. "I remember what you said many weeks ago. That she is a true worshipper."

"I have not changed my opinion." His fist clenched in his lap. "This case grows more complicated every day."

His mother's eyebrows rose. "And what of the

ambassadress?"

His shiver came from more than the drop in the early evening temperature. He clutched the armrests of the chair. "She holds to her position without variance. I have spoken to her numerous times, yet she is unbending."

"She wants Kelli-Layne brought to Xerxes to stand trial?"

"Yes." Zahn's grip tightened. "I am certain she will get the needed support at the summit. I have heard the sentiments of others here. Including those from other worlds. Many believe Terrans hold too much power."

"Though I have felt that way on occasion, I dare not withhold their right in good faith."

"Because Earth is the Planet of Origin?"

"Yes." She leaned forward. "Our sacred writings all point there for our beginnings. Millennia ago."

"Then what the ambassadress desires makes no sense. Spiritually speaking."

"I agree."

"To isolate ourselves would solve nothing." He sliced one hand through the air. "Since we bear the same seed of iniquity, segregation would not solve the corruption she perceives Terrans have brought to our society."

"You are right. But knowing this will not dissuade her. Aeliana is on a crusade for our people. The logic or illogic will not change her mind."

Zahn rose and paced before the screen. "Then I would recommend you put together a court. One that would be fair to Kelli-Layne."

"A wise suggestion."

Again, the conversation turned to other topics while Zahn again sat, risking a glance at the chronometer. He was about to beg off when his mother asked, "And how fares the pursuit of your intended?"

At last, she got to the point of her communication.

Normally, he would be forthright about his plans and

hopes, but this time he resisted. "You are sure that I have time to pursue her?"

"I know you, my son. And I know you would not have agreed so quickly to this mission had that not been an option."

He conceded her point with a nod of his head. "How well you know me."

She folded her hands and leaned closer, inviting a deeper confession. "Tell me more."

Though he wanted to withhold the truth, he chose to share his thoughts. Perhaps if she learned more of Eva, she would grow more supportive of his pursuit of her. "I see a difficult road ahead. She has been deeply wounded."

Her inquisitive expression melted into distress. "And you think to be her savior?"

Her answer was not what he expected.

Defensiveness welled inside him. "No. We already have a Savior. I cannot be that for her. To think and act so would be foolish." He debated how much to say. "I sense she knows Him, but has gotten lost along the way."

Would his mother warn him to give up his foolish goal? Chastise him for not ascertaining her spiritual condition before offering marriage?

She again rubbed her lower lip with a fingertip.

Why strive so hard to convince her? Wasn't God's clear direction enough?

He fought to keep his tone even. "Her mother abandoned her when she was a young child."

"How sad."

"She hides her pain from the world, but I see that she carries it around. Her sorrow defines her."

"You without a father, she without a mother."

He caught his breath at the parallel before hastening to reassure her. "Your bound consort has been my father for as long as I can remember. I feel no lack."

"Yet, that can be a point of bonding between you and

your intended."

Would that knowledge draw him and Eva closer or drive them apart? Zahn refused to try to manipulate her with that information.

"I have pried enough, my son." His mother smiled at him. "I bid you good night."

He bowed to the image as it flickered, then faded.

For a long time, Zahn remained before the screen until his hands began to ache. When he looked down, he saw that his fingernails had dug into the delicate wood of the chair.

He bolted to his feet and slapped off the security field around his room. After pacing a few moments, he slipped outside into the dusky gardens. The lighted dining room announced that the evening meal had begun.

Forget food. Something more pressing beckoned him. In the shadowy gazebo, he knelt to pray.

"What were you thinking?" Director Rosborough's voice continued to rise. For fifteen minutes, he'd let both Eva and Aric feel the brunt of his irritation.

Keeping her expression neutral, Eva stood at attention. Face forward and shoulders back, she stared ahead without really seeing. Beside her, Aric's posture divulged respect, although her stance was a little less rigid. From her peripheral vision, Eva could tell the scientist's gaze followed the director's movements. For a few moments longer, he marched in front of them before repositioning himself behind his massive desk.

As a seasoned agent, Eva had been through more than one verbal thrashing. The chastisement wasn't personal. Any moment she would get her chance to apologize, then the director would calm down.

What disciplinary action he planned was a whole

different worry.

Would he remove her as liaison? She both feared and wished for that.

As he bent forward, fingertips resting on the shiny desk, his glare beat down on them. He finally settled his irritation on Eva. "You met with a delegate. Without a proper escort. In an unapproved area. The Xerxians situation is volatile enough. Then you pull a stunt like that..." He threw up one hand.

"I'm sorry, sir, this will never—"

"It was *my* fault," Aric interrupted.

Rosborough fixed his gaze on her.

She lifted her chin. "His Excellency wanted to see the park. I should have been more insistent on meeting him here."

The director frowned. "I still hold Ms. Hilliard responsible. As liaison—"

"She didn't know anything about the meeting. Until too late."

Disbelieving her ears, Eva shot a sideways glance at the woman. She was standing up to Rosborough? No one did that.

Ignoring Aric, his amber eyes fixed again on Eva. "I'm tempted to suspend you."

Again, she opened her mouth to say something, and again Aric beat her to it. "Then you'll have to suspend us both, Director. She goes, I go." Jaw jutting, she met his gaze squarely.

"You don't work for Intergalaxia."

"It doesn't matter. If you suspend her, then you'll have to find yourself someone else to head up my team."

What? Eva sucked in a slow breath.

With narrowed eyes, Rosborough appeared to assess the scientist's bluff.

Determined to say nothing more, Eva pressed her lips together. Apparently, this wasn't her fight. Besides, Aric wouldn't allow her to get a word in edgewise.

The silence wore on Eva until she began to twitch. Rosborough said nothing. Aric said nothing. Whoever spoke first would be the loser.

Clenching her fingers, Eva sought to control a tremor.

Frowning, the director finally cleared his throat and took his seat. "That is all." He picked up his small comm-unit and turned his chair. *Dismissed.*

Without hesitation, Eva stepped to the door and beat a hasty retreat. Apparently, she retained her employment with Inter-G. And her position as liaison. Only when she escaped his office did she allow herself to breathe. Aric caught up to her in the hallway, but said nothing.

Eva cleared her throat. "Thanks."

"For…?" The scientist appeared serenely unconcerned.

"Sticking up for me."

"I didn't lie." Her tone betrayed an element of defensiveness.

"Yeah, but you didn't let me take the fall. You should have. That incident was my fault."

"Not so." Aric's touched her arm, compelling her to stop. "His Excellency insisted. And, well, he can be a charming and forceful man."

Zahn? Forceful? That didn't sound like the typical male in a matriarchal society. But the charming part did.

"Besides," Aric continued, "how could we have known something would happen?"

"True." All in all, she was grateful that nothing more serious had occurred. Yet, this incident proved to be a foretaste of the growing animosity.

"Tell me…" The scientist ran a hand over the back of her neck. "Why do you think Zahn wanted to meet my daughter? I mean, isn't that counterintuitive? The Xerxians appear to be hostile toward Kelli, yet for him to request a meeting…" She shook her head.

At first, that too had seemed odd to Eva. The answer

was glaringly obvious. "He was genuinely concerned about your daughter being afraid of his people." She'd read the reports. Not only had Ella Reese been kidnapped by men posing as Xerxian, she'd been physically altered so she too could appear as one. Because of that, she and her abductors had blended into Xer society.

"What about when he put his hand on her forehead?" Aric's head tilted.

"He recited a blessing over her."

"Do you know what he said?"

"He…" Eva didn't want to think of what he'd prayed over the young girl. "It was merely an ancient praise text."

The scientist drew closer. "Can you tell me the words? Please. It's important."

Because of how Ella responded? Though the little girl did not understand what he had said, the prayer obviously had affected her at another level.

It did me. Once upon a time.

Closing her eyes, Eva concentrated on the ancient text. The majestic words flooded her mind. "All glory belongs to You, Lord. We continually speak Your praise. Let us magnify and exalt Your name together. We sought the Lord. He heard and delivered us from all our fears and dangers. Our faces are radiant because we take refuge in Him."

The translation was not as elegant as in the original language, but it was close enough.

Eyes bright, Aric stared into the distance as though pondering the words. She seemed to shake herself with an effort. "So beautiful. Would you mind c-mailing that to me? I would love to share it with my husband."

"Of course." Eva bit her lip at the flippant promise. "However, I'm swamped for the next several days."

"With the summit? I'm sorry. I shouldn't have asked."

"Though we're technically 'off' tomorrow and this weekend, we'll still be busy. And we have at least one huge meeting on Saturday. Of course, if the delegates need anything..." She stopped when she realized she sounded like she trying to excuse herself, to get out of the promise.

Aric smiled. "I understand. Whenever you can send it, I'd be most appreciative." She clasped her hands. "I think it's important. We finally are beginning to feel like a family again. And we're healing. That earring Ella got, the blessing. It will be a huge encouragement to my husband. He..." As tears welled, she fell silent.

A family? Once, Eva too was part of a family.

She turned her head, not so much to give the scientist privacy for her emotional display, but to hide her own reaction. They continued down the hallway. "Tell me, how is Kelli holding up through all this?"

Again, Aric seemed to have a hard time answering. "Well enough under the circumstances." Her teal eyes narrowed. "Why do you want to know?"

"I was merely curious."

"If you're asking whether or not she holds you responsible for her incarceration, then no. She doesn't."

They reached the glass-walled elevator. "She told you this?"

"Yes." Aric's chin rose. "Because I asked her." After Eva punched the ground level, Aric reached across her to choose the third floor. "Why such interest in Kelli all of a sudden?"

Eva shrugged, puzzled. "I don't know. I just..." Why did her situation bother her so much? Because a hardened field agent like Kelli Layne had risked everything—her career, freedom, life—to save a child. From everything Eva had read, Kelli had barely known Aric Reese at the time of the kidnapping. And she hadn't met Ella before that night.

What would it be like to have such loyal friends?

The doors opened to the third floor. After Aric got off, she put her hand over the sensor to keep the elevator panels open. "I'm going to go visit Kelli later. Want me to give her a message?" Her head tilted to one side, the gesture displaying curiosity and a challenge at the same time.

"Yeah." Eva straightened. "Tell her…" She paused over her words. "Tell her she did the right thing. And I'm glad I failed on Xerxes."

If she'd slapped Aric, the woman couldn't have looked more startled. "She'll be encouraged to hear that. Especially coming from you." Her voice quavered.

Aric stepped back and the doors closed.

Not until Eva was in her cubicle did she admit to herself that she'd lied. What she really wanted to say was that Kelli Layne was a better person that she.
Unseeing, she stared at her blurred reflection on the virtual computer screen. She spoke aloud. "What would it take for me to give up everything for another person?"

Chapter 16

"Done." Satisfied, Eva pressed the "send" button. The translation of the blessing that Aric requested had harassed her for several days. And finally, Eva had taken the time to fulfill that promise. A weight lifted from her shoulders.

Wasn't that Mother's favorite? She pushed the unhappy memory away.

After rising from the sofa, she stretched and considered what remained on her list of to-dos. Her apartment was clean, but her plants needed care. Knowing she could get lost in the activity, she set an alarm to alert her when it was time to leave for the final prep meeting later that evening.

Tomorrow she could relax, that is, if no one contacted her.

Monday the Terran Summit would begin. After that would come many days with little sleep and unending scurrying to keep all the delegates happy. But all that could wait. Right now...

Foliage scissors in hand, she was bending over some wilting blossoms when her doorbell chimed. Who could that be? Salespeople and solicitors immediately came to mind. How had they circumvented security to reach her door? Eva slapped her hand on the switch to open the panel, bypassing the usual visual check first. Didn't matter. She could handle whoever was at her door.

When she saw who stood in the hallway, she involuntarily stepped back. "Zahn."

With hands folded in the long sleeves of his robes, he inclined his head.

Openmouthed, she racked her brain for the meeting she'd obviously overlooked.

"Delighted to see you." His lips broadened in a smile.

Two neighbors peeked out their doors. Apparently his arrival had not been all that private. "Come in." She grabbed his arm and pulled him into her apartment. The door whooshed closed.

He stood just inside the entrance, glancing around until his eyes again rested on her. Her cheeks grew warm as he took in her T-shirt and shorts. His gaze lingered at her bare legs and feet. Because he recalled her injury or...?

"I'm sorry. Did we have an appointment?" Eva swept back stray hair that escaped her ponytail. In the hallway mirror, she caught sight of a smudge of dirt on her cheek. With vigor, she scrubbed it off.

"I left a message with your assistant. Yesterday, I believe."

"Oh. I–I never got it." She smoothed down the hem of her shirt. Apparently her aide thought that a "day off" really meant that. She'd have to instruct him about Inter-G's definitions.

"I apologize for intruding. Shall I go?"

"No, no." She shook her head for emphasis. Besides, now that he was there he might as well stay.

"I brought you a gift." He produced a softball-sized item from inside his robes, wrapped in what appeared to be white tissue paper.

"Thank you." She took it, fingers trying to ascertain what it might be.

His lips curled in one corner. "You may open it."

Eva carefully peeled back the thin paper, then stared at the ruby-colored fruit. "I should remember the name…"

"*Gazmandashi*. From the embassy's greenhouse. Since you mentioned fruit when you first visited, I looked to see if any had ripened."

"Thank you again. I'll have it for lunch. Or dinner. Later." If memory served, the fruit was extremely juicy. She didn't want to eat it while Zahn watched. Her face grew hot as she imagined the liquid running down her arms. "Excuse me while I put this away."

She trotted down the short hallway to the kitchen. When she returned, he still remained by the entrance.

"Please, come in." Interesting that he would not advance further without an invitation. A Xerxian custom? She didn't remember that one.

"I have long wanted to see your dwelling." His dark eyes glittered.

"Well, here it is. Pretty small." Eva indicated her apartment with a sweep of her arm. Off the short hallway led to the only bedroom. The living room waited opposite. "I'm not here that much since I spend most of my time at work. Or on assignment. But at least it has no foldable rooms. Probably because it's an older apartment." She bit her lip at her babbling.

"May I?" He waited for her to indicate it was okay to walk around.

"Of course."

He stepped to the arched opening of her living room. Pausing just inside, he took in the simple furniture and sparse knickknacks. Over time, Eva had collected a few interesting artifacts from the worlds she had visited, but not many. Strangely, she found herself a little embarrassed about the Spartan look. However, he seemed neither impressed nor rebuffed.

He turned, robes billowing from the movement. "Do you like living here?"

"It's adequate." Eva shrugged. "Although, as I said, I'm not here much."

"It is very small." He made a wry face.

"I couldn't afford anything bigger. Every apartment in New Washington is expensive. And again, since I often travel, it makes no sense to get a larger place."

The living room spilled into a dining room, his next stop. How would he react to what he saw? Plants crammed into every corner of the room. Because she'd collected so many, she'd gotten rid of the furniture. She never entertained, anyway. Her small kitchen with its two seats and table were more than adequate for her needs.

He sucked in a slow breath.

In the dining area, foliage lined the walls on custom-made wood and glass shelving. She had fifty-two plants now, from a newly propagated African violet on her worktable to a flowering gardenia in a bonsai container. When she traveled, a trusted neighbor took care of them.

"You are a botanist?" he finally asked.

"Not really. Just a plant lover." She slipped into English because no Xer words could sum up the colloquialism.

"Plant lover." Apparently intrigued by the phrase, he repeated it. Zahn paused to bend over a flower that caught his eye.

Eva remained quiet, an odd sensation swirling in the pit of her stomach. Why did she feel like a student before a professor? Would he approve of her collection or chide her for her obsession?

"They are flourishing." He carefully touched a succulent. "Yet in so little light."

"Ah, so you think. Watch this." She touched her comm-panel on the enviro-system to activate it from sleep mode. "Open dining room blinds, south and west corner."

The invisible shades in two perpendicular walls slowly parted, allowing in bright morning sunshine. That feature was why she'd chosen the apartment. The outside walls of the dining room had the illusion of disappearing, creating the perfect greenhouse for her. The exorbitant rent for the cramped apartment was worth this one aspect.

Zahn's eyes gleamed as he took in the view.

As she stood beside him, she grimaced over the three freeways that intersected in the distance. "I'd have preferred a view of a park, but this was the best one I could do on my salary. The upside is the city won't be putting up a building right outside my window. So my light will never be compromised."

"You've done admirably." His eyes shone. "And your plants, as well."

Eva swelled with pride at his words.

Again looking at her vegetation, he fingered the petals of a rare golden orchid. "This is exquisite."

"A florist had thrown it away because it was dying. Happily, I was able to rescue it." One of the rare times she'd been home for an extended period.

"The blooms are quite lovely. And so prolific." His palm cupped the miniature gold and fuchsia-colored flowers.

"Nineteen this time. The most I've gotten."

Zahn smiled at her.

On impulse she asked, "Would you care to have it? Since you so obviously like flora."

He hesitated a moment. "I would be pleased to accept such a rare and beautiful gift."

"I'll have it sent to the embassy."

Something seemed to smolder in his eyes. Again, his gaze flicked down her form. An illusory draft of warm air washed over her. She again tugged at the hem of her T-shirt. "May I offer you something to eat? Drink?"

"Yes." He pursed his lips. "If you don't mind, I'd like that morning beverage Terrans so favor."

"Coffee?"

"Yes, I would like to try some."

"That I can do." She moved into the kitchen, bypassing the automatic brewer. Instead, she chose to heat water in a kettle and make it the old-fashioned way.

The way her father used to brew coffee.

Funny how she hadn't remembered that until now.

Sitting at the tiny breakfast table, Zahn watched as she moved about the kitchen. Would he remark about her slight limp? Though her leg felt healed, she still favored it. Only that morning when she'd done her usual exercises, it had twinged in discomfort when she pushed it too hard. Another reminder that her future may have done an abrupt about-face.

As she prepared the coffee, a peaceful camaraderie settled over her. As though this was right. She searched her cupboards for matching cups, but couldn't find any. But did it matter? Her unpretentious life didn't seem to bother Zahn.

"I have a patio, if you would like to sit outside. But the noise is horrendous." Long ago, she had not chosen to waste money on a costly enviro-dome for the space.

"This spot is perfect." He smoothed his hand over the table's surface.

He waited until she took the only other seat across from him before handling his cup. Heat flashed across her face as her knee bumped his. Even when she scooted her chair away, she was aware that her leg was mere inches from his under the small kitchen table.

I can feel his warmth.

He raised his cup. "After you."

As she sipped her drink, she enjoyed the heat and flavor on her tongue. Did the coffee taste extra delectable because they shared this moment?

Zahn merely inhaled the scent, before he sampled his coffee. As though savoring every subtle flavor, he allowed the liquid to move around in his mouth.

"Be careful or you'll turn into a connoisseur." She again lapsed into English. When his brows rose, she explained. "Someone who is an expert."

"That sounds like a wonderful profession."

She grinned. Then she remembered what he'd said about making an appointment with her assistant. "I forgot to ask, did you have an agenda for this morning?"

"Merely to see you."

"I meant, somewhere to go? Someone to visit?"

He remained quiet.

She added, "It wouldn't take me long to change. Five minutes and I'd be ready to leave."

Zahn touched her arm. "No, stay. I did not wish to go somewhere else."

He really only wanted to see her?

"I am glad for an opportunity to speak freely with you." He set his cup down. "Without worry of someone overhearing us."

She sat back, waiting.

"I hesitate to bring this up. Not wanting to disturb this peaceful time." Zahn's brow clouded. "But I feel it important to be honest."

What could he be talking about?

"The day I found you injured." He paused, as though gathering his thoughts. "I need you to know that I had been following you."

She set her mug down with a clunk. "What?" So her suspicions about being watched had been correct.

"I had been tasked by the High Council to find Kelli-

Layne and Jayden-Song while another was to observe the Intergalaxia operatives. Once I located you, I found the ones called 'the fugitives.'"

"I never knew." And she prided herself on her stealth. On her ability to remain invisible, even in enemy territory. How long had he been following her?

A concerned expression crossed his face. "Does this anger you?"

She reflected. "No. I'm merely astonished. It explains a lot, though."

Zahn's shoulders relaxed. "I was worried…"

"You? Worried?" She couldn't help but tease.

His forehead knitted with humbleness. "Yes, I do have faults. Does that surprise you?"

"More like relieves me. I'm not the only one who has failings."

"No, you're not. I could give you a list of mine."

"Hmm." Then she went back to his confession. "You were ordered to do nothing about Kelli and Jayden Song?"

"Correct. Merely observe."

"You didn't merely observe me."

His dark eyes fixed on her. "I did at first. I saw part of the battle between you and Kelli-Layne. I watched her carry you through the woods to the road. When I began to follow her back to Jayden-Song, I felt constrained to return to you."

Reliving that moment, she stared into the memories. "When I first saw you, I thought I was hallucinating."

"And you were frightened."

"Yes."

In retrospect, she'd been terrified of dying. Because she wasn't ready? Or because deep down she knew her life up to that point had been wasted and pointless?

She smoothed her thumb over the cup's handle. For several moments, she fought for words. "Why did you help me?"

His brow tightened. "You called out in pain. I could not

ignore that."

She said nothing. The raw emotions of that day hit her afresh.

"It was your cry, Eva, that urged me to do more."

She swallowed at the look in his eyes.

"And," he added softly, "the God of the heavens compelled me."

No. She couldn't believe He cared. Not after she'd turned her back on Him. Certainly not after she had spent her life running away from Him.

Abruptly Eva rose and put her unfinished drink on the counter. She gripped the edge of the sink, looking for some distraction. Anything. Finally she noticed Zahn's nearly empty cup. "Would you care for more coffee?"

"No. This was the perfect amount."

Pretending she wanted a fresh cup, she ground additional beans.

When the noise stopped, Zahn said, "I need to ask you something, Eva."

The use of her name emphasized the importance of his question. "Yes?" She kept her gaze fixed on the water running into the kettle, even though she had no plans to heat it.

"Have you forgiven Kelli-Layne? For causing you injury?"

Relief washed over her because he'd dropped the subject of God.

She shrugged. "I don't plan to get even, if that's what you mean."

"No, I mean truly forgiven her." He rose and drew closer. "From your heart."

Turning off the water, she stared into his face. "I don't…" His words made her pause. Had she forgiven Kelli? She had visited her in prison. Once. They'd been cordial. Wasn't that enough?

"I needed to bring this up. As a friend." His voice fell

low on her ear. "We Xerxians have a saying, and that is to do good to our enemies. Not necessarily for their benefit, but for ours."

"Kelli isn't my enemy."

"Perhaps not now. But she once was. And you bear her mark on your body. Permanently."

Eva stretched out her leg. Would she really limp the rest of her life? If so, did it really matter now? Whenever she looked toward the future, she sensed that her days in the field had ended.

He tilted his head as he watched her. "Have you done Kelli-Layne any good?"

She was about to tell him about the prison visit. But what was good about that? Eva needed to do more—fight for Kelli's freedom.

"I have said what I came to say." Zahn moved away. "I don't wish to intrude upon you any longer."

"You're leaving?" Disappointment buffeted her.

"I know you have much to do before the summit begins."

"Yes. But…" Eva followed him down the hallway. Her apartment would feel empty after he left.

Pausing at the bedroom door, Zahn merely glanced in. He suddenly turned, astonishment rippling across his features. "I am pleased you gave my gift a place of prominence in your dwelling."

She looked in, recalling that she'd set his carved box on her dresser. With her room so recently tidied, his gift was conspicuously displayed. Only that morning, she had placed a light disc under it to highlight the intricate scrollwork.

While she gazed at him, his eyes grew hooded. She gulped. Her pulse hammered against her throat.

How did he stir her with just a look?

From the recesses of her mind came an awareness of Xer customs. Zahn waited for her to make the first move. In his society, the female dominated the relationship. The woman was supposed to indicate that she wanted a man to prove his exclusive devotion to her—by speaking her wishes, touching him, or sending him a host of nonverbal signals.

Mortification gripped Eva. What must Zahn think as she invited him over and over by her quickened breath and misty eyes? And now, his personal gift sat in a room of intimacy, in a place of prominence. Though her actions betrayed her, he waited for her to speak her intentions.

Yes, her heart whispered, *admit that you are tempted.* Tempted to place her palm on his cheek. To seek a response from him that she knew he would not hesitate to give. Her gesture would grant permission for him to court her. Behind his self-restraint, she sensed a smoldering passion. From his glittering eyes to the tense muscles in his neck, he betrayed his true feelings.

As the floor tilted at the rush of emotion, Eva gripped the doorframe.

He wants me to agree to a formal courtship. The age-old response to desire swept over her. She had never felt this way about any man. The emotion thrilled.

And pained.

Her breath gushed from her as though someone punched her in the stomach.

Zahn stepped back. How wise he was. He knew she needed time. Needed to sort out the confusion in her soul.

He bowed. "Farewell, Eva Daviana. Until next we meet."

Chapter 17

"And finally," the presenter said to the hundred-odd Intergalaxia personnel in the conference room, "we will outline the clothing requirements for the summit's opening night."

Eva stifled her yawn at yet another "final" remark. A peek at the chrono on her virtual memo pad confirmed the late hour. The meeting had gone way past the scheduled time.

When muted chimes sounded, alerting her that several people had questions about the topic, she straightened in her seat and focused. What had she missed?

"Let me repeat," the presenter said with rising terseness, "it was decided that this year we will not favor one race above another. Clothing choices for the reception need to be Terran in design and origin."

The man next to Eva growled, "Xenophobe."

She pressed her chime and waited for her chance to ask a question.

"Yes, Hilliard?"

"In former years, a liaison wore attire appropriate for their delegation. Are you saying that is no longer the case?"

"Correct."

"But to *not* do so," she continued, interrupting him before he could call on someone else, "would insult the very group we are supposed to honor and serve."

Voices rose in support of her objection.

"That makes perfect sense." The man next to her allowed his voice to carry this time. "How're we supposed to—?"

"Order," the presenter demanded when a dozen discussions erupted. "Order."

No one paid him heed. Everyone had an opinion, which apparently disagreed with the new regulations.

Director Rosborough took center stage. Face set, he looked about the room, which grew still in an instant. "Everyone here knows how volatile this year's summit will be because of the Kelli Layne situation. In light of anti-Terran sentiment, we will all abide with this directive."

End of discussion.

Eva rubbed her forehead as she ducked her head. The new rule meant she would not be able to wear the robe Zahn had given her—the one he had crafted with her in mind. Regret warred with relief. However, she hated the idea of disappointing him.

After Rosborough sat down, the presenter moved on to the meeting's wrap-up. In no time Eva rose with the other participants in preparation to leave.

A throat clearing nearby caused her to turn.

Rosborough stood behind her in the aisle. "Please join me in my office."

Without waiting for her assent, he left the room.

"Uh, oh." The man behind her eloquently expressed her sentiment.

Was Rosborough going to take her to task for causing trouble during the meeting? Or bring up that fiasco in the park again?

When she reached the director's office, his assistant nodded for her to go in. Didn't that man ever take time off?

"Sir?" Eva stood before Rosborough's desk aware of the door closing behind her.

"Have a seat." He indicated one of the two chairs before his massive desk. "And remember my asking you to call me Jordan?"

"Yes, sir. Jordan." Perched at the edge of her chair, Eva clasped her hands together. Before he could say anything, she barreled ahead. "I apologize for speaking so forcefully about the dress requirement. I didn't mean—"

"That's not why I wanted to see you." The director came around his desk and leaned against it.

She opened her mouth, then shut it. "Oh. I wanted to make sure I didn't cause you or Inter-G any embarrassment."

"None at all. My agents should feel free to voice their opinion."

Really? Over the years, that's not what she'd observed.

She pressed her lips together. What was this about then? Not known for cozy chitchat, Rosborough was usually direct.

She gazed at his crisp shirt collar, the antique pen and inkwell on his desktop, the expensive *Dindas* artwork. Anywhere but at his face.

"Eva. We've known each other for quite a while."

Already not liking the sound of this, she clenched the

chair's cushion.

"I don't explain my reasoning. To anyone." He paused. "However, in this case..."

Still she couldn't meet his eyes. Eva chewed the inside of her lip.

The director crossed his legs as he remained standing. "I want you to accompany me to the reception at the summit's opening. It would be inappropriate for me to attend solo."

What? She gaped, mind terrifying in its blankness. Why her? Why not someone else?

"I'm honored, sir." The words bolted from her lips. "But is that wise? After all, I—you—*we* both work for Intergalaxia and—"

"That's precisely why you're the perfect choice."

She stared at his shoes.

"You check out. No scandals. No money issues. I anticipate no problems for Intergalaxia. Or for me."

Still, she remained dumb. She checked out? That meant Rosborough had scrutinized her past. It was obvious he had been more thorough than Inter-G's initial background check when they hired her.

Is that why Marshall had been invited to be part of the Xerxian panel? So Rosborough could corner her father and ferret out any secrets?

She stared at the director, unable to shake that belief.

"Come now, Eva. Don't be demure. If you want to believe this is strictly professional, fine." His legs uncrossed. "However, if you think there's something more in my request, I'll leave that up to you."

Glued to her chair, she couldn't begin to imagine the ramifications.

He straightened. "We can explore that possibility once the summit is over. If *you* so choose."

Heat invaded her face as she anticipated her supervisor's snide comments multiplied by hundreds. Despite the director's power, he wouldn't be able to stifle all the gossip.

After holding out his hand, Jordan helped her rise. He gripped her fingers a moment longer before releasing them. "I trust your discretion. Your reserve. As I've already said, you're the perfect choice."

Jordan stepped to the door. "My driver will pick you up tomorrow morning at eight. He'll take you to a clothier, jeweler and so forth. The salespeople have been prepped. No need to worry about anything."

Eva gulped. "But tomorrow's Sunday. Won't some shops—?"

"Taken care of." The director pressed the panel to open the door. "See you early Monday evening. Good night." He ushered her out.

Not until the door closed behind her did Eva realize she'd not agreed to anything. Obviously "no" wasn't an option. Director Rosborough was used to getting his way.

Garbed in a diaphanous ivory gown of silk and lace, Eva felt like a peacock. If a terrorist group stormed the reception, she would be about as useful. For the third time in half an hour, she adjusted the hand-embroidered sash as she greeted dignitaries, ambassadors, and other delegates for the opening ceremony of the Eighth Annual Terran Summit. A dizzying array of hues greeted her as peoples from twenty-three planets converged in Intergalaxia's grand ballroom.

Now she was glad she'd overruled the salesclerk's insistence that she choose something more colorful. Jordan Rosborough had approved her choice, the light in his eyes and smile on his face letting her know he liked what he saw. Fingers shaking, Eva handled the violet Laotiacian diamonds set in the now-infamous Angel Gold around her neck and at her ears. The rented jewelry was worth more than two years of her salary.

She blinked to relieve the discomfort of the contact lens she wore, provided by Inter-G. It gave her a miniature visual printout about anyone on whom she focused. Her earpiece—synced to the lens—provided the proper way to greet the dignitaries, whether a bow, a curtsey or a hand gesture. Now she understood how the director kept everyone straight, not just at this function, but every other one she'd attended. Not only that, but a team of synecologists, anthropologists and others were at their disposal should any difficulty arise.

Her earpiece translated the greetings of the dignitaries, prompting her with an acceptable response. Because every guest had a translator, she was able to speak to them in English. It made her job all the easier.

She caught a glimpse of Zahn as he followed the ambassadress and her retinue. As the only male in the Xerxian delegation, he was last in the lineup as they walked through the main foyer. His gaze flickered to her gown before he looked away. Since her attention was focused on welcoming the ambassadress, she didn't get a chance to greet him personally. Expression impassive, he passed by without meeting her gaze.

I'll explain later. She owed him that.

The opening greeting, complete with celebratory aperitifs, signaled the start of the festivities. Speeches followed, a buffet style dinner. Stomach in knots, Eva picked at her food. All during dinner and afterwards, Jordan kept her by his side as he made the rounds, conversing with everyone he met. He pressed an Irish coffee-type drink into her hand, which she nursed, not wanting the alcohol to impair her in any way. All the while, Eva grew more aware of the number of times the director touched her—his hand on the small of her back, his fingers on her bare elbow, his arm linking hers. More than once, she caught Zahn watching, his eyes glittering with an indefinable sentiment.

As the evening wore on, guests migrated to the open terrace where a dance floor had been prepared. Uncountable sky lanterns bobbed in the gentle autumn breeze while lush blossoming plants graced every table. With the abundance of fragrances and the muted lighting, Eva moved in a dream. As night descended, her senses intensified to an impossible pitch. Time and again, her gaze strayed to Zahn. A desire to be with him echoed through her.

If they were alone, she would no longer resist his wordless call. What would happen then? She remained clueless about the nuances of Xerxian courtship. But her soul thrummed with curiosity. No, more than that. Sang of its longing.

The orchestra played a number of alien tunes, giving participants the chance to dance as their culture permitted. She welcomed the distraction when those of Keelias IV performed their gyrations. Only the men danced, stalking about the floor with heads bobbing. Why did they remind her of chickens as they strutted about? When the music ended, another group took their places. The wild beat of drums and shouts accompanied the participants' prancing about the room.

Jordan stepped closer to speak in her ear. "Do you dance?"

"Only a little. *Very* little." She watched the group on the floor, their bodies bending at impossible angles. "I would prefer a more sedate Terran style."

"How about a good, old-fashioned waltz?"

"I can probably handle that."

He smiled. "Good. It's next on the program."

The cacophonous music ended. Form impeccable, Jordan led her to the dance floor. Now Eva was glad Marshall had insisted she learn the conventional steps. However, the director was an excellent dancer, leading her in such a way that she could not have embarrassed herself if she tried. He was light on his feet, his athletic form a pleasure to move in sync to.

She suddenly felt as if the two of them were alone. The people around her were merely props while he guided her around the floor with ease. The physical cues he gave, in the pressure of his hands and fingers on her back, kept her attention fixed on him.

He met her gaze. "Enjoying yourself?"

"Yes. Thank you."

"I'm glad." He turned his head as though focusing at something over her shoulder. However, the shift made his speech feel more intimate. "I appreciate how seriously you've taken tonight's assignment. I couldn't be more impressed with your poise. You're bearing. I was right in choosing you."

"I'm glad I lived up to your expectations."

"You seem more relaxed." His grip tightened. "I like it."

She wanted to joke about the alcohol she'd consumed, but she squelched the comment. Would he see it as flirtatious?

"You're different, Eva. Ever since you came back from Xerxes." His voice lowered another notch. "More...inviting." He breath brushed her ear.

Could it be because of Zahn? The Xerxian had caressed the imprisoning cords about her heart, gently loosening the strangling pressure. Much like when he'd untied the bandages around her leg because they were too tight. Though keeping her injury immobile, the splint had not allowed healing to take place.

She caught a glimpse of him standing in the crowds, talking to someone. At that moment, Zahn glanced over. Her pulse accelerated a notch as he fixed his dark gaze on her. In that second, Eva forgot the man who held her in his arms as she mentally rushed to Zahn's side.

I want to be with you, her soul whispered across the expanse. *Do you know that?*

A small smile touched his lips. His eyes burned more

deeply. Could he hear the call of her heart?

She wanted him to.

Waltz neglected, her timing faltered. The director tightened his hold to correct her misstep.

Her attention snapped back to him. "I'm sorry."

"Perhaps that last drink wasn't such a good idea." His voice held a hint of humor.

"I probably didn't eat enough dinner."

"Hmm." His fingers squeezed hers. "I should have paid more attention. Not rushed you."

When she glanced again at Zahn, he had turned away. The magical moment evaporated.

She cleared her throat. "Would you mind my asking someone else to dance?"

Would Rosborough accommodate her wish? It would be the perfect opportunity to explain to Zahn about the robe. If she remembered correctly, Xerxians were not opposed to dancing.

"I'm that boring?"

"Of course not." Heat bruised her cheeks. "I apologize. That was badly timed."

Jordan pursed his lips as though in thought. "I don't see why not."

"I didn't want to offend you."

"Only if you performed some of the maneuvers I saw earlier. With another man."

Her face grew hotter. "As I said, I dance only a little."

"Happy for me, then." He smiled down into her eyes.

Her gaze again sought Zahn. This time he stood with a group of delegates who were watching those on the floor. He didn't look her direction. Should she ask him? Even if he declined to dance, it would give her a chance to explain.

The orchestra performed another waltz immediately after the first, not giving her an opportunity to gracefully bow out. Was it because Jordan had signaled the conductor? Holding her hand more firmly, he drew her closer. His breath warmed her cheek.

She moved stiffly. Should she beg off because of her leg? Though an occasional zing raced up her thigh, the pain was minimal. The longer she was in the director's arms, the more self-conscious she became. Like she was betraying Zahn? This waltz went on and on.

When the music finally ended, Jordan stepped away and turned, applauding the musicians like the other dancers.

"Please excuse me." Eva left the director's side, heading where she'd last seen Zahn.

He was nowhere to be found. Though she searched the crowds, he was not on the terrace. Inside then? She looked for him there. Nothing. Snagging an aide, she asked if he'd seen the Xerxian delegates.

"One moment, I'll check." He pulled out his comm-unit and scanned the guest list. Then he headed over to the greeters before returning to her side. "Apparently, the ambassadress and party have already left."

"Oh. Well, thank you." She then realized how late it was. During the last waltz a number of guests had departed.

With reluctance, she headed back to Jordan.

He touched her elbow and drew her closer. "You look tired. Want to leave?"

"I don't wish to take you away from your obligations."

"Already fulfilled."

With Zahn gone, she no longer desired to stay. "Then I'm ready whenever you are."

Not much later, they were seated in the back of an air limo, the director's personal driver up front, privacy mode activated in the back. In the limo's interior dim lighting, Eva leaned back against the leather cushions and gazed up at the star-sprinkled sky through the transparent ceiling. The heavenly bodies danced in the darkness. She sighed. Perhaps alcohol had affected her more than she first believed.

Jordan leaned toward her. "Thank you."

"For? Not stepping on your toes during the waltz?"

His grin broadened. "Yes. And for the whole evening. You're wonderful."

She fingered one priceless earring. "Thanks for being confident that I wouldn't cause a galactic incident. Or embarrass you in any way."

"I had no doubts." His amber eyes flickered downward. "And I wanted to commend you on your choice of gowns. Not one I'd picked but your taste won out this round."

This round? Eva gulped.

Hand resting between them on the seat, his gaze fixed on her. "I want to do this again. With fewer dinner guests. Two to be exact."

She didn't know how to answer. An intimate dinner would be impossible. How to refuse?

"But," he drew out the word, "if I remember right, we talked about waiting on that topic. After the summit." He looked down at his hand, then reached for hers.

Eva sucked in a slow breath.

His chin puckered as he studied her fingers in the dim blue light. "You have lovely hands. I've long admired them. I've long admired a lot about you." Jordan's voice grew husky. "You didn't know, did you?"

Words blockading her throat, she shook her head.

"Good. I don't care to be the topic of gossip." He tilted his head to one side. "And you don't either."

"No." She spoke a little breathlessly. What had started out as *official* was quickly becoming personal.

He suddenly tugged on her hand and scooted closer. The next moment, his lips enveloped hers. Though not unexpected, Eva was still shocked by how they felt. His feral-like kisses very much invited—no, demanded—she submit. Jordan Rosborough refused to take no for an answer.

Almost apart from herself, she felt her head tilting back as she yielded to the growing pressure on her mouth.

Without warning, a bubble of energy burst inside her.

Buried passion—long suppressed—gripped her and conquered any reticence. Jordan grunted in surprise, then responded with greater fervency until his panting breath resounded in her ears. She fought the overwhelming need to dominate him. To take this intimate moment to its logical conclusion.

Cold reason finally rescued her. When his lips pressed just below her jawline, she struggled upward.

"Stop…" Her hands shoved against his chest. "Stop it."

He sat back, eyes wide with surprise. And simmering desire. "I—I'm sorry. I didn't expect you to…"

Eva ducked her head, furious not with him, but with herself. And terrified that she had not anticipated or controlled that part of her being.

The limo hummed as it rested on the aeropad. At her apartment? How long had they been there?

"I need to go. Let me out." She slapped at the door panel.

"Wait." Jordan's hand gripped hers as he too reached for the release. "Let me." He opened the door, then helped her out.

Mustering every ounce of willpower, Eva stopped herself from running headlong to her apartment. She fumbled in her clutch for her electronic key. Finally, the panel unlocked. "Open."

Get inside. Lock the door. Hurry.

"Lights," she rasped. The inside hallway lit up.

"Eva." Jordan grabbed her arm.

She stiffened, again fighting the emotion that rose again. The desire to either assault him or pull him into her apartment raged in her.

Digging fingernails into the palms of her hands, she struggled with the tremors that shuddered through her. She remained rooted, feet as heavy as boulders.

He studied her, brow drawn. "I only wanted to say good night."

"Good night." She kept her face turned away. As long as he had a hold of her arm, she couldn't move. Another shudder ran through her.

She must resist.

If he insisted on coming in, she didn't know what she would do. Fear rippled through her. Not of him. Of herself.

Keeping her head ducked, she squeezed her eyes closed.

Leave. Before I do something awful!

As though she'd screamed the words, he suddenly withdrew.

Eva stepped backward across the threshold and hit the palm lock. As soon as the door clicked shut, her knees gave way. She sank to the floor.

Chapter 18

I burn.

Zahn paced in the darkened garden, fists clamped, jaw clenching. Never had he felt so out of control. Never had he known such fury towards another being. Images from the reception barraged his mind—the human male standing beside Eva, his possessiveness, his hand on her elbow, the way he held her when they danced, the look in his eyes.

That director of Intergalaxia had laid a claim on Eva. And Zahn could do nothing about it.

More than once, the man had glanced at Zahn, the challenge—no, the triumph—unmistakable in his thinly disguised smirk. Somehow Rosborough had sensed a connection between Eva and Zahn. The human made it clear, in his lifting chin and narrowed eyes, that he would conquer her. She would belong to him.

She already did.

Zahn hit the marble bench with his bunched fist. And again. However, the bruising of his hand could not overcome the pain of his powerlessness. Blinded by everything but his own passions, his soul raged.

I want Eva. He desired her like nothing else in his life. He had been so certain that her heart had begun softening, even increasing in affection for him. He had grown confident that by his quiet and devoted persistence, she would agree to his proposal of marriage.

A source he'd not anticipated demolished that hope.

A rival. A dominant, human male.

Leaning against the gazebo, Zahn buried his forehead against his tense forearm. The look in Eva's eyes when she had smiled into the face of her dance partner seared his mind. She had blushed in his arms. What had they been talking about? What had the director said that made her grow soft-eyed? She had looked toward Zahn, then forgotten him the moment Rosborough had drawn her attention back. Had Zahn merely imagined the tender glance he and Eva had shared?

That she was flattered by the attentions of the director appeared obvious. Rosborough was a man of power and persuasion, one who would take what he wanted. And yes, Zahn knew he wanted Eva. Jordan Rosborough would pursue her until she surrendered. Eventually, he would coerce her into choosing him.

That was not the way of the Xerxian.

In quiet faithfulness, Xer males won the hearts of their chosen. In keeping with his culture, Zahn had let Eva know that it was not just because of his declaration that he had proposed, but that he truly cared for her. In a short amount of time, the seed of affection had sprung into a mature and deepening love.

But merely in his own heart?

"Why, God of the heavens? Why?" Zahn cried aloud, not caring that any might hear.

But no one shared the darkened gardens with him. He was alone in his misery.

Above, the unfamiliar constellations glittered, raining down weak light. As he tilted back his head, the words grated through his throat. "Why did You command me to offer her marriage? Why stir my heart when You knew she would choose another?"

No response came. Zahn stalked through the gardens. Round and round the perimeter of the gazebo he went, no closer to an answer than when he'd descended upon the enclosure.

The words of the sacred texts came to him.

O God, everything I desire is before you;
You hear my every sigh.
My heart pounds, my strength fails me;
There is no longer even a glimmer of light in my eyes. It is gone!

He continued to pace, but rest would not come. Instead, his anger smoldered, searing the full measure of his soul. Hour after hour he pleaded for relief. He prayed for deliverance from the emotions that racked him. Nothing eased his torment.

As the impending dawn lit the sky, Zahn made a decision. While his soul roiled in torment, he could not stay on Earth. He needed to leave before he did something that would embarrass his homeworld and dishonor God.

Nothing remained here for him. Xerxes IX was where he belonged. He must return home.

A man was kissing her. Alone, secluded, and uninterruptible. Half reclining, Eva melted under caresses that grew more passionate. She ran her fingers through his hair. His lips were on her neck, stirring passions that she had long suppressed. Forbidden emotions.

Then she realized the hair she touched was finer than silk.

Zahn.

He was the one who held her. In his arms, she sighed. Her fingers again sought his hair. Wanting to learn his features, she traced his eyebrows, his chiseled cheeks. She felt his strong jaw. The curve of his soft lips.

"Zahn!" Eva bolted upright in bed. As she grew more wakeful, trembling seized her. Though the room was dark, she could see the details of her furniture. Even without the lighted disc, she could see his gift—the carved box on her dresser. Gulping air, she tried to understand what she had dreamt. And why.

Jordan may have awakened desire, but her heart had fled to Zahn. Even now, fully conscious, she thought only of him. Wanted only him.

"But I...I can't." She whispered the reproof into the darkness.

Slowly, she reclined. The images would not leave her. Fantasy competed with reality, then the two merged. She remembered Zahn's gentle touch. His black-inside-black eyes. His soft smile.

"His love." The wistful confession, spoken aloud, filled the void.

If only...*if only* she could fully love him in return. Agree to his proposal. Give herself to him. But that was forbidden. Eva had long ago learned that she could never belong to a man. *Any* man. If Zahn found out the truth about her, she could not bear his rejection. She would not open herself up to that possibility. Would not let him, or anyone else, discover she was an accident of nature.

"I'm a freak." The sorrowful plaint echoed in the dusky room. "I can never forget that. *Never.*"

She must remain alone. Forever.

After rising, she positioned herself in front of the mirror and lifted her shirt. The lack of light was no hindrance. The Xerxian inside her had no need of more. In the reflection, she saw her navel, positioned high on her abdomen. Too high for a human...a visible deformity that proved her abnormality. A mistake of engineering.

For years, she'd successfully hidden the secret. With her blood stirred, her dual natures warred. The Xerxian domination threatened to overcome—swallowing her and everyone around. It promised only agony. Even now it raged in her.

She closed her eyes, seeking the ancient chant.

"Pain *can* be controlled," she whispered. "I will master it. I *will* conquer it."

More important, she must master that hidden half.

"God?" she dared whisper into the darkness. "Please..."

But what could she ask for? Would He even listen after all the years she'd rejected Him?

She crawled back into bed and closed her eyes. But even as she commanded herself to sleep, the longing for Zahn's phantom lips haunted her.

"I see no way around it." Thom Marshall stood beside the virtual projection in Aric's office. The bland, gray wall was a perfect backdrop to display the lighted hologram of the treaty. "See here? This verbiage leaves no room for other interpretations."

"Amplify translation," she commanded the computer. The Xerxian text darkened as English script filled in below.

Two-inch letters scrawled across the wall.

"Yes, there." Thom pointed. "The law is specific. Disguising oneself as Xerxian is a crime. We can't get around it."

Dismay gripped Aric as she stared at the screen. "I'm getting that from all the other team members as well." Her heart broke for Kelli.

"You've heard about the kidnapper?" His bushy eyebrows clashed over his nose. "He was executed yesterday. On Xerxes."

Sick to her stomach, she nodded. "One other as well." The bodies of both men had been transported to the space station, then jettisoned toward their solar star to be cremated.

As if the Xerxians wanted no human remains to taint their soil.

"The High Council focused on that one issue of their assuming a Xerxian disguise." Thom sunk into a chair. "Nothing else seemed to matter."

Aric had read the reports. They'd not focused on Ella's kidnapping, but rather stuck to that point only. Their decision set the stage for Kelli.

If she stood trial on Xerxes IX, she wouldn't have a chance.

With hands resting palm-up in his lap, Thom asked in a low voice, "What about the summit? Any support there?"

"Everything I've heard tells me that a majority of the council members will favor Kelli's extradition to Xerxes. Intergalaxia will have to comply or else risk an interstellar war."

"When's the vote?"

"Tomorrow at one. I was praying we could come up with something before then." Aric rubbed her temples as she slouched in her chair.

The older man reached across the space and patted her arm. "Don't give up hope. Even if she stands trial in Xer

Prime, the court may be lenient because of the extenuating circumstances."

"I'd like to believe that." However, Aric had been monitoring an isolationist movement that had been gaining alarming popularity. Several large clans on Xerxes supported it. They wanted all Terrans off their world. Permanently.

Thom sat back in his chair, looking tired. Like the rest of the team, he'd been putting in long hours. All of them were weary. All of them felt as though they'd failed.

How would she be able to hide this the next time she visited Kelli in prison? Her friend was expecting something hopeful. But Aric had no idea how to manufacture false optimism.

Regardless, she needed to put on a brave face for the sake of her friend.

Thom passed a hand across the back of his neck. "Have you made plans if Ms. Layne is extradited?"

"I'll go to Xerxes IX to testify. With Ella." She was prepared to petition the First Chancellor for permission. "You?"

"I don't…" He fell silent, then seemed to struggle within himself. "If I could be sure I'd do more good than harm…"

"You'd go?"

He shifted in his chair. "I'll make a few careful inquiries, but I don't know if…" He again fell silent.

Had he made enemies on Xerxes? Was that the source of his reticence?

As his shoulders sagged, he appeared older. Aric no longer saw the esteemed scientist, but a lonely man. He'd told the team that retirement was wonderful, but admitted he missed interacting with people. One specifically.

"Forgive the question," she said, "but have you had a chance to visit your daughter yet?"

"No." His grimace betrayed only sadness. "She's busy with this summit. I checked with her aide, but her schedule is packed."

Aric took a deep breath. Would he resent her prying into his personal life? "I urge you to make time to see her." When he frowned, she added, "Though my father's death wasn't unexpected, I regret the things we never got to talk about. So much I wish I'd said."

When he didn't answer, she added, "I'm merely trying to save you—and Eva—the remorse."

Thom's gaze flickered to her, then away.

Was that begrudging assent? She dared to add, "Your hotel reservations are good until the day after tomorrow, right? I'd be pleased to offer you our guest room after that. We have a large house. Plenty of room." She saw him begin to weaken. "And I have an eight-year-old who would love a chance to talk your ear off. And draw you pictures."

He sighed. "That sounds great."

"Then you'll stay?"

Eyes crinkling in the corners, he nodded.

Aric leaned forward. "Good. I'd love to hear stories about my father if you're willing to share. I know Ella would like them."

A smile appeared. "Since he's not around to contest them, I can slant them any way I want."

She managed to chuckle. "True." She rose. "I need to get home to my family. Thanks again for all your hard work."

"I wish I had better news to share." His eyes seemed to burn more brilliantly. With tears?

Stepping out of her comfort zone, she laid a hand on his shoulder. As an encouragement to herself, not just Thom Marshall, she said, "We need to trust God for the outcome."

He ran his knuckles across his chin. "Yes. We should."

What was up with Zahn? Eva watched him attend to the

ambassadress at the luncheon, but not once had he glanced over. Despite the fact that she—and most of the liaisons—pulled double duty to beef up security, he had no reason to ignore her. She got the distinct impression he was avoiding her. Though Eva attended the gathering, he'd not made one move in her direction. It was markedly different from his first days in New Washington.

Her earpiece chimed, alerting her of an incoming call. However, the preprogrammed tones indicated that she needed to be able to speak freely. She moved outside the room and into the nearby corridor. Once more she glanced at Zahn, but he was deep in conversation with another delegate. Though he must see her in his peripheral vision, he didn't look her direction.

She wanted to linger, but the call couldn't wait. Before speaking, she parked herself outside the room and signaled her team leader.

"Sir?" She spoke in her concealed mike in her badge, wishing again for her sub-dermal chip. But those were reserved only for field agents.

"Change of plans. You are to meet in second-floor conference room in fifteen."

"Yes, sir." Eva resisted the urge to ask him what this was about. After the luncheon concluded, she was supposed to escort the delegates to the general assembly. They were about to vote on Kelli's fate.

But he had already clicked off the call. She would have to comply. Besides, she would hear of the results soon enough.

First things first. She had to make sure all the delegates found their way to the general assembly. When Eva returned to the dining room, most of them had already departed through another set of exits. She checked for stragglers, then headed toward the conference room. On the way up the stairs, she observed the demonstrators at the outskirts of Inter-G's grounds. Their number had almost doubled since that morning. A long line of picketers pressed against the wrought iron fence, waving a plethora of signs. Their expressions projected anger. Hostility. Despite the distance and the barrier of glass, she understood their unified chant. *"Free Kelli Layne. Free Kelli Layne."*

"They don't look real happy." One of her colleagues rushed up the steps as well.

"No, they don't."

"I'm betting they're gonna be downright ugly after the vote."

Eva slowed. So that's why they were there? She'd been so busy with the summit that she'd not monitored the news.

By the time she arrived at the conference room, the meeting was already in progress. She stood by the door while the head of security went over plans for mob control should the crowd outside get unruly. A number of agents had been called in to help handle the situation, as well as many extras conscripted from other organizations. It didn't look good.

Extra protection had been assigned to the delegates, particularly the Xerxians. After being specifically prepped, she went back downstairs. Before she'd even reached the general assembly room, two aides burst through the doors, their faces grim.

"What was...?" Eva's words died.

They were already out of earshot, hurrying to some unknown destination.

When she reached the main doors, they again opened, spilling out an assistant she recognized.

"What happened?" She sought for the answer on his face. "What was the vote?"

"Six against, two abstain, fifteen for."

"Which way? What was decided?"

He paused, face grave. "Kelli Layne is to be extradited to Xerxes IX in five days."

Zahn observed the crowds swelling outside Intergalaxia with interest. Humans were so unpredictable. Then he laughed mirthlessly to himself. How well he knew. Through the massive glass windows on the second story, he watched as dusk further inflamed the protesters. The darker it grew, the more their boldness mushroomed. As though the mask of night and their sheer numbers made them more volatile.

The hour was late. He was tired. Tired of the city. Weary of the failed attempt to influence Xerxian sentiments since that no longer seemed to matter. He longed for the quiet of his home.

No, he chided himself. His heart had grown sick. Despair colored all other emotions. All other thoughts.

The rest of the Xerxian delegates joined him as they waited for instruction about their transportation back to the embassy. Extra security guards crowded around them. All were heavily armed with neuro-guns and extra energy packs. Because of the general assembly's vote? No doubt, Kelli-Layne's extradition was the first step in moving toward greater restrictions for humans on Xerxes. The ambassadress had even hinted that new technology would soon be available to screen all travelers. Those in disguise wouldn't be able to hide their planet of origin.

Perhaps this would be a good time for Zahn's traveling days to end.

"Ready?" Sounding a little harried, Eva approached his group. She glanced at him, but her attention was already drawn to someone talking in her earpiece, evidenced by her depressing her fingertips to the side of her head. "Yes, sir. Understood." She again addressed Zahn and his group. "We will be taking two cars with escorts. The ambassadress and three others in the first. The rest in the second."

In respect to the women in the delegation, Zahn chose

the latter group. Eva fell into step beside him as they headed toward some unknown destination where limos waited.

She appeared nervous. Her eyes darted about them as they hurried to the aeropad. Determined to keep from reassuring her, Zahn clamped his lips together. He had no right to offer comfort. Besides, it would only distract her from her job.

The ambassadress and others entered the first limo and departed with escort vehicles and security. Eva had them wait until she got word for the second group. After their limo descended from the aerial highway, she ushered them inside.

Though the view from above was spectacular, Zahn stopped looking once they were airborne. He stared at the back of Eva's head as she sat in the front seat. She appeared to receive continuous information in her earpiece, because she kept touching the device. More than once, she directed the driver to turn onto some prearranged route.

Apparently, the airspace in the virtual highway was not much safer than ground travel.

Zahn could not help but admire her. Dedicated to her job, she displayed amazing skills. Her attention was completely focused on the task. She allowed no distractions. Not even him.

It was just as well. Without seeing, he looked out toward the blurring lights of the city as the limo sped by the sights. New Washington's nightlife had begun, the amount of traffic considerable despite the time. *She belongs here.* Eva would never be content with the slower pace of Xer Prime, even though it was considered a modern city.

They reached the embassy. As the car lowered onto the aeropad, he scarcely paid attention to the mob that pressed against the fencing at the entrance. The blue force field that protected the compound had not yet reactivated. Eva leaped out and opened the door closest to the building, ushering the women in first. Lastly, he climbed out, taking a moment to bow in thanks. Unspoken words pressed against his throat, demanding he explain why he must leave Earth. When he straightened, her eyes widen in alarm.

"Run!" After shoving him, she thrust herself in the way of whatever approached.

She would not face it alone. Zahn turned, determined to meet the threat with her.

Two men came at them, one brandishing a club. One assailant swung at Eva, while the other fixed his eyes on Zahn. She grappled with the first while he readied himself for the male who rushed him—the one with the cudgel. As Zahn protected his face, a blow caught his arm. Fury drove the assailant who swung at him again and again. Zahn wrested the club from the attacker's hand and grabbed him around the neck in a chokehold. His opponent struggled, then collapsed, unconscious from his expert pressure.

Eva dispatched one man, however more protesters breached the embassy's wall. "Zahn, go!"

He knew they weren't after Eva, but him. After hesitating a moment longer, he sprinted toward the building. Other agents were running toward him from the structure, but he knew they wouldn't make it in time. Behind Zahn, three men were hard on his heels. One grabbed his robe, the material tearing in his hands. It didn't stop Zahn, but slowed him enough for the others to tackle him.

Aware that Eva and the other agents were only seconds from them, he fought the attackers. But these three men needed little time. Raw hatred filled their faces, their expressions easy to read despite the lack of light.
One of them raised his arm. Zahn saw the glint of metal.
Heard Eva scream his name. Something struck his head.
Then again. Warm stickiness blinded him, then he knew no more.

Chapter 19

"No one should have gotten hurt." Eva could not squelch the bitterness in her tone. Pacing before the director, she ignored the pain shooting up her infirm leg. For countless minutes, Rosborough had allowed her to castigate herself while he leaned against his desk and merely listened.

She marched back and forth over the soft Orienz carpeting. Good thing he stood five feet away so she wouldn't strike him as her gestures punctuated her points. "His Excellency was *my* responsibility."

"No. He was mine." Jordan crossed his arms. "I should have better prepped you."

"We should *all* have been better prepared. More guards should have met us at the aeropad. And the technicians should have been quicker redeploying the force field." She slumped in a chair and passed a hand over her forehead. Her skull throbbed and eyes burned. She'd not slept in over twenty-eight hours. Leaning back, her spine popped in release.

"Have you seen a medic, Eva?"

"No. I'm fine." She'd been too busy securing the Xerxian embassy. Too busy to stay by Zahn's side after the medics arrived. Too busy to accompany him to the hospital—not the one in New Washington. No, anti-Xerxian sentiment ran too hot here.

I don't even know where they took him.

Jordan scooted a second chair closer and sat beside her. "Quit blaming yourself."

"I can't—"

"That's an order."

He meant it as a joke, but she could not respond to his teasing. Closing her eyes, she sought to avoid Rosborough and his attentions. If he would just stay professional *this* time...

The brightening day vied with the harsh lights in the office. The pleasant view outside the window was preferable to the cold sterile night she'd just been through. But Eva couldn't relax. Not until she was sure Zahn would recover.

Her presence in the director's office felt surreal. She inhaled sharply when Jordan took her hand. *No. Not again.*

"Your wrist hurt?"

"Yes." She clung to the lie, the lifeline to sanity. Anything to get him to release his hold.

"That decides it. Go to the clinic and get checked out. Thoroughly. I don't want to see you for a couple days. Got it?"

She nodded. "Any word how...how His Excellency is?" She stumbled over Zahn's designation, catching herself before she called him by name.

"I heard mild concussion. Nasty wound. I'm sure mended by now."

"Good." Eva would never forget the pool of blood in which he lay. Would never forget the sound of her own scream. The fear that he was dead.

The fear that she'd lost him. Forever.

Her oversight had almost killed him. Her selfishness. Wanting to be close, she had chosen to ride in the second limo with him.

Rosborough's mouth pulled to one side. "Don't you want to know how the demonstrators fared?"

Out of the corner of her eye, she met his gaze. Briefly. "I suppose."

"You took out five of them, Eva. *Five*. By yourself."

She shook her head, remembering little more than cries of pain, bones crunching, and grunts. None of the sounds were hers. The picture of Zahn—prostrate on the ground, three men above him, a large gash on his forehead—burned into her memory. And she would never forget the blood. His blood. Everywhere.

Only later, pain visited her hands, neck, leg. That meant nothing compared to his life.

"Good news—you didn't kill anyone." Rosborough lowered his voice. "I'm glad you restrained yourself."

He meant to lighten the mood, but she couldn't get there yet.

Zahn could have been killed. And it would have been my fault.

Expression tightening, Jordan tilted his head. She sensed his desire to comfort her but knew it would involve an intimacy she could never welcome.

As Eva rose, the director did as well. His hand curved around her back. Rooted in one spot, she could not fathom how to excuse herself. Her brain thrummed with fatigue.

She had to get out of there. If necessary, she would shove him aside.

His hand moved slightly. A gentle caress. An invitation for her to melt, just a little.

"I'm glad you're okay." His voice grew husky. "I can't explain what went through my mind when I heard…"

Eva cast down her gaze, afraid he would take any reaction from her as encouragement for a greater affinity.

If he attempted to kiss her, she would snap. A mental picture of him, lying on the floor, lip split, pulsed through her imagination. What about the words that would follow? Harsh. Expressions of betrayal and pain. Unforgivable confessions…

Chest rising and falling even more slowly, he drew closer as though preparing to kiss her. She had only seconds.

Squeezing her eyes shut, she swayed on her feet.

"I'm a cad." Jordan's hand disappeared from her waist as he stepped away. "You're ready to pass out." He tapped the polished surface of his desk, activating the command system.

The miniature hologram of his assistant shimmered on the desk. "Yes, Director?"

"Get Ms. Hilliard a car." His voice had again grown cool. Professional. "The driver is to take her to Prime Medical Clinic. Secure an appointment with my personal doctor. No excuses."

"There's no need to…" Eva broke off, knowing her protests would go unheeded.

He snapped off the holo and moved toward her. "After you're cleared by my medic, head home. Get some rest."

"Yes, sir." Realizing that she had not used his name, she bit her lip.

He merely grinned. "That's more like it."

Of course he would assume her acquiescence meant to be playful, not subordinate.

The intercom chimed. "The car is here, Director."

He pressed her hand one last time. "Call me later."

Zahn left. He didn't say goodbye.

Confounded, Eva pressed her hands against the window at her apartment, staring out at the black, rainy night. Why had he gone without explanation? Despite his injuries, his life had not been in danger. He had no need to rush to his homeworld for additional medical attention. Within hours after his release from the clinic, he was on a transport ship leaving Earth. The summit had been cut short because of rioting.

Why had he not contacted her? His abrupt departure made no sense.

Now he would be incommunicado for three days as he headed home. Eva had a feeling she would never see him again. Never hear from him again.

She leaned her head against the cool glass, watching as rivulets of water ran down the window.

Did he blame her for his injury? Did he blame all humans? Though Terrans made up the majority of demonstrators, they weren't the only ones. Other races had joined in the protests.

She jumped when her door chime clanged like an alarm. Who could that be? It was nearly eight in the evening.

Not Rosborough, surely.

The chime sounded again. Suppressing a tremor, she pressed the visual.

Thom Marshall stood at her door.

Her heart pounded. She considered not answering, then discarded the childishness. Hand poised over the lock, she hesitated. Then annoyed at herself, she punched it.

"Hello, Eva." He greeted her after the panel slid open. "Am I disturbing you?"

The smell of his shaving essence hit her. The one he used to wear when she was a child.

"No. Come in." She backed away so he could pass by. And to distance herself from the fragrance—one of rugged mountains and uncut trees. A memory of his cuddling arms as he read to her struck Eva so hard she nearly staggered.

She clenched her hands so tightly that her fingernails dug into the palms. Had he worn it to soften her up? That along with his crisp shirt and slacks—like he was planned to go on a date?

"The director said he'd sent you home for the day." Marshall followed her mute indication for him to go into her living room. "I hope you don't mind that I checked with him."

Yes, she *did* mind. Were they getting chummy now? Perhaps Marshall's coming to New Washington had less to do with the Xerxian Problem and more to do with prying into her life. And what was Jordan's part in all this? She had no doubt the director took full advantage of the opportunity to ply her *ex*-father with questions. What had Marshall admitted to him?

"Have a seat." She pointed. "Want anything to drink?"

"No." He shook his head, lowering himself to the chair opposite her.

"Aren't you leaving town tomorrow?" Eva bit her lip, realizing how callous that sounded. Like she wanted to get rid of him as soon as possible.

So true. She didn't want to see him again. Hadn't they once agreed?

"Actually, no. I've been invited to spend a few days at the home of Sean and Aric Reese."

"Oh?" Surprising news. Marshall was a known recluse. His accepting an invitation, even a fellow scientist's, unsettled her. Why had he agreed?

He cleared his throat. "You up for dinner? I know of this nice café..."

"No thanks." She struggled with the rude rebuff, but lost. "I've been ordered to stay home and rest."

"Of course." After adjusting the pillow behind his back, he settled in his chair. "I, um...I was sorry to hear about your injuries. Are you okay now?"

Minimal. Not worth mentioning.

"Yes. Fine." She crossed her arms as she remained on her feet, leaning against the sofa's armrest. "All in a day's work."

"For you, perhaps." He studied her a moment. "You take after your mother more in that regard."

Her heart hardened. "Can we not talk about her?"

"Don't you think it's time?"

"We already did. Nine years ago. There's no reason to dredge up everything again."

He remained quiet, giving time for the creases on his forehead to multiple. "Nine years. Feels like an eternity." His mouth moved before his neck muscles tightened, as though he attempted to swallow something too large. "I was hoping you might have softened toward your old dad a little."

Old dad? She clamped her jaw to keep from railing at him. Didn't he understand anything? Why she had legally changed her last name to Hilliard, his bitterest enemy? Eva Marshall no longer existed. That's why she had dropped her pursuit of theoretical math and blown a priceless opportunity in the science community. Didn't he remember their last argument before she'd stormed out of his life forever?

She opened her mouth to blast him when a memory silenced her in an instant.

"Has it ever occurred to you that your mother chose to leave?" Zahn's quiet challenge slammed into her mind. And extinguished her anger.

What if *Emaa* had voluntarily left? This was Eva's chance to find out. She wrestled with herself. Yes, she *had* to know the truth. It was time.

Eva planted herself before the man she had once called

Daddy. "Did you drive *Emaa* away? Or did she leave because she wanted to?"

His brow clouded as he stared into the distant past. He took a long time answering. "Honestly? I don't know anymore." His lower lip quivered. "It no longer matters. All I know is…" He shrugged.

"It matters to *me.*" Voice quavering, she spoke more forcefully than she intended. "I need to know if my mother turned her back on me and walked away. From us both."

His bleary eyes focused on her.

She knelt by his chair. "Tell me the truth, Daddy. I need to know."

His Adam's apple bobbed several times, gaze sidling away from her again. "After…after you were born, things got complicated. We realized—too late—that we could not raise you together. We could never be a normal family. Your mother and I started arguing. Our fears spiraled out of control. Hiding the truth got to be too much. It tore us apart. I had my work. Your mother and I saw less and less of each other." His eyes swam with tears. "We drew only one solution. The only one that would solve everything."

"So she left." Eva sat back on her heels, unable to stifle the next question. "Why didn't you stop her?"

"Believe me, I tried." His shoulders slumped. "But we kept returning to the same solution. Her staying wouldn't solve anything."

"So obviously you were the only one who could raise me. Without repercussions."

"Yes." His word came out barely a whisper. He ground his palm against his forehead. "But, oh, how I miss her. I loved her more than life." He raised tortured eyes to her. "I still do."

Eva stared at him, suddenly seeing him as the lonely man that he was. He said he still loved his wife. Present tense. Twenty years of living apart had not changed his feelings.

"Where is she?" She fought for an even tone. "Where is *Emaa* now?"

Her father seemed not to hear her.

She gripped his arm. "Daddy, where is my mother?"

"I don't—don't know. I wish I did." He took a shaky breath. "I've tried to reach her. More than once. But I haven't…haven't been able…"

Eva rose, turning away from him.

"Tnara asked me to never search for her. To never contact her again." His tone carried the finality of defeat. "She made that quite clear."

As Eva moved away, his chair creaked. Fingering the stiff leaves of a plant, she tried to sort through all her father had told her. With her back to him, she heard him sniff, heard him fumble for his handkerchief.

He expelled a deep breath. And again.

The silence wore on. What was left to say? They had nothing in common. He knew little of her life while she knew nothing of his. Years before, she'd chosen a career that was as far removed from the science world as she could get. Now, they had only the abandonment of a woman in common. Not enough to sustain a relationship.

It would be better that anything left between them die a natural death.

"I see you have quite a plant collection," he said, his voice close as he stood behind her. "Your mother had a green thumb. Could make anything grow."

Eva nodded.

"At our cabin, she transformed that dead yard into a field of daisies. Thousands of them. And behind the cabin were tulips and hyacinth. Every season she made certain something was in bloom. The cabin was always filled with plants. But she loved those daisies the most."

"I remember." Throat tight, she turned.

Her father drew nearer. "We never meant to hurt you, Eva Daviana. You are a precious gift. That's why we chose to give you a middle name that means *beloved*." He shook his head, mouth turned down at the corners. "I wish things could have turned out differently."

She knew she should hug him. To tell him that she forgave him. But too many years had passed, cementing the wall between them, now impassable. It would take too much work to deconstruct it. And what would be the point? She saw no future with him.

She saw no future for herself.

As she met his gaze, Eva straightened. "Thank you for telling me the truth."

The muscles of one cheek quivered as he fought to speak. "I'm glad you were able to accept it."

Accept it? Yes, she had, but it didn't lessen the heartache. The wounded child in her still cried for the loss.

Couldn't they have found some way to keep their family together? Couldn't her father, with all his influence, all his genius, overcome every obstacle they had faced?

It occurred to her that the mess with Kelli Layne might have been mitigated if her parents had pushed harder for acceptance twenty-six years ago. Humanity had not progressed that far in all those years. Prejudice—across the universe—still ran deep.

"I'd better go. Let you get some rest." Her father's quiet voice interrupted her thoughts. At the door, he paused. "Thanks for letting me barge in on you this evening. Perhaps sometime before I leave we can go out for dinner?"

"Sure." Eva would agree to anything if it meant she wouldn't have to hug him goodbye. As long as Marshall thought he would see her again, he wouldn't feel compelled to touch her.

She couldn't bear that. Not now.

"Until next time then." He managed a small smile.

She tightened her lips in response. Just enough to fool him.

After he departed, she released a long breath.

Instead of being distraught over his visit though, she felt strangely at peace. As though she had opened up another part of her life, sorted miscellaneous pieces, then reshelved it. She would never again have to examine this pain. She could move on to the next item, until she tackled all the odds and ends.

Then she would be done. Permanently.

"Emaa."

Snuggling against her mother, Eva pressed her nose against the soft neck. She loved the way her mother smelled. Like grassy fields before it rained. And something else. Perhaps lilies? Emaa's hair fell across her cheek, tickling her skin. Eva reached upward and fingered the silky strands, loving the glassy smoothness.

"Time for bed, small one." Her voice was soft, soothing.

"Can't I stay up for one more minute?" Eva continued to caress the hair strands, fascinated by the texture. Emaa's hair was thick. So beautiful. Would Eva's be like that someday?

Oh, how she wished.

Her mother laughed, a throaty sound. "You ask that every night."

How did she remember? Eva only knew that to be parted again would be torturous. Even in sleep.

"Please, Emaa?" She again pressed her nose against the soft skin and wrapped an arm about her mother more securely. If only she would stay until Eva grew sleepy. Daddy would carry her to bed and tuck her in. Before she dozed off, Eva's last memory would be a gentle hand on her head. Or perhaps the quiet murmuring of her parents as they prayed over her. Or even the soothing hum of an ancient tune.

"Very well. A little longer."

Smiling, she snuggled against her mother's soft breast. She reached up to touch her face...

"Emaa!" Eva bolted up in bed, looking wildly around.

Reality closed around her. She was alone. Again.

Tears ran down her cheek. Silent. Burning. Torment gripped her.

Bending forward, she pressed her hands against her abdomen as though staunching blood from a wound. No good. Slipping from the entangling sheets, she clutched her side as she tried to walk off the pain. Back and forth across her dark living room she paced until her leg ached. Weary to the core, she slumped next to the soft chair where her father had sat the night before.

"God, please..." Eva buried her face against the pillow, not knowing what to pray. Would He even answer?

A faint scent rose up in her nostrils, of rugged mountains and uncut trees. Her father's essence. Her eyes stung anew. She threw back her head as the truth shuddered through her. "It wasn't his fault *Emaa* left," she whispered. "All those years, I blamed him. And You, God."

Tears ran down her cheeks. "Forgive me," she said with a sob.

A huge, crushing weight disappeared. She felt like she could finally take a deep breath. Pain dissipated. As she sat back on her heels, her arms fell to her sides.

Light gradually seeped into the dusky room. The sounds of voices in the hallway and the muted roar of traffic let her know that morning had arrived. The population geared up for their day.

And for her...a new beginning.

She rose to open the door to her balcony—a place she rarely visited. Faint pink tinged the sky, fading into golden light. The traffic's deafening roar washed over her. In each passing minute, she grew more detached from the city. From the planet.

I am finally beginning to see life. No, to really see my life.

Not just what it had been, but what it should be. Everything came into focus. With Zahn no longer on Earth, he was no longer a distraction. No longer a possible dream.

For a time, she had toyed with the idea that he could be in her future. A foolish wish. Now that he had departed, her path became clear. He had served a purpose—showing her the impossibility of ever having a normal life. Of being in love and marrying. Having children.

Now that Jordan Rosborough had made his intentions known, her career too, was ending. Not only he, but her infirm leg, would be a hindrance to any advancement. That door closed.

She had settled things with her father as much as she wanted. And now, the door to her mother—to both her parents—shut and locked.

Eva gripped the railing. Where could she go? What new future awaited? Lifting her head, she whispered, "What would You have me do?" The moment she spoke, an unearthly peace settled over her soul. She could no longer stay on Earth. That left one choice—she must go to Xerxes IX.

After she arrived, God would lead her to the next step.

Contented, she sighed. Her future lay in that planet of origin. What it involved, she didn't know. Didn't *have* to know.

"I was born for a purpose. The answer must lie there." She prayed for the courage to not waver from the path set before her. Wherever it may lead.

Chapter 20

"Eva, what are you doing here?" The director's miniature holographic image appeared on her desktop.

"Just finishing my report. Sir." She plastered a tranquil expression on her face as she smiled. If she were to pull off this charade, she had to let him think she was happy to see him.

"I made it clear you were to take today off as well."

"I'll have the weekend to rest up." The summit was over, cut short because of the unrest in the city. Her obligations there were done. Time to tie up another aspect of her life.

"Okay, then. I will *allow* you to stay at headquarters. Today." He glanced down at something, then back up at her. "My assistant said you wanted to see me this afternoon?"

"Yes. About fifteen minutes of your time, if you don't mind."

He crossed his arms. "Care to give me a hint what this is about?"

"No." Relaxing her body, she smiled again. "You are busy until one-thirty. I can wait."

"Well, I can't."

"You will have to. Sir." Eva instilled a little teasing into her tone.

He let out an exasperated breath. "Very well. I'll let you get away with it. This time."

"Until then." She switched off the communication and let her expression settle back into the grim resolution that consumed her. Leaning back in her chair, she pressed her palms and fingers together. Eva closed her eyes, feeling like she'd passed a minor test. She'd never been very good at acting. But in order to get her way, she had to let Rosborough think everything was back to normal. Otherwise he would try to stop her.

She concentrated on the reports before her, the ones her father and the rest of the SARC team had created. Then she dug a little deeper, researching Xerxian laws and even the results of the first contact between Earth and Xerxes IX. As expected, there was no precedent when it came to a situation like hers.

The event she planned to instigate would be a historical first.

That is...*if* her meeting with the director went as planned. *If* all her arrangements were not thwarted. Otherwise...

Eva could not entertain the idea of failure. Not for one moment.

Before she knew it, an alarm beeped, indicating that her

meeting with Rosborough was in ten minutes. The day had flown by. She rechecked her appearance. Had she put on too much makeup? She didn't want him to think she was falling for him. He would see right through that.

At the last minute, she put on lipstick, then wiped it off. That had been okay for the reception. Not now. She smoothed down her suit, concerned anew that the skirt and heels might be over the top. Too late now to change her mind.

She arrived a few minutes before the appointment, but ended up waiting another twelve before he bid his visitor farewell.

"Sorry to have kept you." After the director ushered her into his office, he closed the door.

"Does this cut into my allotted time?" Eva hoped she struck the right tone.

He grinned. "You can have the rest of my afternoon. The senator can wait till tomorrow."

As she took the seat he indicated, she managed to chuckle. But instead of sitting beside her, he leaned on his desk. She could tell he was being cautious. This wasn't normal behavior for her and he knew it. As Jordan pressed his hands to the edge, his amber eyes narrowed. She willed her body not to tense, knowing he would detect that in an instant.

He glanced down at what she wore, gaze lingering at her legs. "I get the feeling I'm not your only appointment today. Perhaps you have one later?"

Was that jealousy? Interesting.

"Not at all. This is my only meeting for the day."

"Ah." He smiled, obviously reading plenty into what she said. And what she implied.

Before he assumed it an invitation to get cozy, Eva plunged in. She needed to be direct. "I want you to assign me to the Kelli Layne case. I'd like to be the one to escort her to Xerxes IX."

His eyebrows rose, but he appeared to consider her request. "I had already made up my mind."

"I know." She clamped her mouth shut. Best not to appear too eager.

His fingers tapped the desk's edge as in thought. "Why should you be the one to go?"

She had a list prepared. Of all Inter-G's agents, she was the most experienced when it came to Xerxians. That she had been their liaison. That she, of all people, had the biggest possible vendetta against Kelli since she was responsible for Eva's limp. Because of that, she would work the hardest to make certain Kelli got delivered into the hands of the Xerxians.

But he knew all that.

Instead, she said, "I am hoping my presence will have a positive impact on Terran-Xerxian relations." She paused before adding, "Since I plan to support Kelli."

He frowned. Was that a good sign or not?

"I took the liberty of drawing up plans to get her safely to Xerxes with as little civilian interference as possible." Without rising, she held out an info-chip.

The director hesitated before stepping forward and taking it from her. "I see." He studied the silver square, turning it over in his hand before setting it on his desk.

She remained silent. Nothing else could be said.

His amber eyes fixed on her. "And afterwards?"

Eva inhaled slowly. Her instincts told her to lie. To tell him what he wanted to hear. That she looked forward to exploring a relationship with him. A personal one.

But she couldn't.

"This assignment will be my last in the field," she said slowly, with all sincerity. "For several reasons. After that, I'd be open to discussing a desk job." She felt herself blushing as she said it, because of the fiction imbedded in her words. "Or another line of work."

Unable to maintain eye contact, she looked down at her

hands.

He knows something's not right. Jordan Rosborough didn't get to be the director of Intergalaxia because he was stupid. He'd perfected the art of reading people, of many races. And he must see that she withheld something.

"Who will your partner be?" he suddenly asked.

Flustered by his bold question, her head shot up. It took a moment to realize Rosborough wasn't asking who her life partner would be her when she returned to Earth. Rather, he wanted to know whom she had chosen to accompany her to Xerxes IX. As per regulations.

"I thought, perhaps, a goodwill gesture to USF. One of their agents."

His lips pursed. "Interesting." He sauntered away to look out the window. "You've spent quite a bit of time thinking this through."

He had no idea.

Eva felt like her life had crystallized to this one vital moment. A chance to change history. A chance to change the course of her own life.

What was left of it, anyway.

Regardless of whether he said yes or no, she *would* go to Xerxes. It would be easier and less hassle if he agreed. But she wasn't going to let Jordan Rosborough—or anyone else—stop her.

She rose and moved closer to the desk, glad for the barrier between them. Knowing the director didn't like his hand forced, she vacillated between asserting what she wanted and playing a more passive role.

The former won out. It just felt right.

"I need your decision soon, Jordan. In order to put my plan into action. If I'm not the right person for the job, then tell me. Right now. I don't want this hanging over my head all weekend." Sensing she'd said enough, she pressed her lips together.

Her alternative plans barged into her mind, but she

banished them as soon as he looked her way. He would know. He would guess by her expression that she wouldn't give up. If he didn't let her travel to Xerxes IX in an official capacity, she planned to find a way to the planet herself.

Eva pressed her fingertips to the edge of the desk, willing them not to tremble.

"Okay." He drew out the word. "You have my approval. The orders will be in the system before you leave work."

She couldn't stop her body from nearly wilting with relief. "Thank you."

Jordan nodded. "Safe journeys."

Determined not to betray herself with an extended farewell, she managed a nod in return. Then she walked out.

If her plans succeeded, she would never again visit his office.

Like a caged animal, Aric marched back and forth in the tiny meeting room at the prison. However, she reminded herself that compared to Kelli's cell, this space was probably huge. She stopped briefly before the small table and two chairs before resuming her pacing.

"You're going to wear a hole in the floor," Sean chided without looking at her. He stood with their daughter Ella as they looked out the room's tiny window. Probably watching the demonstrators outside the prison walls. The crowds had made it difficult to make it to the parking lot. They should have brought their aero-car.

Ella studied the thin carpet with wide eyes. "Can Mama really put a hole in the floor?"

Sean answered before Aric could. "If she keeps walking on the same spot over and over she will." When he chucked their daughter's chin, she giggled.

Good thing. Aric felt like she was about to lose it from

the inactivity and small space.

A few weeks before, Sean alerted her that their friend had been moved to a maximum security facility in the middle of the night. For her protection? Riot police had been on guard around the clock. Since Kelli wasn't a criminal, she had to be locked up where she would be safe from real criminals.

But the result was much stricter security. Visiting hours were a joke. Kelli was continually kept in isolation. No contact except for the occasional guard. When she was allowed "exercise" outside, she was alone in a caged off area.

How was she not going insane?

Unable to help herself, Aric again strode across the room. A noise at the door caused her to swivel.

"Ten minutes." The stern voice of a guard sounded as the panel slid open. "When I chime, you get back to the door immediately. Got it?"

"Sure, Giorgio." Kelli smiled impishly up at the tall man. "You know I'd do anything for you."

"Kelli!" Ella squealed. Before Aric could stop her, the little girl ran and threw her arms around her friend's waist.

"Whoa." Garbed in prison orange, Kelli staggered back from the enthusiastic welcome. It seemed to take her a moment to register who assaulted her. With one hand squeezing Ella, her blue eyes filled with tears as her gaze met Aric's.

With a word, she went to her friend and hugged her. Sean's arms embraced of them.

"How...?" Kelli started to speak, voice muffled. She took a ragged breath, but seemed unable to finish her sentence.

Ella was the first to break from the group hug. "Look, Kelli. I drew some pictures for you." She ran to her tablet that was sitting on the table and scrolled through several drawings.

After they moved more deeply into the room, the door

slid shut.

"They are beautiful." Swiping tears from her cheeks, she shot a glance at Aric before speaking again to Ella. "Can you keep them for me? Until I can come visit you in your house?"

"That'd be a great idea." Sean chimed in as he put his hand on his daughter's shoulder. "We'll print them and put them in a special spot for Kelli in your room. 'K?"

"Okay." Ella looked up at the blonde beauty.

Kelli tilted her head. "I think you've grown taller, Ella."

"She did." Aric laughed. "I had to buy her a new wardrobe. She grew out of everything from last year."

"Are you still trying to be my height?" Kelli asked with a mock frown. "Regardless, I think you're going to be taller than your mom someday."

Ella smiled shyly.

"Five feet ten I could handle. Just as long as she's not as tall as Sean," Aric said. "I don't want to be the only midget in the family."

At six-two, her husband towered over her.

Kelli smiled, the gesture tight as she glanced between them. "What's the occasion? Not that you need a reason to come visit. It's just...just nice to see all three of you at once."

"We're making a speech later on." Aric glanced at her husband. "Sean arranged it. We're holding a press conference to spread goodwill. Ella agreed to let reporters take pictures."

"Ah. Fun." Understanding flitted over Kelli's features. "Was that in trade for this visit?"

"Something like that."

"You probably could have bargained for an exotic vacation instead. This isn't exactly a luxury hotel."

"It's the perfect place for us." Aric squeezed her hand.

"Sweetheart..." Sean glanced pointedly at his comm-unit, obviously referring to the fleeting time.

Aric took a deep breath. "Ella, could you show your dad

the pictures while I talk to Kelli?"

The little girl nodded, studying the two of them.

"Over here, Sweetie." Sean sat, taking Ella onto his lap while Aric grabbed Kelli's arm and pulled her to a corner.

"I need you to promise something." Aric kept her voice low.

Kelli tensed, but answered quickly. "Anything."

"Promise—no, swear—that you will not try to escape if you get a chance."

"From here? No way."

Aric shook her head, the weight of her request pressing down on her. "From anywhere." She took a quick breath. "I can't say anymore, but I need your promise."

Kelli stared at her a moment. "I swear."

"And you'll willingly stand trial at Xerxes IX? You'll go all the way?"

Biting her lip, Kelli hesitated. Her pale face faded into a deeper pallor. "Yes. I'll stand trial. Whatever happens, I want this over with. Legally."

Aric let out her breath. "Good enough."

Sean shot a look at them. "Ok, Sweetie. Give Kelli a quick hug. She needs to go soon."

"We have one minute before the guard returns." Aric glanced at the door.

"I have a great suggestion." Sean took Kelli's hand and his wife's. "How about we pray?"

Kelli's mouth trembled. "I'd like that. A lot."

While he asked the Lord for mercy and peace, tears flowed freely down her friend's face. Aric fervently hoped God was listening. And that He would intervene.

Chapter 21

"Are you sure? You don't want them anymore?" Eyes wide, Eva's neighbor stared at her as they stood in the hallway.

"Yep. My mind's made up. Any that you don't want, feel free to regift."

"Your plants are worth thousands of dollars. I know. I've priced them."

"Eh." Eva shrugged. "I know you'll give them the care they deserve. You always have, every time I traveled. I'll give you my apartment key before I leave. You can go in anytime and get them."

"Sure." Her elderly neighbor still couldn't seem to grasp what was happening. "So where are you going, anyway?"

"Work. And then a long vacation."

"Then I'll just take care of them until you get back."

"In the time I'll be gone, you will have earned every one of them." Wanting this conversation to end, she pulled out her mini comm-unit. "I'll drop off my key tomorrow morning. That work?"

"Absolutely. And thanks. So very much."

Eva smiled and turned on her heel. One last thing to do and she'd be ready. She tapped out the phone number to the USF agent who would be traveling with her. He answered on the second ring just as she reentered her apartment.

She identified herself. Then they exchanged pleasantries before he asked, "Why are you doing this?"

"I think we can discuss that later." She took the lead in the conversation, realizing that someone could be listening. "You got my instructions?"

"Yes."

"Any problem following them? And I mean *exactly* as I've laid them out."

Silence came from the other end of the line. Finally, the agent answered. "No, no problem. I'm not stupid."

"Good. Then welcome aboard. I'll see you tomorrow." Eva disconnected.

Mind numb, she sank onto her sofa. Everything was in place. She'd paid the final months of her lease and donated everything of value. The remaining items—furniture and household goods—would stay in the apartment. The landlord could do whatever he wanted with them.

Nothing was left to do but get ready in the morning.

As Eva relaxed against the cushions, her body begged for rest, but she knew she wouldn't be able to sleep. She had not the night before and probably wouldn't this one either. She was too keyed up.

Closing her eyes, she leaned her head back. So tired…

She skipped as she headed out the cabin's door, toward their field of daisies. The flowers rippled and waved in the blowing wind.

But she stopped after picking only a few. Turning, she looked into the dark living room. She could see every detail, even in the gloom.

Her mother, hair black as the night, stood next to the wall lined with books. Her eyes were large, unfathomable. Her skin, dusky and beautiful in the dim light, shimmered, soft as silk. Eva always loved snuggling before she fell asleep each night.

Her mother reached for a suitcase. Tears slipped down her cheeks. "I love you, Eva Daviana." She mouthed the words. "Never forget. I love you."

The front door banged from the wind that whistled through the cabin, drawing her attention away from her mother. When Eva looked back, the room was empty.

"Don't go!" Crying the words out loud, she awoke. The cushion under her head was soaked with tears.

Eva bent forward, crushed under the weight of emotions.

"God, please…"

She didn't know what to pray. What even to ask for.

Eva marched down the endless prison corridors, blinking to relieve the discomfort of contacts. Today, her eyes were green instead of her usual brown. But the clothing she wore could have come out of her own closet. The royal blue blouse and taupe pants were perfect for a winter complexion.

Per orders, a tall, brown-wigged woman walked beside her, head low. A beefy guard escorted them, also silent. He was a no-nonsense Greek with a neck so massive it melded seamlessly into his shoulders. In the solitary confinement section of the prison, they didn't mess around.

Behind solid panels, prisoners apparently sensed the quiet trio and catcalled or shouted obscenities.

Walking with determination, the guard led Eva and her

companion through multiple security doors. They finally reached their destination. He pressed a chime and the door slid open.

An orange-clad blonde lay curled up on the cot, facing the wall. She didn't even bother to turn. "What'd'ya want, Giorgio?"

"Visitors."

"Again?"

Finally Kelli peered over her shoulder. Eyes widening, she leaped from the cot.

The guard spoke to them all. "Five minutes." Without another word, he stepped outside the cell. The panel shut.

Kelli glanced between Eva and the woman who began to undress. The prisoner frowned.

"You need to change." Eva tapped the imaginary watch on her wrist. "We don't have much time."

"What's going on, Eva? And what's with the green contacts?"

"You're mistaken. My name is Aric Reese." Eva's mouth tightened. "Please hurry."

Still, Kelli didn't move. Finally, she shook her head and stepped back. "Sorry. I gave my word I wouldn't try to escape. I'm not going anywhere."

Eva smiled. "Glad to hear it. But this is not what you think. This is a *get off Earth with our skins intact* plan."

Kelli absorbed the information a second longer, then stripped out of her prison garb. In moments, she was dressed in the agent's clothing while the other woman wore the bright orange jumpsuit. With a cosmetic towelette, the woman removed all her makeup, then took her wig off and shook out bleached tresses.

Kelli slipped the brown curls onto her head and tucked telltale light-colored hairs out of sight. "Okay?"

Eva nodded as she handed Kelli some face powder and the bright-colored lipstick her companion had once worn. In no time she was ready.

"Thank you." As Kelli ran her hand over the shirt's soft fabric she sighed in pleasure. "Silk blend. These feel wonderful."

The tall impostor grinned as she curled on the cot, back to the door.

Straightening, Kelli assumed the slightly crooked smile of her replacement. "I'm ready, Aric."

Eva pursed her lips, admiring Kelli's ability to instantly change her persona. The former USF agent even struck a pose like the other woman.

They didn't have to wait long for the guard who opened the door seconds later. Without a word, he led them out of the cell. They marched down the long corridors.

Out of the corner of her eye, Eva noted how Kelli kept her head down, especially as they neared cameras. The walk back took forever. Not that Eva worried about herself or Kelli. She fervently hoped that none of the numerous guards would suddenly make a comment about her companion looking like Kelli.

The only way to assure this charade would work had been to alert as few people as possible. Only Giorgio, the warden and a select few knew about the swap.

They retrieved their belongings from the last stop and signed out. However, instead of heading out the front doors, they went up a set of stairs.

Giorgio paused in front of a door with a plaque on it. "I'm sorry, I just received news that the warden will not be able to see you today, Mrs. Reese. Please follow me back to your vehicle."

Eva felt the stares of people in adjourning rooms. "We'll try again Monday," she said, lowering the pitch of her voice to match Aric's. "Thank you."

She turned, shielding Kelli from the curious.

When they reached an exterior door, Giorgio held it open for them. "Just be careful of the demonstrators." The panel closed behind them. An electronic lock clicked into place.

Kelli paused outside, turning her face to the warm sunshine. A long sigh escaped her.

Hating to interrupt her companion's obvious pleasure, Eva spoke low. Urgent. "We need to go."

Disappointment flitted over Kelli's face, but she obeyed. As Eva started the car, her companion blotted her lipstick.

Eva glanced over. "Good idea." She pressed the door locks, ensuring they wouldn't have any unexpected or additional passengers as they exited the prison grounds. "To keep things as normal looking as possible, we are traveling by ground car."

"'K." Kelli pulled some of the wig's curls across her forehead and ducked her head. A tissue to her face completed the picture of a distraught visitor. As the vehicle neared the first security force field, she slid down in her seat to disguise her height.

"You're good." Eva spoke with unconcealed admiration. No wonder the USF agent had fooled a whole world.

A muffled snort responded. "You're not bad yourself."

A mob waited just outside the second force field. Voices rose in protest, demanding the release of Kelli Layne.

As security guards approached the car, Eva rolled down the window on her side. She gave their names and ID's while Kelli cried into her tissue. One of the guards scrutinized them before signaling to his partner to deactivate the first security force field. Beyond the second, a wall of people waited.

Eva put on dark sunglasses and handed Kelli a pair. "Okay. Here we go."

The first gate snapped on behind them before the second was released. Reporters and protesters poured into the space between the checkpoints.

The vehicle rocked as bodies pressed against it. Blinding camera lights glared into the interior. Kelli kept her face down, tissue against her nose. Fists thumped the sides of the car. Some people tried the door handles to get in.

"Aric Reese! Aric! Were you able to see Kelli Layne?"

"Over here. Look over here."

"Who's your companion?"

"What did Kelli Layne say?"

"Is she ready to be extradited tomorrow?"

"What happens if the Xerxians demand her execution?"

A hundred questions were fired at them while Eva shook her head, refusing to stop and answer questions. Her car moved steadily forward as they plowed through the massive crowd. After they broke free, some reporters followed on foot for a few yards before turning back to the prison.

"I can't imagine what it'll be like tomorrow," Eva said. "You've caused quite a bit of trouble, you know."

"I had no idea there were so many protestors."

"This isn't the half of it."

Kelli shook her head. "Who knew doing something right would turn out so wrong."

"Oh, no. Not wrong."

"Nice to have you believe me."

Out of her peripheral vision, she watched Kelli study her. What was she thinking? Probably wondering why Eva was the one to escort her back to Xerxes IX. She didn't have time to explain as she watched a vehicle behind them make all the same turns.

Before she could say anything, Kelli tilted her head. "We've got a tail."

"So I've noticed. Shouldn't be too much trouble to lose him once we reach the city."

"I've no doubt you are quite experienced at fixing that."

"Not as good as you, I hear." Eva shot her a glance.

Her companion laughed. "I'd love to swap stories with you sometime."

Eva grinned.

After a moment, Kelli added, "When this is over, we

should start a business. Maybe a self-defense club or investigative service."

Eva's throat tightened. How this ended would be completely different for her and Kelli. However, she managed a small smile. "I'd like that."

They traveled toward the city, Eva switching her route several times to shake their follower. It wasn't long before they lost their tail. Several checks in the monitors confirmed that.

"Where are we going to hole up for the night?" Kelli asked.

"We're not." Eva switched directions again. "We're going to the ship. Too dangerous to wait another day. Everyone is expecting us to depart tomorrow."

A frown tightened Kelli's forehead. "Can I make a phone call?"

Eva shook her head. "Sorry." She hated to disappoint the agent, but couldn't say anything more. Secrecy and speed were vital.

A small sigh and quivering mouth betrayed how her companion felt about the refusal. An emotion tugged at Eva's heart. Regret? She couldn't say anything in case plans had changed. It would be awful to raise the woman's hopes only to dash them later.

Yet she knew Kelli longed to see the man she loved. How well Eva understood that.

She clenched her teeth and tightened her grip on the steering wheel.

Hours passed as they traveled toward the terminal. Eva remained silent while Kelli seemed lost in thought. The evening descended upon them as they drove on and on.

Kelli straightened. "We're not going to the spaceport in New Washington?"

"No. A smaller one outside the city. We'll be checked through and can bypass the main terminal. Safer this way."

By the time they arrived, darkness enveloped the sky. A

light drizzle glazed the landscape under the lights.

Eva pulled out two new ID's for them as they passed through the small, nearly empty terminal. They boarded a private plane that took them to the port at New Washington.

"We're ready to board," Eva explained. "And we need to hurry. We don't have much time before the ship departs."

They rushed through the port, Kelli taking only a few minutes to hit the restroom and clean up her face. By the time they reached their shuttle, they were breathless, having jogged a good part of the distance. Soon they were on their way. Their shuttle would meet their ship at the station that orbited Earth.

Inter-G had conscripted a private vessel for the voyage through the space corridors. The three-day journey would be safer that way. Already Eva had seen and heard glimpses of the furor over Kelli's extradition. It was a wonder no one recognized her, considering how many photos of the heroine flashed across the monitors. Perhaps the repeated mantra of her scheduled departure for the next day threw everyone off. Eva couldn't imagine what would happen on the morrow.

While they rode the shuttle, she watched the passengers around them, but no one paid them any attention in the premier-class section.

"We're here." Eva tensed, planning to elbow everyone out of the way so that they would be the first to disembark.

The shuttle jarred as it made contact. A faint *clink* alerted her that the airlock clicked into place.

Eva unbuckled her seatbelt and shot to her feet. "Stay close."

"Will do." Head down, Kelli kept her voice low.

After the shuttle door chimed, the flight attendant pressed her hand to the lock and the panel slid open. Kelli stayed on her heels while swarms of passengers hurried about them. No one tossed a second glance their way.

When they reached the ship, Eva stepped away from the

doorway. "You first."

After hesitating a moment, Kelli passed through the portal and into the ship. A second set of double doors hissed open. The ship was small, with room for only about ten passengers, if that.

Had the USF agent arrived yet? With Kelli in the way, Eva couldn't see if anyone else occupied the cabin.

Kelli stopped so abruptly that Eva nearly ran into her.

"Jayd?" The blonde swiveled, openmouthed, as she stared at Eva, then back at the Asian man who rose to greet them.

"Jayd!" In two steps, Kelli leaped into his arms.

Chapter 22

Eva dozed, then awoke to the sound of her traveling companions' low voices. Straightening a fraction, she surreptitiously peered at the chronometer on the wall. Five hours had passed since they'd departed Earth's orbiting station. While they sped past the stars, she sensed the pull of the space corridors, as though unseen forces were about to rip the ship apart. Normally, she couldn't sleep during flights, but this time was different. With all her ties to Earth cut, she could look forward to Xerxes IX with a calm heart.

Again, she closed her eyes as she unkinked her neck. Without looking, she knew Kelli and Jayd sat diagonally across the aisle. Side by side, they held hands. Pretending she was resettling to sleep, she squirmed a little to readjust her pillow.

Let them believe they had all the privacy in the world. They needed it for what lay ahead.

She relaxed her face while she heard the sounds of a quiet kiss and their soft murmurs of love for each other. Then the loud clearing of a throat. A man's.

"Okay, Eva." Jayden Song, the USF operative, spoke. "It's safe to open your eyes now."

"Hmm?" She blinked and yawned, acting as though she was just awakening. When she stretched out an arm, the joint popped in release.

Kelli was grinning. "I should have warned you. Jayd has the world's most accurate baloney detector. You can't fool him."

Eva sat up. "Ha. *You* did." She'd read how Kelli had eluded a host of agents, including Jayd, when she had escaped surveillance and traveled to Xerxes IX. The woman was already a legend.

"Only because he was temporarily blinded." Kelli didn't complete the thought as she gazed dreamily into his eyes.

By love. Eva silently finished the sentence.

The way Jayd was looking at Kelli reminded her of…

Eva shut the door on her memories, but they still barged in. Zahn had once looked at her like that.

Did he think of her at all? Did he miss her? He would never withdraw his vow, but did he regret having made it in the first place?

She scolded herself for the questions. It no longer mattered what he had once thought.

"I'm starving. Anyone else want food?" Eva rose and stretched backwards to relieve the last few kinks. "No elite attendants on this flight, unfortunately. I think all we get are cold sandwiches, some fruit. Maybe a snack bag or two."

"Sounds perfect." Kelli rose. "I'll help."

"No need. Besides, there's only room for one in the

galley."

"Then I'll check with the pilot. See if he wants anything." She sauntered in the opposite direction.

Jayd followed Eva to the back, leaning his hands on the doorway. While she searched cabinets, he merely watched.

He didn't speak until she looked at him. "Thank you."

She knew what he was grateful for. A chance to spend time with the woman he loved. Before she answered, she bent to retrieve prepackaged foods from the cooler.

"Eh, t'was nothing." She waved off his gratefulness. "Since I was going to Xerxes anyway, and needed another agent along."

"I meant, for not killing me when you had the chance." His eyes glinted with humor.

If circumstances had been otherwise, she would have. Eva had been fully prepared to take his life if the neurotoxin had not been enough to stop him. "Oh, *that*. Well, I guess I was having a bad day."

"Good thing for me."

As she set out wrapped sandwiches and grabbed a few snack bags, she debated about how to bring up the next topic. The clock was ticking. If Eva's plan didn't work perfectly, Jayd and Kelli didn't have much time together.

Best to be direct. "Have you proposed yet?"

"To Kelli?" His mouth tightened, but he answered. Slowly. Painfully. "No."

"You should. Don't wait."

Knuckles whitening as he gripped the door, he shook his head. "With everything up in the air like this—"

"That's why it's imperative. She needs hope, Jayden."

Expression grave, he seemed to consider her words. Yes, he must know the possibilities. The Xerxians were out for blood.

"I'll think about it." He glanced over his shoulder as Kelli joined them.

As she ducked under his raised arm, she slipped one

hand about his waist. "Think about what?"

"Whether I want chicken or turkey." His arm rested on her shoulder as he grinned.

"What did the pilot say?" Eva didn't miss the frown on Kelli's face as she glanced between the two of them.

She *knew* they'd been discussing something else.

The blonde fixed her eyes on Eva. "He said he'd wait on food. But he would take coffee."

"That I can make." Well acquainted with the small craft, Eva found everything she needed and prepared a pot. In no time, the three of them were sitting in a cozy group and having dinner. Or was it breakfast?

"So, Eva, I have to ask." Jayd wiped his mouth with a napkin. "How'd you manage to involve USF in this extradition?"

"Magic." She smiled. "Don't you know Inter-G uses it on a regular basis? That's how we perform our amazing feats."

"I hope you use some when it comes to my trial." Though Kelli forced a smile, her tone remained strained.

Eva looked away, feeling like it might very well get down to that.

"Inter-G's director called USF." Jayd's dark eyes studied her. "Personally."

She shrugged. "I had the best plan. Jordan liked it."

"Jordan?" His eyebrows rose.

Eva couldn't suppress the heat that rose to her face. "Director Rosborough."

"Ah, I figured that's who you meant."

Kelli was right. Jayden Song was too stinkin' perceptive for his own good.

He pinned Eva with his gaze. "So what's going to happen when we reach the Xerxian Outpost?"

"Depends on the general atmosphere when we arrive. I'll monitor the news waves to see if anyone's caught wind of our early departure. I'm guessing Director Rosborough will let the public think that he'll delay Kelli's extradition.

Throw as many people off as possible."

"You know Inter-G put a stop to all travelers to the outpost." Jayd was looking at Kelli as he spoke.

"Good. I really don't want to be mobbed."

"Unfortunately, that order only affects commercial ships." Eva brushed some crumbs from her shirt. "I've no doubt their mandate had little effect on private ships."

Kelli nodded. "I'm betting somebody's making money hand over fist selling seats."

"No kidding." Jayd agreed.

The former agent shook her head and frowned. "It's going to be a three-ring circus."

"They won't be able to get to Xerxes though," Eva said. "Inter-G put a hold on all shuttle flights off the outpost. And the Xerxians are on guard for extra 'tourists' that are already in the city. Any trouble and they'll be bounced off the planet."

"That's good to know." She sighed. "I don't want anyone getting hurt because of me."

Too late, Eva wanted to say. A bloodied Zahn, lying on the ground, again flashed through her memory.

They finished their meal in silence.

"You know USF has been approached about installing security scans on the outpost." Jayd looked at Eva. "To 'ensure the bloodlines of all visitors,' I think is how they put it."

That was news to her. "Who requested it?"

"The ambassadress."

Eva let out a long slow breath. "Makes sense."

"Tell me if I'm wrong," Kelli inserted, "but I get the distinct impression that she would like to take over control of Xerxes."

Jayd nodded. "It would answer a lot of questions I've been having recently. Although I'm not an expert like Eva is." He glanced at Kelli who held his hand, then back. "I think this trial is just a cover for a power play."

"That thought has crossed my mind. More than once." Eva pushed her plate away. "The First Chancellor does not have a direct female descendent. And her only male descendent cannot be the next ruler."

"Only females?" Kelli asked.

She nodded.

Eva, along with the rest of the experts, knew little about how precisely the line of succession worked in Xerxian society. It was still a well-guarded secret. However, based on the historical research she'd done, the ambassadress could conceivably be the next ruler. Unless…

The speculation crystallized—unless Zahn married a full-blooded Xerxian female of the highest rank. A perfect solution to keep the line of succession in his clan.

But he would never propose marriage to anyone else as long as he maintained his word-bond to Eva.

"Suddenly, you're way too quiet." Jayd broke into her thoughts.

"I'm just thinking through what you've suggested. I believe you're right about the ambassadress. She is going to make a power play during or after Kelli's trial."

With her in power, what would happen to Xerxes? No doubt, the woman would remove "alien contamination" from her planet. Eva had heard the speculation around Inter-G. Had seen firsthand her thinly veiled hostility toward Terrans.

Jayd added his own thoughts. "If she becomes ruler of Xerxes IX, she will destroy everything we've gained in space exploration. Even with the best of intentions. We don't call her the 'Dragon Lady' at USF for no reason."

"Then we've got to find some way to stop her." Kelli's eyes gleamed.

Eva nodded. If she could ensure the continuation of the First Chancellor's lineage, then balance would be restored to the universe. Ileya had always been Earth's staunchest ally.

Only one way to accomplish this—Eva would release

Zahn from his vow.

Chapter 23

Eva smiled at the light in her friend's face. Even before getting the thumbs up from Jayd, she knew he'd proposed and Kelli had accepted.

They deserved a long and happy life together.

Again, she felt like her whole life boiled down to this one moment—a future that only she could ensure. Eva had finally found the purpose for her life. A blessed and perfect mission. One that would make the God of the heavens smile.

By the time they reached the outpost, she settled her mind. Determination encased her soul. Another thing to cross off the list. Not many items remained.

Hair now covered with a dark brown wig, Kelli waited

until they'd docked before releasing her fiancé's hand.

"Don't run off so quickly. You have bags to carry." Eva pointed to some closed bins.

"I don't have luggage," Kelli answered. "All I've got is what I'm wearing."

"That's what you think." Eva grinned. "Jayd picked up some of your things before we left."

"Really?" Kelli threw her arms around him. "I so love you."

"I know." He grinned and winked at Eva. "That's why you said yes."

She managed a tight smile. If she failed, their happiness would be short-lived. Before they departed the ship, she withdrew a cloth-wrapped item from a storage bin—Zahn's gift, which she planned to return to him.

Eva joined the couple at the airlock. "Let me lead the way."

They crossed the promenade. As she'd guessed, the space station didn't show any evidence that tourism was down. The opposite was true. Dozens upon dozens of people milled about, especially at the docks.

Keeping her head down, Kelli clung to Jayd's arm. If anyone was on the lookout for armed guards escorting a blonde in handcuffs, they wouldn't see it in this trio.

"One stop before the hotel," Eva said.

Jayd adjusted his bag. "We're not going directly to the planet?"

"Nope. Not till tonight. Late."

At all costs, they had to avoid being mobbed.

She knew the station well, leading them in the general direction of the hotel. First, she paused before a small shop. "Outpost Weddings" was prominently displayed in garish neon green on a black background.

"What...?" Jayd peered at Eva.

She shrugged. "I thought we might stop here for a few minutes. If you wanted to."

Kelli was gazing at him, a pretty blush splaying across her cheeks.

"I'll give you a minute to decide how long we'll be here. But it's totally up to you." Eva wandered into the chapel. After verifying the receptionist was the officiant's wife, she flashed her badge.

The woman's face brightened. "Oh, yes. You're the agent I talked to? Everything is prepared."

"Great. We merely need to wait for the couple to arrive." From where Eva stood, she could see Jayd and Kelli talking outside the shop, their heads together. She had no doubts about their agreeing to her suggestion—the whole reason she had made the appointment in the first place.

Her confidence gave her pause. How had she known Jayd wanted to propose? And that he would respond to her prodding? Eva knew Kelli would accept. Just as she knew they would decide to go ahead and get married while they had the chance.

"I wanted to thank you again for choosing Outpost Weddings," the woman behind the desk gushed. "We pride ourselves in confidentiality."

"And I appreciate that." Regardless of the woman's assurances, Eva had already done a thorough background check on the small operation. They had an impeccable track record, despite one irregularity in their paperwork from their earliest days. Though loathe to use that against them, Eva wouldn't hesitate if it helped protect Jayd and Kelli's privacy.

After a few minutes, the couple entered the shop. Hands clasped, both wore huge smiles.

"I guess that's a yes?" Eva asked.

"Not hard to figure out." Jayd's eyes shone as he gazed at his soon-to-be bride.

The receptionist rose. "We just need you to complete the license application and the minister will meet you up front."

"Complete?" Jayd frowned at the woman.

Eva cleared her throat. "I took the liberty of filling out most of your information already." She pointed to the electronic tablets that required merely their names and signatures. Before departing Earth, she had provided all other details.

He gaped. "You filled them out already?"

"Mostly. But I doubt these good people believe Antony and Cleopatra reside at your addresses."

Kelli laughed. "Remember my warning, Jayd? To never get on Eva's bad side?"

His widening eyes met hers. "I believe it."

The officiant emerged from a back room to greet everyone. As prearranged by Eva, he secured the doors and pulled shades across the windows to prevent prying eyes.

Jayd paid the fees for the ceremony, which included genuine Xerxian bonding rings, made from an unidentified metal.

"I'll get you something nicer when we get back to Earth," he promised Kelli.

She shook her head as she fingered the ring. "No way. I'm keeping this one forever."

"Just to reiterate." Eva leaned toward the woman at the desk. "You and your husband pledged to not upload their marriage record into the system for exactly one week. Correct?" She included the minister in her glance.

The woman gasped as she viewed the signatures. As she stared hard at brown-wigged Kelli and Asian Jayd, she sputtered, "You're...?"

Her curious husband peered over her shoulder and blanched.

"And in exchange for your full cooperation," Eva said in a calm, but firm tone, "you are allowed the exclusive story and photos. Remember?"

The woman's head bobbed. "Of—of course."

Eva fixed her gaze on the officiant who didn't appear as agreeable. "Think how great this will be for business.

Especially as word gets out that you protect your clients' identities. No matter what."

"We've given our word." He drew himself up. "We don't intend to break it."

Eva smiled. "I had no doubts." She ushered Jayd and Kelli to the front of the chapel.

"If I were them, I wouldn't even consider crossing you," Kelli spoke in a low voice. "No matter how sweet you sounded."

"Learned your lesson, eh?"

The tall woman chuckled. "Oh, yes." She massaged her jaw as though recalling how it felt to get punched by Eva.

The minister joined them up front.

Jayd held up his finger. "One request before we begin."

"And that is?"

He turned to Kelli. "Would you mind losing the disguise?"

Chuckling, she removed the wig and shook out her fair tresses.

The officiant studied them both. "Ready?"

Expression serious, Jayd took her hand. Together, they faced front.

"Dearly beloved..."

After the first words, Eva found herself blinking several times. And swallowing hard. She thought of Zahn. Thought of what *might* have been if circumstances were different. Were Xerxian weddings like those on Earth?

If Eva were getting married, she would choose daisies. And wear the beautiful robe Zahn had woven for her.

After several photos, Kelli again assumed her disguise while Eva stopped at the desk. The receptionist managed a tight smile.

"Press your thumb right here." Eva pointed to the small screen on her comm-unit. "My system will automatically send the images in one week. This way they'll be able to find you wherever you may be."

Hand trembling, the woman complied.

"And yours." She told the officiant. "I included a thank-you bonus which will be available in a week. Pleasure doing business with you."

After they departed, Kelli chuckled. "That was *almost* mean."

"I have no idea what you're talking about." Eva lifted her chin. Truth was, the owners of Outpost Weddings might be shocked at the hefty bonus she had left them.

"Requiring their thumbprint? They obviously know Inter-G can now track them anywhere in the universe."

Eva stopped and held up her hands. "I didn't threaten."

Smirking, the tall blonde crossed her arms.

"Okay, maybe just a tiny bit. But if I were as tall as you, I might not have turned out so rotten."

Jayd laughed.

"Oh." Eva paused to steady her voice. "May I be the first to congratulate you both, Mr. and Mrs. Song?"

"Thank you." Eyes misty, Kelli leaned against her husband. "I like the sound of that."

"Me too." Jayd slipped his arm about her waist.

Eva checked into the hotel. Unfortunately, because they were there on official business, they had to share a room. However, she chose a suite. Let Inter-G complain. By the time Rosborough fussed it would no longer matter.

When they entered the rooms, she set Zahn's gift on a side table, then slung her backpack off her shoulder and dropped it on a chair.

Jayd's head swiveled as he looked around. "Wow. Maybe I need to start working for Intergalaxia. Their agents get much nicer hotel rooms than we do."

"And don't forget that private ship," Kelli added.

Eva tapped the electronic key in her hand. "I have some errands. Be back in a few hours."

"Hours?" Kelli pulled off her wig and tossed it onto her bag.

"Yeah. Probably two—no, make that three hours." She winked at Jayd. "Minimum. I've got lots and lots to do. Tons of souvenirs to buy. Shopping."

He grinned, eyes twinkling. "Sounds busy. I'd agree—definitely three hours."

Having missed Eva's wink, Kelli glanced between them. "What're you talking...?" Her face reddened in understanding. "Oh."

Grinning more broadly, her husband laced his fingers through hers. "And we are grateful, aren't we, Kel?"

"Yes." She cleared her throat. "Thank you, Eva."

Laughing, she exited the room and shut the door firmly behind her.

It wasn't much, but privacy was the only wedding gift Eva could give the newlyweds.

Chapter 24

Standing on the patio of his home, Zahn closed his eyes. Ever since his return to Xer Prime, he had sought serenity. Today, he sensed it was within his grasp. A tentative peace flowed over him as he crossed the flat paving stones into his gardens. Despite that, overpowering loneliness echoed through him. The dream of sharing his home with a wife—with Eva—had vaporized, leaving a dull ache in its place.

How could he have been so wrong?

The question had nagged him since his departure from Terran soil. Zahn had been so certain God had told him to ask her to be his wife. Why, if she was being courted by one of the most powerful men on Earth? The way she reacted to the director proved she would accept him. How could she not? Zahn had witnessed the dozens of small ways Rosborough displayed his devotion to her.

The traditions of humans were different than Xerxian. Terran males pursued females. And human women, he'd observed, enjoyed the pursuit. That Eva would respond to the director's advances he had no doubt. How could she not be captivated by Rosborough's power, charm and aggressiveness? She was human, female. The Creator had designed her to be attracted to her own kind. Her nature longed to be won over by a man like Rosborough. To be courted, flattered, bent to the will of a dominant male.

Not like the men of Xerxes. They proved themselves with patience and fidelity, a practice that ensured a lifelong, unbreakable bond.

As Zahn paced over the white stones, it dawned on him that he had been obedient to the call of God. He *had* asked Eva to be his wife.

"Does this mean I should wait for her?" He lifted his whispered prayer to the heavens. He might never see his dream fulfilled.

But he must obey. And continue to do so, even for the rest of his days.

He sat on a bench under an arbor and stared at the scrollwork. If God wanted him to remain unmarried, who was he to question the Lord of the universe?

"Do I interrupt?"

At the voice of his mother, Zahn shot to his feet. "Not at all. Would you care to sit?" He indicated the bench.

After she took her place, he perched beside her and stared across the gardens. She seemed in no hurry to explain the purpose of her visit. Breathing deeply, she closed her eyes. "This is a wonderful place you've created. It feels so full of joy. And of peace."

Yet it lacked a wife. His bound life-mate.

He gazed at the woman who'd borne him, still beautiful.

Age had marked her face and hair with a benevolent touch. Only a thin band of silver trailed its way through her black hair, proof of the passing years. Zahn shot up a prayer of thankfulness for his mother.

"I've missed seeing you since your return." Her gentle voice softened the rebuke. "But I realize that you are a man with many cares. Many responsibilities." She turned her dark eyes toward him. "So I decided I should come to you."

Unable to bear her kindness, Zahn looked away.

"I sense you are hurting, my son. Please, let me share your burden." She put a soft hand on his shoulder.

He took only a second to consider. "The woman to whom I made a vow…" He paused, trying to find the best words. "She has accepted the attentions of another man."

"A human male?"

"Yes."

Her brow wrinkled and she pursed her lips. "Has she formally refused you?"

"No." He added slowly. "Not yet."

"I would not be so cruel as to suggest that this may be for the best. For her to mate with her own kind."

"The thought occurred to me. However, I believe she and I would have been well suited." More than well suited. Zahn had grown to love her. He dared admit to himself that he had seen a reciprocal emotion in her. He was certain of it. Was it merely affection? The fire he'd seen in her eyes had given him hope.

His mother folded her hands. "For your peace of mind, get a release of vow from her. Soon. Your heart will be more settled afterwards."

Again Zahn stared out across the garden, sensing the wisdom of his mother's advice. It would be only fair to Eva as well. As per custom, he must ask her to liberate him. Then he would give his blessing and a promise of prayers for the relationship she would pursue with Rosborough. "As usual, you are prudent, *Emaa*. I will return to Earth as soon as possible."

One piece of information he kept to himself. He didn't tell her that though Eva released him, he would remain steadfast to her. Zahn would not declare himself free to marry anyone else.

No, Eva was the only woman for him.

"What else troubles you, my son?"

He could not hide a small smile. "I am always amazed at your perception."

"It is sometimes helpful."

He fingered the hem of his sleeve, wondering how best to voice his concern. "How do you feel about the rulership passing from our clan to another?"

His mother sucked in a long, slow breath. "Why do you ask?"

"I discern it has crossed your mind. That you see the possibility."

Her face grew stony.

"I know it is not my place to speak of this to you. But I am concerned for my people."

"Which is why you can be the one to solve this dilemma." She gripped his hand. "Choose a wife from our people. From a strong clan. Bring forth a daughter who will carry on our lineage."

Zahn wanted so much to please her, but he couldn't disobey God. "I cannot."

"You *must* break that oath."

He shook his head. "I am—and will remain—bound."

"To a human!" Her mouth turned down at the corners. "Can you not see the folly of your choice?"

He gave her a moment before speaking in a low voice. "She was not my choice, but our God's."

"Consider." Her expression grew implacable. "Was that not your own emotion, sweeping you away? Could you not have been blinded by desire?"

For his mother's sake, Zahn did not protest. Yes, he had

been attracted to Eva from the moment he had seen her. From when he had first carried her in his arms. She felt small, frail, so very vulnerable. He recalled the vivid rush of protectiveness that had swept over him.

But he had restrained himself. Even while in the cabin, he had been continually on guard. Furthermore, he had not tried to appear in the most favorable light. He had withheld his identity so as not to sway her with his position.

The memories of their hours together focused on and distilled to one comet-like incident that could not be explained away.

Eva wept. She offered her tears. For me alone.

Never would he forget her response. And the overwhelming rush of emotion. Her weeping had been a holy sign that he had done the right thing. He had obeyed the call of God.

Zahn raised his eyes to his mother, the First Chancellor of their world. Everything in him wanted to assure her that he would do what she asked. He would lay aside his desire for Eva and bow to what she wanted.

But he could not. The Lord of heavens was the greater authority. God was above the First Chancellor of Xerxes IX. They were both answerable to Him.

"Could I have been blinded by desire?" He repeated her question.

Expression eager, she nodded. "Yes. Is that not possible?"

He paused, considering how to word his question. He knew it would sound harsh, but it had to be asked.

They had never spoken of his biological father. It was time. All he knew was his father's name and that he had died before Zahn was born. His parents had never married.

With care, he chose his words. "And what of you, *Emaa*? Were you blinded by desire the night I was conceived?"

She recoiled from him as the full weight of his questions hit her. A moment later, she slapped him.

The sting on his cheek hurt less than the burning in his soul. How could he have so wounded her by his cruel questions? Never before had she struck him.

"Forgive me." Seeking to somehow make amends, Zahn slid off the bench to kneel, head bowed against her knee. "Forgive me, *Emaa*. Forgive me." Though he didn't understand why she'd slapped him, she was under no obligation to explain.

She was his mother. Not only the ruler of Xerxes but the head of their clan. He should have treated her with more respect. Should not have asked the question that had burned in his heart for years. Should have accepted her silence on the matter and let it be.

For a long time, he remained submissive before her. Contrition ate at him. Once again, he murmured, "I am sorry. Truly."

When she touched his head with a hand of mercy, he dared raise his face. Her eyes swam with tears...tears she did not hide from him. Because of the pain he had caused? Or for another reason?

Regardless, remorse ground into his soul. "Forgive my lack of compassion." He kept his voice to a repentant whisper. "Forgive me, *Emaa*."

"I regret..." Voice quavering, she stopped to take a deep breath. "I regret now that I never told you." She looked away, mouth trembling. Cheeks dark with torment, she seemed to fight for control of her voice. "You deserve to know everything. It is time." She rose, turning away from him. "The night you were conceived..." Her shoulders tensed. "I was not carried away by desire, but naivety. Without the consent of my parents, I met him—your father—foolishly believing that he held the same values as I." She turned to Zahn, face hard, yet painfully vulnerable. "Know this. I did not give myself to him. He *took*. I fought him. But he was too strong. He—he took..." Her voice drifted off as she stared into the agonizing memory.

For endless moments she gazed into the past. Finally, her eyes flicked to Zahn. "Something else you must know. Your father did not go unpunished. That very night, he died when his shuttle crashed. Afterwards I saw no reason to renounce him."

Zahn felt as though Xerxes should split open and swallow him for being blind and heartless.

His mother slipped her hands into the sleeves of her robes, letting him absorb the vast, painful truth. "Be certain of this, Zahn." She met his gaze squarely. "You do not bear the shame of what happened. The shame remains on him." She returned to his side and rested her hand on his shoulder. "Only my parents knew the truth. They took it to their graves. No one else knows but my consort. And now you."

His eyes stung, lashes growing wet. His mother's face grew more compassionate as his tears betrayed the proof of his parentage.

Lifting the hem of her robe, Zahn kissed it.

Chapter 25

Eva's comm-unit beeped, waking her as she lay on the hotel room's sofa. Three a.m. Shaking sleep from her head, she rose and tapped at the closed bedroom door. "It's time." Without waiting for a response, she packed her belongings.

Intergalaxia had arranged a private shuttle since no other transports were allowed from the space station to Xerxes IX without authorization. With the outpost on Xerxian time, not many people should be up, even the dedicated partiers.

She'd been monitoring the space station's messages and news streams, glad of the confusion about Kelli's location. Some believed she was on Earth, still in prison, while others speculated that she was traveling. True to their word, the Outpost Wedding couple had not gossiped. However, rumor had already placed Kelli on the Xerxian space station. Eva hoped they would encounter no trouble boarding the shuttle, but she wouldn't assume that.

Jayd and Kelli emerged from the other room, bags over their shoulders, looking as alert as possible for the middle of the night. The blonde was again wigged.

"Wait." Jayd stopped Eva as she reached for the door.

"What is it?"

"One minute of your time." He grabbed her hand and Kelli's, then bowed his head. "Whatever Your will is, Father, let it be done. For Your glory. Amen."

Eva stared at Jayd. "Thank you."

"And thank *you*." Kelli gave her a quick hug. "I'm ready."

But now Eva lingered. "Whatever happens," she said as she drew a shaky breath, "I wish the best for you both." Without another word, she yanked open the door and walked into the bright hallway.

They crossed the promenade without mishap, but lingering people noticed as they headed toward the shuttle bay area. Obviously, some had designated themselves as lookouts.

"Hey! That them?" a burly guy yelled.

Several men hurried their way.

"Go. And take this." Eva pressed Zahn's gift into Kelli's hands. If they stuck together, they would never make it. While they ducked down the narrow hallway, Eva stood guard. The shuttle couldn't be used as a getaway vehicle. Even jetting out into space.

If Kelli and Jayd could reach it while Eva kept the loiterers busy, they could break port. The crowd would bottleneck at the hall's entrance.

The first man came at her. "You're not turning Kelli Layne over to those greenies." His jaw thrust out as he prepared to attack. Eva dodged his blow, then struck his chest. It had little effect on the huge man.

She didn't want to seriously injure him. Just buy Kelli and Jayd time.

As the man swung at her again, she ducked. Next thing she knew, he sprawled backwards and fell.

Fists raised, Jayd readied his stance.

Eva shot him a glance, then at the gathering crowd. "Nice timing."

"You shouldn't have all the fun." His face hardened with determination.

She grinned. "If you insist."

Another man came at them and a third while they backed steadily down the hallway. Beyond them, she could see more people running their direction. Word was spreading. Fast.

"We can't fight the whole outpost." Jayd grunted from grappling with his opponent.

"If you're trying to bug out, fine." Eva bloodied the nose of a man. "I'll hold them."

"Stop it." Kelli's voice cut through the noise of the scuffles. "I said stop it. *Now!*"

The six people who were gathering to take their shot at Eva and Jayd dropped back.

Kelli pulled off her wig. "All of you. *Back off.*"

Surprise rippled across the faces of the growing crowd.

"Kelli Layne?" one person asked. "We're not going to let them sacrifice you—"

"I *choose* to go to Xerxes," she interrupted. "Do you hear me? I want to go."

Several muttered in disbelief.

"You're going to turn yourself over to them?" someone said. "They'll crucify you."

"We don't know that." Kelli stared him down. "I want this...this *prejudice* to end. Once and for all." She planted fists at her hips. "You are not going to use me as an excuse to hate. Not you, not anyone."

Eva stood ready, not convinced Kelli had defused the crowd's mood. But she wasn't done yet.

"Go home. Get out of here and let my friends be." She appeared to grow taller by several inches as she straightened, taking on the expression of a stern teacher. "Go on. I said beat it."

Some looked sheepish, some still looked angry. Kelli stared them down until they backed off. Several ducked away.

After waiting a moment longer, she turned and stalked toward the waiting shuttle.

Eva glanced at Jayd. What would his reaction be?

"Don't look at me." He grinned without meeting her gaze. "She surprises me. All the time."

Together they backed down the hall, still keeping the lingering crowd in sight. Many had dispersed, but not all.

After securing the shuttle door, Eva relaxed. She slouched in a chair across from Jayd. "Your next fifty years together ought to be a real trip."

After grabbing his wife's hand, he kissed it. He was looking at Kelli when he said, "I'm counting on it."

Eva leaned against the garden's fence, watching the Xerxian who contemplated the stalk of a flowering plant. After studying it, Zahn clipped some withered leaves. His fingers caressed a few petals before he moved on. He appeared so peaceful that she could not make herself interrupt him.

Content to merely gaze, she rested her hand on the gate.

She'd brought his gift back to him. But cowardice had forced her to leave it by his front door. She'd nearly slunk away, but something had drawn her to the side of the house.

Just as she suspected, he was working in his garden.

Now she couldn't tear herself away.

What sixth sense caused Zahn to look up? Her heart faltered at his expression. Of all the possible reactions, she'd not expected the joy that infused his face.

He set down the clippers while she remained rooted, unable to escape. His dark eyes fixed on her, smile softening as another emotion amplified the radiating gladness. Love?

After opening the gate, he bowed and waited for her to enter.

Eva finally found her voice. "I'm sorry to barge in on you." She stepped onto the cobblestone path. "An official at the terminal gave me directions to your home."

"I bid you welcome."

Now that she was inside the fence, her mind lost the ability to function.

"Come. Let us sit over here. I hope you will find the scenery as delightful as I do." Zahn's voice sent chills skipping down her spine.

She'd always loved that about him. For a moment, she was back in the tiny cabin they'd shared. In the middle of the night, when pain had robbed her of sleep, his soothing tones had eased her torment.

What would it be like to have him read to her? Or recite poetry with his deep calming tones? To have him again sit at her feet as when they had first met? When he had asked about her life.

She so wanted to tell him all that was in her heart. All her plans.

That would not be wise.

Perched at the edge of a marble bench, Eva jammed her thumbs under her thighs. With his house tucked at the plateau's border, his garden appeared to trail off into space. The massive fence that guarded the edge remained out of sight on a lower cliff. She had an unimpeded view of the plains below.

The scenery did delight her, as he'd said. Yet, she couldn't allow herself to relax. Not yet. Perhaps never.

She spoke first. "I was glad to hear you recovered quickly from...from your injury."

"Inhale the scent of the *gazmin* blooms. Does it not stir your soul?" Zahn raised his chin as though drinking of the fragrance.

He wasn't going to make this easy. How could she be so foolish as to assume that? She sighed in frustration.

With one corner of his mouth curving upward, he studied her. "Whatever it is you came to say can keep for a few moments. I urge you to allow the beauty and tranquility to minister to your soul."

How silly to refuse his invitation. Still resistant and a little impatient, Eva leaned her head back and sucked in several deep breaths. Noisily. Rebelliously. However, the garden began to work on her.

That scent–*gazmin?*–reminded her of her mother's garden. Yes. The memory settled in the recesses of her mind as she closed her eyes. Her mother had grown a plant indoors. One that might have been a transplant from Xerxes. Had it been the same genus?

A sweeter fragrance tickled her nose, vying for attention. But the subtle perfume of the *gazmin* won out. Its palliative scent enchanted her. This time she inhaled slowly, truly enjoying the fruity fragrance.

Tension seeped from her. Worry and stress melted away. Future plans ebbed in favor of the seductive present.

"It is good to see you again, Eva Daviana." Zahn's voice cocooned her in warmth and safety.

Willing her eyes to remain closed, she pushed away the impending hurt she must cause him. She held the pain at arm's length.

The gentle breeze played in her hair, blowing a strand across her cheek. When Zahn's fingers gently smoothed it off her skin, she gasped. Longing shivered through her.

As she opened her eyes, the sensation morphed into remorse.

"You have nothing to fear from me." He met her gaze steadily. "Not now. Not in the future."

"I know." She could barely speak.

How she wished…

Steeling her mind to what must be done, she ducked her head. "I accompanied Kelli Layne to Xerxes. We arrived just this morning."

"I guessed that was the reason for your presence."

Eva clenched her hands, hearing what he did not say: *"I know I am not the primary reason for your visit to my planet."*

Ashamed now, she turned away.

A chirping green bird flitted nearby, drawing her attention. Eva sighed yet again, feeling as though she slipped into a new level of relaxation. What was it about this place that compelled her to lay aside all that troubled her?

Or was Zahn the source?

"I could stay here forever," she whispered. Then she bit her lip. Why had she voiced that fantasy aloud? How imprudent.

His smile softened. "You are welcome any time. No invitation needed. Come and take your pleasure."

"Thank you." Eva grew solemn. If she knew which day would be her last, she would spend it here. After her final hours in Zahn's garden, she could leave this life in peace.

His robe rustled. "I wanted to tell you about the gift you gave me."

She blinked. What was he talking about?

"The golden orchid, I think is the name you gave, is doing well. Most of the blossoms are still intact." Zahn indicated the open door of his house. "I have it in my study."

Ah. She'd forgotten. "I'm glad."

It was fitting he should own that one plant of hers—the only thing she could give him. She noticed the space between them on the bench had shrunk. Had he scooted closer?

After rising, Eva sauntered through the garden. She paused beside a small pergola, made of intricate latticed scrollwork. Had Zahn carved these panels? She ran her fingers over the curling patterns, their satiny smooth finish a pleasure to touch. No doubt he had spent a considerable amount of time sanding down the rough wood, even into the small crevices.

What would her life have been like had she been raised on Xerxes instead of Earth? What would *she* have been like? Useless speculation. But perhaps her being raised on Earth made her more appreciative of the beauty and serenity of this place.

"I am sorry that I did not bid you goodbye." Zahn drew nearer. "Before I left Earth."

"Understandable. You'd been injured and—"

"No. That is no excuse."

Eva turned to him.

"I must explain." His brow grew troubled. "I was jealous."

"Of what?"

"Your director."

"Jordan Rosborough?"

"Yes. I recognized the source of his attentions toward you. And…" He paused, jaw tightening. "And I became jealous. A new and very uncomfortable sensation."

Eva clasped her hands behind her.

"I saw the way you responded to him. And thought, perhaps, you returned his affections."

"No." She shook her head for emphasis.

How could she explain that though the director imposed upon her, she had thought only of Zahn? He was the one who had awakened her senses. Her emotions. Not Jordan Rosborough.

"There is nothing…" She again shook her head.

"Rosborough desired something more between us. But I don't share his feelings."

"Then you have no intention of welcoming his courtship?"

"Absolutely not." Jordan's kiss flashed through her mind. Her response had been instinctual. She had given in to compulsion—to her dominant side that she had not yet conquered. Had he suspected something between her and Zahn? Then taken advantage when she let down her guard? No doubt. The director did nothing without an agenda. And he was used to getting his own way.

Regardless, her culpability crystalized with painful clarity.

"I should have refused to accompany him that night— and been more concerned about my reputation instead of Intergalaxia's." She shuddered in disgust with herself. "I'm more than sorry now."

One thing she must do before Kelli's trial began—send a letter to Jordan, telling him they had no future together. And at the same time, resign from Inter-G. Eva determined to take care of that as soon as possible.

Zahn's expression grew bemused as he laced his fingers through the lattice's scrollwork. "Then my jealousy was for naught. A wasted emotion."

"It's a natural human feel—" She pressed her lips together. "Or rather, it's normal for humans. But not for Xerxians?"

Brow furrowing, he looked away. "Not usually."

"Forgive me for causing you discomfort." She rested a hand on his arm. "Director Rosborough is a forceful man. Very controlling. I would not—*could* not—be happy with him."

Before she said something more, something she would regret, Eva walked away. Zahn followed. Ever aware of him, she paused to bend over a bloom and inhale its fragrance. So many wonderful and strange smells. She fingered a few blossoms, enthralled by the velvet feel of one and the delicate, curved spikes of another.

One flower, on a long stem, stood apart in its own plot. When she reached for it, Zahn grabbed her wrist.

"That one is not to be touched."

"Oh, I'm sorry." Was it sacrosanct? She should have guessed since he'd planted it apart from the others.

"It would harm you." He spoke softly, brow wrinkled. His fingers loosened, but he did not release her wrist. Instead, his fingertips slid across her forearm. His breathing slowed.

Mesmerized by his touch, Eva couldn't move. The planet's rotation seemed to decelerate, sky hushing and all nature focusing on this one caress. Entranced, she watched his long fingers.

"Eva..." He said her name low.

Her heart thumped in her chest. Dizziness—no, something else—throbbed through her. Was it longing? With unhurried deliberation, he held up his hands, elbows bent, palms facing her.

An invitation?

She took a slow breath. His pose called to her. Perhaps their touching hands would be considered more intimate— more sacred—than a kiss.

Eva couldn't stop herself. After raising her hands, she rested her palms against his. Luxuriating in the warmth of his skin, she released a pent-up breath. A sense of belonging, of utter contentment, flowed over her. Was he somehow conveying emotions to her? Yearning, and so much more, cascaded through her, reaching out to him and multiplying.

A jolt of pleasure speared her. Zahn's dark eyes widened. For a moment, she felt as though their souls touched.

Eva jerked back. As reality hit, panic coursed through her. What was she doing?

She shrank away from him. "Stay away from me, Zahn.

You'll only get hurt." The pain of self-loathing returned in full force and shattered any lingering dream. The old mantra played again in her mind.

I'm a freak. I have no future with any man.

"I release you from your vow." Her voice rose. "I returned your gift. Please, *please* don't ever talk to me about marriage again."

Before he could stop her, Eva turned and bolted.

For two days, Eva waited. She, like many others, anticipated the trial of Kelli Layne Song. Something held up the Xerxian court. Each passing hour stoked the growing bias against the former USF agent. Many clan leaders had traveled to Xer Prime to witness the proceedings. And yet, they too, waited. It was as if the judges wanted to fully rouse Xerxian hostility against all Terrans.

One benefit was that Inter-G had allowed others to travel to Xerxes IX. With the approval of the High Council, they came to give testimony on Kelli's behalf. Eva heard that Aric Reese and family had arrived, and even her own father. She avoided them all.

Finally, the tribunal began. No outsider was permitted to view the full court proceedings. The panel of five judges called in witnesses, both human and Xerxian. One at a time they entered the lofty circular chamber to give testimony. Eva had no idea what anyone said. Had no idea which way the Xerxians leaned—whether they were biased against Kelli or in support of her. Though Eva made herself available, no one called for her testimony. Because it was irrelevant? No matter. Her plans would not change.

Once the giving of evidence ended, the court would hear Kelli's final comments. Then they would pass judgment. Xerxian law, in its beauty and simplicity, expedited justice without the entanglements of lawyers or jail time.

While Eva waited for news, she wandered the streets of Xer Prime. The whole city felt subdued. As though everyone was aware of history being written. Irrevocably.

Eva traveled to the very edge of the Great Plateau, having walked the length of the city. There she found a small temple and paused on the threshold, looking into the gloom. An altar, with sunlight spilling down from the open skylight, glowed in the center of the t-shaped building.

She gripped the doorpost, overwhelmed with trepidation, yet drawn to the quiet. No one else was there. She stepped inside and walked toward the center. A memory of her mother praying flashed through her mind. Without circumspection, she fell before the altar, stretching herself out on the steps. Words, long abandoned, but never forgotten, poured out of her mouth.

"Hear my prayer, Lord, listen to my cries for help. Do not be deaf to my weeping. I am a stranger here. I don't know my way."

She repeated the prayer, and again. Realization finally hit her that she prayed in Xerxian. Her mother had uttered these very words. Often. And aloud.

Now I understand. Oh, how I understand...

Eva remained prostrate on the floor until shadows lengthened and the building plunged into darkness. Other petitions bubbled up in her memory and she gave voice to every one, faltering over words. Deep inside she knew she couldn't leave until she recited them all. Hours later, body stiff and spirit weary, she rose.

Before she exited the temple, she looked back at the altar. The darkness was no hindrance to her sight, thanks to the ability she'd inherited from her mother. In the starlight, the altar dazzled with supernatural light.

Peace washed over Eva. God had heard. He would answer.

In the hour of her greatest need, He would give her

Anna Zogg

strength.

Chapter 26

Avoiding the main streets of Xer Prime, Eva hurried to the great chambers in the early morning hours. Today the courts would hand down Kelli's verdict. Before spectators were barred because of the overly packed room, she entered the circular chamber and found a place along one aisle.

Adjusting her hood to hide her face, she pressed herself into a corner and remained standing on the ground floor. Two hundred and fifty seats on three tiered sides began filling with Xerxians, humans and those of different races. The spaces along the fourth wall were reserved for the five judges and esteemed members.

The First Chancellor's chair remained empty for now.

From Eva's vantage point, she saw Aric Reese enter with her daughter. Her husband nodded for them to find a seat while he remained standing in an aisle. Before they parted ways, he spoke to his wife. Eva had no trouble reading his lips from across the room.

"If this goes bad," her husband said, "I'll come get Ella. We'll go for a walk or something. Okay?"

Aric nodded before taking their daughter to a spot not far from Eva.

The room hushed when the First Chancellor entered from a private door with her bound consort and son. They took the three chairs closest to center stage. Dyn'Perzsi Aeliana followed. She also took a front row seat.

Eva stared at Zahn who appeared more subdued than she'd ever seen him. Did he too sense the impending disaster?

Forget me, Zahn. She closed her eyes, willing for him to hear the plea of her heart. *Find a woman worthy of your love. Build a life with her.*

The room suddenly grew hushed as another side door opened. Everyone stood in deference to the five judges who swept in. After they seated themselves, a quiet murmuring arose while the spectators settled.

An imposing Xerxian woman stepped forward and hit a wooden square with a heavy pockmarked ball. "This court is now called to order. Silence!" She turned and bowed to the First Chancellor before uttering the opening prayer.

As she spoke and welcomed different heads of clans, Eva looked about the room. It appeared as Xerxians had come from every part of the planet. From their simple robes to the elaborate, everyone apparently wanted to be in on the court proceedings.

Those from Earth included the Reeses, Thom Marshall and even the new director of SARC. Obviously Rosborough wouldn't attend for political reasons. Across from Eva sat Jayden Song. He pressed his fingers against the translator bud in his ear as various Xerxians took turns pontificating. His jaw alternately flexed and loosened.

Eva listened as they not only reiterated ancient laws, but their intent. Some spoke in Xer that was so archaic she doubted the translators would know what to do with the obscure phrases. During each recitation, she concentrated on the panel of judges. All of them wore impassive expressions. However, she sensed their resistance to the leniency some speakers proposed.

"Mama, you're squeezing me too hard." Ella Reese's young voice rose above the speaker's, interrupting her for a moment.

The woman turned and looked at the girl, face softening in indulgence before she went on.

After she sat, the room grew quiet. The court convener rose and asked if any final witnesses were to be called. After the recorder stood to respond in the negative, the tall woman nodded.

First Judge rose and spoke to two women by a side door. "Bring in the accused."

As they waited for Kelli's arrival, Eva noticed a small commotion as Sean Reese entered to escort Ella from the room. So she wouldn't see the tragedy yet to be played out?

Kelli entered shortly afterwards. Though she appeared exhausted, she walked with confidence. Dressed modestly in Terran fashion, her natural blonde hair shimmered in the illumination that streamed through a skylight.

Eva's heartbeat hammered. It would not be long now. She prayed for the courage to follow through with her plan.

"We will hear your final statements, Kelli-Layne," the lead judge said in English. Impatience flickered behind her expressionless mask. Because she wanted this farce ended? And soon?

Others might be fooled by her supposed objectivity. Not Eva.

Many onlookers leaned forward in their seats. When a

tall woman stepped in front of her, Eva elbowed her way toward the front once more.

"First Chancellor, honorable judges, women and men of Xerxes, guests…" Kelli paused.

Eva realized with a start that she spoke in Xerxian, her intonation nearly impeccable. Murmurs of surprise, and scorn, rippled through the room.

Kelli waited until the murmuring died. "You have heard many testimonies of my actions while I was on your planet. I thank everyone who spoke kindly on my behalf and with truth. I have nothing else to add in my defense when it comes to the facts of my case. However, I feel it important to speak of my intent."

"We don't have all day," the ambassadress grumbled, the acoustics carrying her voice.

"Silence." The lead judge glared not only at her, but others. "This is the right of the accused. We will honor her with our full attention."

Though the judge appeared polite, Eva knew the courtesy was a sham.

Kelli bowed to the judge before turning to speak to the ambassadress. "I will be brief, for your sake as well as others." She pressed her lips together as though gathering her thoughts. "I am sincerely grieved for the offense I have caused all of you. In my anxiety over the fate of my friend's daughter, I thought of nothing but her safety. I thought of nothing but my ability to rescue her from the hands of the wicked. This does not excuse me, but perhaps helps you see that my motivation was not based on selfishness or disrespect."

The ambassadress made a small sound of scorn.

Kelli waited a moment, her expression revealing no impatience. "It is true that I broke laws, not only here, but on Earth. I am willing to pay the penalty for my actions. I freely submit to whatever punishment you deem is just and fair. I ask only one thing—that it be clearly understood that, though I broke humanoid-made laws, I obeyed God and my conscience. On this I rest." Kelli bowed low to the judges, holding the submissive posture for many moments.

A buzz of approval rose from the audience.

Eyes burning, the coil tightened inside Eva. Despite Kelli's eloquent speech, the results would not change. The ambassadress and the First Judge controlled the court, therefore the outcome.

"We must take time to deliberate." All five judges rose and filed out of the room.

Eva shifted the weight on her feet. They could pretend to deliberate. She knew they had already made up their minds.

As she had made up hers.

While they were gone, the volume of chatter increased. Kelli remained standing in the center of the room. She turned and gazed at Jayd who managed a smile. At the look that passed between them, Eva's heart swelled.

Please, God, regardless of what happens, let them have many years together.

The chatter died off as the side door creaked open and the women reentered.

"We have reached a decision. Though not unanimous, the judgment is based on superior numbers." The First Judge waited until the room grew completely quiet. "By a majority vote, we find Kelli-Layne guilty of violating our most sacred laws."

The hum of vocalization swelled. Glaring about the room, the judge waited until the sound died down.

"Given the seriousness of her offenses, it is fitting that the punishment fit her crimes. Tomorrow morning at first light, Kelli-Layne will be executed."

How could they?

In grief, Zahn bowed his head at the pronouncement of judgment. Kelli-Layne guilty?

Yes, that was possible. But her punishment?

He could not recall the last time a woman, *any* woman, had been executed on Xerxes. The evil men who had kidnapped the young girl had paid for their crime, but what had Kelli-Layne done to deserve the same fate? The more devastating question rang in his mind. What had his world come to?

God of the heaven, please intervene. Not only to save the life of this human, but to save the consciences of everyone here.

Voices, which had begun to rise, suddenly dropped off until the room became utterly silent. Zahn raised his head and studied the players in this tragedy. The shock and pallor of the one accused. The grief in her friend, Jayden Song. The grim satisfaction of Dyn'Perzsi Aeliana, the ambassadress.

Why? What did she hope to gain in alienating the Terrans? Was not her job, her sacred duty, to ensure the harmony of their relationships?

In the deafening roar of silence, Aeliana's eyes narrowed as she studied the ruler of Xerxes. Lips white, Zahn's mother stared ahead as though not seeing. Then her head slowly turned to her one-time friend. As children, they had been very close, but over the years, something had come between them. Zahn had never known what caused the breach. Such information had never been shared with him.

What are you thinking, my Birthing One?

The ambassadress seemed to be waiting. Did she expect the ruler to countermand? To denounce the judgment?

As First Chancellor, she had the right to appoint a new panel of judges and begin the proceedings again. She had the authority to override the court, but in doing so, she risked alienating many clan leaders. She would lose their support. And likely her rulership before her time.

Had this been Aeliana's plan all along?

Not only he, but the entire room seemed to fix their

attention on the First Chancellor. Expression betraying her torment, she moved her lips as though struggling to speak. She rose to her feet. Unsteadily.

"I demand to be heard. I invoke the Law of Mishk'n for the accused." A woman's voice, coming from a doorway, rang throughout the room.

Eva! Before his eyes identified her, his heart recognized her. She spoke in Xerxian, using an archaic speech pattern. It took him a moment to recognize the law she invoked. Mishk'n? The ancient law of sanctuary?

Around him, women and men craned to see who spoke.

Eva walked into the center of the room and stood next to Kelli. Though Zahn willed it with all his heart, not once did she glance his direction.

He had seen that look on her face before. Those first days after they'd met. In the cabin.

One of steely determination.

Yet, something more. Sorrow upon sorrow emanated from her. He knew the meaning. This lamb was going to lay down her life for another. Zahn's throat tightened, choking him.

Eva bowed to the First Chancellor then to the officials.

First Judge glowered. "Who are you? And by what authority do you claim to address us in this manner?"

"I invoke the ancient law. It is clear. If a woman is found guilty of a crime punishable by death, a willing substitute can take her place. I claim the Substitution Prerogative of Mishk'n."

The ambassadress bolted to her feet. "You have no right to invoke that edict."

"Yes, I do. It is your law. Do you not recognize it?" Without fear, Eva met her opponent's scowl. She would not be beaten down by the woman's authority or height.

"Eva. Please, don't." Kelli spoke in a strangled whisper.

Face rigid, Eva ignored the plea.

"This is a Xerxian court of law," the judge said.

"But the accused is human. As a human, I can speak on her behalf." Eva stood her ground.

The ambassadress again spoke. "If we were on Earth, perhaps. But we are not."

Eva's jaw jutted. "I have the right to speak. And offer myself."

"You are in the employ of Intergalaxia. You cannot interfere with our proceedings."

"As of two nights ago, I resigned my position. I am here as a free person."

"We are on Xerxes," Aeliana countered. "You have no rights here. *Human.*"

Others in the room apparently agreed. Voices rose. First Judge glared to squelch any discussion, but she allowed the ambassadress to speak for the court.

Eva waited until the murmuring died down. "I do have license here. I claim my birthright."

"Birthright? Based on what?"

"My bloodline. I am not only human, but Xerxian as well."

Zahn grunted as Eva's confession hit him like a physical blow. Could this be true?

The ambassadress sneered as she looked Eva over in an insulting manner. "You lie."

Jaw tightening, she again waited until silence reigned. She spoke with meticulous deliberation. "My mother's name is Qeturah Aaliyah Tnara...Marshall."

Face haggard, the ambassadress staggered to one side. She clutched at the railing. "Impossible. *Impossible.*"

Understanding dawning, Zahn stared at his beloved.

Eva's mother was Aeliana's older sister? As the ambassadress's niece, Eva's mixed blood would be an abomination to the one who hated all Terrans.

Aeliana rallied, speaking more forcefully. "You lie! What you say is impossible."

"Not impossible." Another woman, from somewhere in

the room, now spoke. "She speaks truth, my sister. And that you know."

Zahn looked for the new speaker. A Xerxian woman rose from her seat. As she strode toward the center of the chambers, she pushed back her hood. But she was not looking at the ambassadress. Her gaze fixed on Eva.

Despite the differences in race, the likeness between them was unmistakable.

The older woman slowed, lips curving in compassion as she studied the young woman who stared openmouthed at her.

Her daughter.

Eva had gone white. Her legs buckled and she slumped to the floor. One word escaped. *"Emaa!"*

My mother...my mother is here?

Collapsed on the floor, Eva stared at the woman who walked toward her...a woman she'd not seen in twenty years.

Was it really *Emaa?*

Her face was as she remembered, hair long and black, skin a beautiful, dusky teal, mouth softening with love—and sorrow. Expression lined with compassion, she extended her hand. Eva squeezed her eyes shut, hardly daring to believe this wasn't a dream.

"Eva-Daviana." The voice—so long remembered, so deeply cherished—reached across the years.

Eyes burning, she placed her fingers against her mother's and stood. The next moment she melted into her arms, heart almost breaking all over again. Had they found each other only to be rent apart? Eva fought to control her tears. A deep sigh erupted from her chest, settling yet another piece of her life.

Thank You, God.

Though she would only greet her mother long enough to say goodbye, it was enough. Eva's course had not changed.

The court had yet to decide whether or not they would accept the Substitution Prerogative of Mishk'n. If needed, Eva would force their hand by petitioning the First Chancellor. By Xerxian law, the ruler would have to accept the offering.

When she pulled back from her mother's embrace, puzzlement flashed across her face.

"I must see this through, *Emaa*," she murmured. "You know there is no other way."

Mouth quivering, she nodded. As she smoothed back Eva's hair, Eva leaned into the caress. Oh, how she had missed her mother's gentle touch.

Then with clasped hands, they turned toward the stone-faced judges.

Looking around, Eva realized the courtroom had cleared. Only a handful of people remained—the judges, First Chancellor Ileya, Ambassadress Aeliana, Kelli Layne Song as well as her husband.

And Daddy. Eva's heart tightened as she met his gaze. For his sake, she smiled at him. At last he would no longer be alone. Another worry removed.

Then there was Zahn.

Swallowing hard, Eva determined to not look at him.

Nothing had changed between them. Her course was set.

Out of the corner of her eye, she watched the ambassadress who still slumped in her chair. Though she might appear defeated, Eva knew better. Jayden Song had been right—Aeliana had made a power play for rulership. Despite being sidetracked, she would not give up.

First Chancellor nodded to Eva's mother. "You wish to add your testimony, Tnara? This is your chance to speak."

Still standing beside Eva in the room's center, she

straightened.

"I loved a human." Eva's mother spoke quietly. "There was—and still is no law against that. And yes, I married him. Secretly. That man." She pointed. "Dr. Thomas Marshall." She paused, chest heaving with emotion. "He was with the group of scientists who were our first contacts from Earth. I traveled with him back to his homeworld. But we feared the prejudice of both our peoples. Using his skill as a scientist, Thomas altered the DNA of our unborn child so that she would look human, not Xerxian. We lived on Earth, the wisest choice at the time." Her hand tightened in Eva's, eyes bright with unshed tears. "For six standard years we kept our marriage and our daughter concealed. But the hatred, the bias, became too much."

"How so?" Ileya asked.

"I was treated with contempt. Spoken to with disrespect as though I were a lesser being. Most thought I was a servant in Thomas' home. Or a loose woman." She glanced at Eva. "I couldn't allow my daughter to suffer the anguish of rejection and hatred. I saw only one solution—leave my daughter to be raised by Thomas while I returned home."

Tears gathered as Eva listened to her mother's narrative. Across the room, her father was openly crying.

"If I am guilty of any crime," *Emaa* continued, voice trembling, "it was the crime of giving into fear. I believed I had taken the best course of action for my daughter and my husband. Believe me…" She paused as her voice broke. Her shoulders shook as she bowed her head. "Believe me, I have suffered greatly because of my decision."

Eva clasped her mother's hand to her chest.

"Not just you," Aeliana now spoke. "Your *selfishness* made our whole family suffer. Our mother died of a broken heart."

Pulling away from Eva, she stalked toward her sister. "Don't you think I know, dear one? Do you doubt my deep regret for the pain I've caused? Countless times over the years I begged our mother for forgiveness—which she gave only on her deathbed. You didn't know, did you?"

First Judge now spoke. "We appreciate your sharing this difficult truth, Tnara. It verifies your daughter's right to Substitution Prerogative. But it does not change the verdict of this court."

"How can you be so blind?" Her voice reverberated with passion. "Do you not see how the prejudice that tore my family apart is the same hatred that now condemns my daughter? When will it end?"

"We have not yet voted on whether we will accept her substitution." Mouth rigid, the judge flexed her shoulders. "Besides, we must uphold the laws of our people. The Terrans have corrupted our ways and even our citizens. You are proof of that. Choosing a mate outside your race..." Her mouth curled in disgust.

Tnara's hands clenched. "Don't you hear yourself? You are as bigoted as the ones who destroyed my family twenty years ago."

"Peace, Tnara." The First Chancellor now rose. Her soothing voice settled the rising emotion in the room.

Hands pressed together, Eva's mother quieted herself and bowed in honor.

"Please, sit. All of you." The ruler of Xerxes IX tucked her hands into the sleeves of her robes and waited.

Gripped by uncertainty, Eva loitered in the middle of the room. Her mother solved the dilemma by slipping an arm about her and ushering her to an empty section of the chamber. Together they sat side-by-side, opposite the judges and the remaining spectators. No one could miss the meaning. Regardless of the court's decision, *Emaa* would face it with Eva.

First Chancellor remained standing as she spoke. "You have brought up some excellent points, First Judge. I respect your wisdom. However, you err in one vital point." She paused. "You say that the Terrans have corrupted us. Do you not remember the sacred texts that say we have all descended from the same parents? Our God placed us on Xerxes, yet we come from the same seed?"

Though her eyes narrowed, the judge had no response.

"Corruption dwells in every heart. We may have a different society and varying laws, but our nature is still inclined toward rebellion. And we ourselves opt for evil. It was not brought to us by another race. *We* are the ones who choose because corruption is already present in us all."

In the quietness of the room, Eva's heartbeat pounded like a drum in her ears.

"We have one God and one Savior whom we must profess in order to be cleansed." The chancellor looked about the room. "And though we may be clean, we can continue to choose wrong. We can continue in our hatred toward our kinsmen because they are of another race. Or another socio-economic level. Or..." She took in a slow breath. "Or we can stop the hatred. Here and now."

"Thus condescends a pristine tapestry to common cloth." Aeliana rose and pointed at Eva's father. "That human stole my sister's affections. *He* broke the hearts of our parents. It is *his* fault. Terrans have no place in our world. The sooner we rid ourselves of them, the better off we shall be. All our world's troubles began the day we signed a treaty with them."

The ruler of Xerxes smiled sadly. "There you are wrong."

"You don't know what it's like to suffer at their hands." Aeliana gripped the railing. "You cannot understand the ruination at the core of these Terrans. How they can inflict pain and destruction."

"Again—I say, you are wrong." The First Chancellor looked at her son for many moments, then back at the ambassadress. She took a shuddering breath as though the burden of her thoughts was too great to bear. "Before the first official Terran contact, a shuttle landed on Xerxes. My parents welcomed the men—humans. This was just over thirty years ago."

Thirty? Eva shivered as the number of years struck her. When she looked across the room at Zahn, he did not meet her gaze. Rather he was staring up at his mother, compassion and love etching his face.

"How is this possible? I have not heard this before." The First Judge half rose in her seat. "Why was it not made public?"

"Their visit remained secret to protect our people from panic. My parents believed we were not yet ready as a race to accept beings from another world. As ruler, my mother made that decision. But there is more you must know." She raised her chin, pausing to take a deep breath. "The captain of the ship lured me from my home. From the safety of my parents. When we were alone, he assaulted me. The result of that violation is my son."

Stunned silence met her pronouncement.

"Zahn," Eva whispered, pressing her fist to her heart.

As though he had heard her, his head turned her direction.

Overwhelmed by the truth, she lowered her head.

If I'd only known...

But would that have changed anything? Her course was set. Eva would not waver from it now.

Zahn's mother continued, her voice almost matter-of-fact. "My son is half human. And half Xerxian. But I gave him a name that means *Gift from God,* because truly he is." She settled her gaze on the ambassadress, face growing hard. "For you to say that I do not understand suffering at the hands of a human is groundless. However—*hear me clearly.* I *chose* to forgive. I *chose* not to condemn the whole human race because of the actions of one man." She paused. "And now I adjure you, all of you, do not condemn Kelli-Layne. Or Eva-Hilliard, should you accept the Substitution Prerogative of Mishk'n. Do not allow your hatred of one

Terran—or for the whole of their race—to destroy your consciences before our God."

The ambassadress shot to her feet. "Are you exercising your privilege as First Chancellor? Are you overruling the court?"

In sorrow, Eva sighed. Apparently the chancellor's confession had not mitigated her aunt's hostility.

The ruler of Xerxes ignored Aeliana and spoke to First Judge. "I call for a revote. Right now. Which any may implore after new evidence."

They stared at each other for a long moment before the magistrate inclined her head.

"It is within your rights, First Chancellor, to seek this." She and the other four judges again departed.

Eva glanced at Kelli. Which of them would die in the morning? If the court rejected the Substitution Prerogative, Eva resolved to appeal to First Chancellor. As ruler, Ileya must uphold the law and therefor grant Kelli her freedom.

No one will stop me. Determination coiled in every fiber of Eva's being.

She studied the others in the silent courtroom.

The ruler of Xerxes IX sat with hands folded in her robes, face serene with lowered eyes. Was she praying? In contrast, the face of the ambassadress showed no softening. Relentless anger marring her brow, Aeliana scowled at Eva's mother.

Oblivious to her sister's fury, *Emaa* focused on someone across the room. It was not hard to guess whom. Mouth trembling, Daddy gripped the chair's armrests, expression full of longing as he gazed at his wife.

Eva's eyes filled with tears at the love she beheld. *Please, Lord God, please let them reconcile.*

And where did Zahn fix his attention? Unwilling to meet his stare, Eva bowed her head. Regardless of what happened in the courtroom, her course was set. In the morning, she would welcome her end.

Hadn't God created her for this purpose? At the perfect time, He had revealed His will for Eva's life. This was meant to be.

The Xerxian in her rose to dominate and confirm her choice. Nothing and no one would stop the Lord God, or Eva as His instrument.

Her heart calm, she lifted her head as the side door flew open and the judges returned.

The magistrate bowed to the chancellor. "By unanimous vote, we have rejected the Substitution Prerogative of Mishk'n."

Eva leaped to her feet. "You cannot deny me. By Xerxian law, I demand—"

"Peace Eva-Hilliard." First Chancellor held up her hand. "Allow First Judge to finish. Please."

Biding her time, Eva sank back into her seat.

The judge met her gaze, eyes cold. "We elected to revisit the original charge against Kelli-Layne. The split is now four to one."

The ruler of Xerxes inclined her head. "And what is the verdict, First Judge?"

"By majority vote," she spoke through clenched teeth, "Kelli-Layne is pardoned."

Chapter 27

"Eva...Hilliard." His mother spoke in low tones as they traversed the echoing corridors to her chambers.

Zahn's step faltered. His mother had not run her name together as so many of his world did. Because Eva deserved the respect and honor due one so brave?

His throat tightened until he could barely speak. He would not answer until he could trust his voice. "She is...a courageous woman."

His mother stopped and faced him. "Eva is the one you love. She is your heart's desire."

He clenched his jaw. How did she know?

She rested her hand on his. "Is this not so?"

"Yes. You have spoken true." He bowed his head, unable to meet her gaze.

Her grip tightened. "She is worthy of your love, my son. I have no doubts, now that I know who she is. Do not be ashamed of your feelings for her."

Emaa's acceptance soothed his soul. Yet, he could not confess that his chosen had released him from his vow. In honor, he could no longer broach the topic of marriage ever again. Not even to Eva. "I am pleased she meets with your approval."

She responded with a low laugh. "Oh, more than approval. My heart sings with joy for you."

Did it? What had she seen in Eva that up to his point only he knew? It no longer mattered. Yet, he would treasure her words the rest of his life.

As they walked on, his mother slipped her arm through his. "You did not tell me, Zahn, she was half-Xerxian."

"Until this evening, I had no knowledge that she was." Now he understood the conflict he always sensed in Eva. The carefully constructed walls of protection. Despite their reconciliation, would she continue to limp through life? Or could her soul finally heal?

Emaa made a small sound of amusement. "I gather she knew nothing of your heritage?"

"No." He had never thought to share that with her. Though he knew about his human father, Zahn had no other information until his mother provided details.

What might have happened if he had told Eva while they were on Earth?

His mother squeezed his arm. "I commend you for keeping silent when it came to my dishonor."

"As you once said, the shame remains on the one who violated you."

She bowed her head in acknowledgement.

"Tell me, *Emaa,* what will happen to the ambassadress? Especially now that her older sister has returned from self-exile?"

Her answer was slow in coming. "With their mother's death, Tnara is rightfully the clan leader. Whether Aeliana submits or not. Her sister's marriage to a human does not alter her position of authority. She was correct in saying that she has broken no Xerxian law."

"I now understand the vendetta of the ambassadress against humans."

"As do I. Yet I grieve to see a house divided. Until the sisters make peace, animosity may rule."

"But the younger must serve the law, and therefore submit to the elder."

"You are correct. However, Aeliana must first reconcile the conflict in her own heart. I suspect she will soon resign as ambassadress." A speculative look settled over his mother's face. "Perhaps you know of another who would be qualified?"

"A male cannot hold that position."

"True." Her lips curved up at the corners, but she would say nothing more about whom she had in mind.

Pushing away hypotheses, Zahn refocused on what he'd heard in the courtroom. How would today's events affect his world? When they reached his mother's chambers, he stopped before the door. "Here I will bid you good night."

"You will not stay for repast?" She laid a hand on his arm. "The hour for the evening meal is long gone. You must be hungry."

No food could satisfy what gnawed at him.

"I wish to be alone and ponder all that has happened today."

She studied him. "I see your heart grieves still. Yet I know not the source." He thought she might demand an explanation, but instead she kissed his cheek. "Humble yourself to our God. Let Him soothe what troubles you."

He bowed over her hand and left her side.

The triple moons of Xerxes rose above the horizon when Eva opened the gate and walked into Zahn's garden. Though it was late and she was weary beyond comprehension, she had to come.

Her heart could not be denied.

She had no trouble making her way along the dark path. As the moons ascended, her vision would only improve. The heavenly orbs painted the landscape in purple and gold.

I feel as though I am reborn.

For years she had suppressed who she was, *what* she was. That was no longer necessary. Could no longer be hidden even if she wished.

If she had one tear left in her system, she would have wept. But not from sorrow.

Eva let her fingers linger on the scrollwork of the pergola, as though feeling it for the first time. Peace washed over her, cleansing her soul. So much had happened in the last few hours. So much pain swept away.

But even more important, a limitless exultation had rushed into the vacuum. Her spirit soared to the sky.

"I thank you, God of the heavens." Eva tilted back her head, allowing the light of the moons to drench her face. She lifted her hands in worship. "I thank You."

For a long time, she did not move. Then from the fringes of her consciousness, she sensed she wasn't alone. Without turning to face him, she said, "Peace be to you, Zahn." She lowered her arms.

His steady footsteps drew nearer. "And peace to you, Eva."

Heart full, she turned to him.

After Kelli's pardoning, he had left, along with others who congregated outside the building awaiting a final decision. Zahn had not seen the many tears, the smiles, the forgiveness, and yes, the hope in those who released the past, as well as the pain that had crippled them for decades. Others had come forward who, like Eva's parents, had intermarried. The news of what had happened in the courtroom obliterated their fear and shame.

"Are you well?" His quiet voice bathed her soul.

"Very. My mother…" Eva couldn't control her voice for a moment. She swallowed before slowly answering. "My mother asked me to wish you good health."

"And your father?"

"He says the same." Eva drew in a deep breath, the image of her parents searing her mind. When she had left them, they sat close to each other, their body language betraying how tenuous they still felt. They would need time to overcome twenty years of separation. But the love in their eyes encouraged her that they would succeed. When they had reached for each other's hands, unspeakable joy had rushed over her.

Yes, they would succeed.

"I see that you are happy for them."

"I am. And for myself." She turned her face, emotion overwhelming her once again.

Zahn lifted her chin. "Do not look away. Let me share in your happiness."

"It's hard to overcome years of habit. I'm sorry."

"There is no need to apologize."

Words could not express the depth of her happiness. God's grace flowed over a gaping wound, not just soothing, but healing. So much, so quickly.

She felt more alive than ever before.

After Eva took a seat on the bench, she waited for Zahn to join her. They had so much to talk about. But where to start? "Your life will be different now, won't it? Once more Xerxians find out about your history? About your heritage?"

"I don't believe things will change much. Those who are inclined toward prejudice will act it out. Those who have no problem with my mixed blood will behave as before." He gripped his knees, tension rippling through his body. "What about you, Eva? What will your life be like?"

"I don't know. Until an hour ago, I had no tomorrow." She stared into the star-sprinkled sky, overcome by the idea of living. *Really* living for the first time. "I feel like I'm starting over. In a new life. A new future." She turned to Zahn. "I was prepared to take Kelli's place. To die. I had no thought of what would happen beyond the trial."

"You were convinced the judges would find Kelli-Layne guilty?"

"Yes, I knew they would. Without a doubt. I knew the ambassadress would make sure Kelli was condemned. And that she would press for her execution. I don't know how."

With an astute expression, he smiled. "A gift from our God."

Eva shook her head. The thought had never crossed her mind. Yet the truth humbled her. After her mother abandoned her, Eva had rejected God. She recalled her childish raging against Him as she blamed Him for all her disappointments. Yet, He had never turned His back on her. He'd always been there, waiting with open arms.

And Zahn followed this God. He had modeled his faithfulness after the ever-faithful One.

She looked down at her clasped hands. "Do you...do you really believe God told you to propose to me?"

"Without a doubt. Everything that has happened since that day proves that He did."

Even if she discounted divine guidance, she and Zahn were made for each other. Both half-human, half-Xerxian. Truly designed to be each other's perfect match? She was not a freak of nature. Or a mistake. She could finally banish that lie. Now and forever.

But it was more than that. Zahn had demonstrated over and over that he was the kind of man she longed for.

"However..." Zahn bowed his shoulders. "At the time I

proposed, I did not know how you would respond."

"Yet you still obeyed."

"Yes." He turned to face her. "And though you refused me, I will stand by my vow."

"Until...I depart from Xerxes?"

"No. Until the end of my days."

She caught her breath at his resolve. "You would live alone, unmarried, for the rest of your life?"

"Yes." He nodded. "I would. And I will."

His simple confession stunned her. And even more, his self-sacrifice. "That kind of obedience is costly."

"The price of disobedience is far greater." Face set, Zahn gazed into the distance. "Of that I have no doubt."

Afraid to speak, she left him to his thoughts. Because she had rejected him, would he now reject her? Perhaps the pain of living alone would be preferable to the suffering she might cause him. Or could he overlook her flaws? Endure her baggage?

Eva pushed her fears away. She had to know. *Had* to ask.

"What if I changed my mind? About my decision?" Pulse pounding against her throat, she fought to utter the breathless words. "Is it permitted for me to ask you to be my husband?"

Do you still want me, Zahn?

Her heart surged as hope dawned on his face.

"It is permitted." His whispered words hung in the air between them.

As he had done a few days before, she held up her hands, palms facing him. Her fingers shook in the ever-brightening light of the moons.

"Then I ask." Her voice cracked. "I choose you to be my husband. If you will have me."

"And my answer is..." Zahn rested his palms against hers. "My answer is yes." His fingers folded over hers, locking their hands together.

She closed her eyes. The air in her lungs grew heavy,

expanding into every space inside her until she thought she would burst. The beat of her heart slowed, marching in cadence with his. Again, she felt as though their souls touched. Together, they sighed.

A hushed reverence filled the universe. Eva opened her eyes and smiled at the man she loved with all her being. His eyes glittered with an intensity that made her heart nearly stop.

"The Xerxian in me says this is enough for now." His voice grew husky. "But the human in me…"

Scooting closer, he gently cupped her jaw with both hands. When he leaned forward, she met him halfway. Their kiss quaked her to the core of her being. It was not the stirring of her passions that astounded her, but the deep contentment that rushed through her. When she pressed her palms to his chest, the wonder only intensified until she had to draw back. She felt as though she had sampled a heady drink. But she would indulge no further until she was his wife in truth, the vow fulfilled, before God and those of the flesh.

Zahn's arms relaxed. "Remain with me until morning, my love. If you would."

"Here in the garden?"

"Yes. It is permitted." A smile tugged at his lips. "Besides, I could not sleep. Not now."

"Nor I." She lifted his hand to kiss it.

He gripped her fingers. "Then you will stay?"

Was that uncertainty she heard in his voice? She spoke with care, seeking to ease any lingering doubts. "I will stay, Zahn. For the rest of my life."

He caressed her cheek. As his thumb stroked her skin, she tilted her head to lean into his touch.

"I love you, Eva Daviana."

"I don't deserve you, El-Abiri Zahn." Serenity rippled through her. "But I am honored. Beyond words." She hesitated to speak of her love to him. Someday soon, she planned to show him the depth of her passion.

They sat in silence as the garden blooms released their fragrances into the warm air. As she drank in the perfume, Eva contemplated her future, contentment and anticipation dancing in her soul.

As the night waned, she and Zahn talked of many things. Aspirations, dreams, desires. Again she was struck at the breadth of his knowledge. She grew awed and humbled by his desire for the wellbeing of the Xerxian people.

My people.

In awe they watched golden light streak the sky, heralding the approach of morning. A new beginning for them.

A new beginning for both their worlds.

Epilogue

Wearing the royal purple robe that Zahn had given her so long ago, Eva followed the two tall women who led her to his home. The wedding ceremony had been new and strange, yet beautiful in its simplicity. However this custom, with the mothers of both bride and groom escorting her to her husband's house, filled her with disquiet.

As they trod toward his doorway, Eva paused and stared at the numerous items lining the path.

Both mothers stopped and turned.

"What are these?" She pointed.

The women grinned at each other before her mother explained. "Wedding gifts."

"From many peoples," Ileya added. "A tradition that was not explained to you?"

"No." Eva shook her head. Of the million things she and her mother had discussed, they'd missed this one.

Ileya smiled. "You and Zahn will spend a month of privacy. Gifts of food and goods will not cease during that time."

"You need not venture out unless you choose," her mother added. "No one will approach your door, providing the privacy you will—no doubt—desire."

Heat scorched Eva's face as a knowing grin passed between the two women.

They continued to the house. Their task was to prepare the bridal chamber. Once the mothers departed, Zahn would come to her.

Up to the second floor they ascended, Eva hardly glancing at the beauty of the home that would be hers now. When they reached the chamber, she gasped. Filmy white material draped each window and the French-style doors. Hundreds of tiny lights dotted the ceiling by some unknown Xerxian technology. Dozens of blooms filled the room with their scent, while the floor was covered with large petals that reminded her of roses. The sound of wooden wind chimes resonated through the room as they danced in the breeze. Had she stepped into a magical dream world? On one table rested a huge vase of daisies, the only adornment she would wear besides a simple gown this wedding night.

Zahn's mother smiled. "I think she likes the room, Tnara."

The other woman nodded.

Eva realized that she had been staring, openmouthed.

Her mother helped her remove the purple outer robe while Zahn's mother turned down the linens. In no time, Eva was undressed in preparation for the gown in which she would meet her husband.

"Ha," Ileya said as she studied her.

Eva's cheeks grew warm under the woman's inspection.

"If there is any doubt you are Xerxian, you bear the visible proof."

Confusion enveloped her. What did Ileya mean?

"The mother's cord attaches here." She touched Eva's abdomen. "The navel of Xerxians is placed higher than on humans."

Astonished, Eva looked down at herself. All her life she had thought she bore a deformity. Ashamed because she was different, she had hidden that and many other supposed imperfections.

Relief washed over her. And gratitude to her mother-in-law for disclosing this was normal for Xerxians.

The two women helped her slip on the simple robe, then Ileya gently removed the clips from her hair. As Eva sat at a mirrored table, her mother brushed out the strands. Together, the women wove daisies into her locks and re-clipped them into place.

"You are ready." Ileya's smile grew wistful.

The Xerxians grasped her hands and led her to the middle of the room.

Zahn's mother spoke first. "May you love fully and deeply, my daughter. May your home be filled with the laughter of many children." After she kissed Eva's cheeks, she departed.

Emaa squeezed her fingers. "I'm so proud of you." She spoke in a whisper, eyes bright with moisture. "May the joy that only God can give fill this home. May His love abound in you and ever increase as you begin a new life with your husband." She seemed to want to say more, but changed her mind.

"Thank you, *Emaa*." Eva hugged her.

She held on an extra-long time before pulling away. "I must go. A young man I know is anxious for me to depart."

Before her mother left the room, she pressed her hand to the wall. The hundreds of lights in the ceiling dimmed in response.

She listened as *Emaa* retreated out the door. Long before Eva heard Zahn, she sensed his approach. She smiled as he took the stairs two and three at a time. Then he slowed as though he knew she was listening. His steps grew closer, almost cautiously. Wanting to see his expression as he stepped through the doorway, she turned.

She expected him to stare in wonder at the transformation of the room as she had. Or smile at the lights and flowers. But no, he had eyes only for her. The look on his face made her throat tighten.

"May I?" he said, after an impossibly long moment.

"Of course." His question confounded her. "This is your home."

"Custom dictates it is yours now." He took one step in. "I must ask permission to enter the bridal chamber."

"Please." Palms extended, she held out her hands.

He moved closer, but surprised her by kneeling as he slid his fingers across hers. Another cultural convention?

She looked down at his bowed head. Many weeks ago, she had settled her dual heritage. But what about Zahn? Did his two natures battle like hers had? She vowed to help him overcome his ambiguity.

As Eva slowly knelt, his gaze met her, eyes widening.

She spoke softly. "You realize that my very appearance may offend people? And not just me, but wherever we go as husband and wife, we will face censure because we look dissimilar?"

He nodded.

"Then let us vow—right now—that nothing will come between us. We will first consider each other before everyone else. That includes cultures, our upbringing, even long-held customs. This very night we must start our own traditions."

A smile flickered over his lips. "I agree. However, I urge caution. Let us begin at home before we try to change society." He laced his fingers with hers. "We don't want to alienate the matriarchs of both families."

True. Yet she knew difficult times lay ahead. They would meet bigotry, not only on Xerxes, but on Earth.

But let the universe sort itself out—Eva had done her part to foster peace.

She shivered from the sensation of his palms against hers. "Right now I'm not interested in anyone else. I'm only concerned with your feelings."

Zahn's eyes smoldered. "As I am with yours, my lovely one, my bride."

His captivating voice wrapped around her like a silken garment. Giving into impulse, she entwined her arms about his neck. His slow intake of breath told her that yet again, she had broken tradition. Still tentative, his hands encircled her waist.

"I love you, Zahn." As she had done so long ago in her dreams, she tangled her fingers in his hair. "Never doubt that, no matter what. As long as we both live."

Though his embrace tightened, she still sensed his uncertainty. Not with her, but with himself? He shuddered as though his human side—long denied—was breaking through.

"Don't be afraid." She smoothed fingertips across his cheeks and chin. "Trust in me. Trust in my love."

Groaning, he crushed her lips with his. The kiss not only flamed her passions, but his. Mouths still pressed together, Zahn lifted her in his strong arms and carried her across the room.

As the night darkened and Eva fully became his wife, she knew the God of the universe smiled down on her. On them both.

Author Note

Though the characters in *The Terran Summit* are fictional, some of the themes are found in the Bible. Just like Kelli Layne broke Xerxian Laws, we all have failed to perfectly keep the law of God. Like her, we deserve punishment. We have earned condemnation and an eternity of separation from God. Like her, we are powerless to do or say anything in our defense. All of our good deeds cannot wipe away our guilt. Just as Eva offered to take her friend's place, so Jesus took our penalty by dying on the cross and rising from the dead. God exchanges our guilt (sin) for Christ's sinless perfection (righteousness), not because of anything we have done, but because of His unfathomable love and mercy. He extends this gift of grace to anyone who believes on and trusts in what Jesus has done on our behalf.

For more information, check out these Bible passages: John 3:16, Ephesians 2:11-13, Titus 3:5-6, Romans 3:23, Romans 6:23. I would love to hear from you. Write to me at anna@annazogg.com.

Scripture quote in Chapter 15: paraphrase of Psalm 34:1-5

Scripture quote in Chapter 18: paraphrase of Psalm 38:9-10

Scripture quote in Chapter 25: paraphrase of Psalm 39:12

Don't miss the other books in the Intergalaxia series.

Stranded on a primitive planet light-years from Earth, bio-scientist Aric Lindquist struggles to survive in the hostile environment. When a new assistant finally arrives, she suspects he is not what he seems to be. Is he truly there to help her…or to kill her?

USF special agent Kelli Layne has one goal in life—find the girl who was abducted on her watch. Confident and self-sufficient, she doesn't need anyone. Including God. But to rescue the missing girl, Kelli must become a fugitive from the law. Can she save the child without forfeiting her own life?

Also by Anna Zogg

Breath ragged, Lindsey Hayden clutched her side. As her feet sank into soft sand, she felt as though she jogged through wet concrete. Each lift of her legs took enormous energy. A steep embankment rose before her like Mount Everest.

You can do it.

The ocean growled, reaching out with foamy fingers as though to pull her back. It seemed to roar in disappointment as she escaped its grasp. A million bubbles shattered along the shore. Hissing filled the air.

She shuddered at the sound. All day she expected melancholy over her husband's death to hound her, not this relentless anxiety. Today would have been their tenth anniversary. Before dawn, Alex would have awakened her with his lavish gift. How had she survived nearly four, long years alone?

The reminder should have made her weepy, however sorrow didn't dog her. Never before had such unease gripped her soul.

Sunlight erupted between the clouds and horizon, splashing crimson across the landscape. She stopped and turned. Normally, the beautiful panorama would cause her heart to swell in worship. Not today. Why did it look like the ground bled?

"Enough." The word burst from her mouth. For a few moments, irritation overrode all other emotion.

What was wrong with her? Earlier, a brooding tension had caused her to pace at home, driving her to ignore the threatening weather. After slipping on running shoes, she skipped her usual dynamic stretching. Before she'd jogged a half-mile, she sensed she wasn't escaping the source of her apprehension, but running headlong into it.

Whatever *it* was.

Panting, she reached the road and paused to bend with hands on knees. Spatters of chilling spring rain struck her exposed neck. Lindsey straightened. The red landscape morphed into purple, appearing bruised as the sun slowly sank below the watery horizon. In moments, light would skitter away. She would be shrouded in a night as dark as the blacktop of the Oregon highway. How foolish to have left the house without reflective clothing or a flashlight. Isolation clung to her like a bad dream.

Her heart slammed against her sternum.

I have to get out of here.

Irresolute, Lindsey gazed back to the barely visible shoreline. The wheezing tide made her shiver. *Not that way. The road will be faster.* She started walking, and then sped up when raindrops pelted her. Ignoring her burning side, she pushed on and crested one hill.

In the distance, the lone light of her cottage glimmered. Soon she would reach home. Soon she would be safe.

Rain began to fall with determination. The soles of her shoes squeaked on the wet pavement while droplets pattered in hypnotic repetition. Several times she stopped, gasping for breath as the ache in her side grew. The recent injury to her right knee flared, reminding her she pushed too hard.

Again she stopped. As she peered through the darkness, she measured the distance. Not much further. The bright bulb on her front porch…

When the light suddenly blinked out of sight, Lindsey gaped. That wasn't a welcome beacon shining in the distance, but an oncoming car. The single beam split into two blurry headlights. In a flash, she realized the danger.

On one side of the coastal highway a deadly chasm of tangled brush awaited, while on the other a sheer wall where it cut into the mountain. Not only that, but the road had narrowed. No room for both her and a fast-moving car. The thin strips of reflective tape on her socks provided pitiful help against the rain and dark.

She estimated how far to where the lane widened. Ignoring pain, Lindsey broke into a dead run. Now she could hear the car's engine, whining and fading as the driver alternately accelerated and braked around the curve of the mountain. Too fast for this road. Much too fast for the slick darkness.

Nearly there. Rock Pointe lay ahead. Just beyond, a scenic turnout. If she could arrive before the car…

Gulping wet air, she reached the near-hairpin turn. Her calves protested. A ghostly cross glowed at the fringe of the road, a reminder of the last fatality before the county erected a metal barrier. Countless motorists, misjudging the sharpness of the curve, had already mangled the guardrail.

She gasped. The white cross didn't glow on its own, but reflected the light from the car. The engine howled as the driver flew up the steep incline.

Too soon!

She lurched forward. *Hurry.* On the other side of the hill, headlights slashed the glittering rain. What should she do? The vehicle roared like an angry dragon.

I'm not going to make it.

The realization slammed into her mind. Her heart froze and her legs locked.

As she hesitated, dazzling brightness suddenly burst before her. Lindsey shielded her eyes. A giant rectangle of light appeared, two feet off the ground. The illumination didn't saturate the area, but focused a spotlight like she was a performer on stage.

A door? In the middle of the road?

Impossible.

When a dark form inside the doorway loomed into view, a squeak of terror escaped her. The figure, clearly a man, paused on the non-existent threshold. She staggered back.

A moment later, the car swung around the curve. Headed right for her.

Lindsey screamed.

Time slowed. Tires squealed. Burnt rubber and the smell of ozone scorched her nostrils. The vehicle fishtailed. She tensed, anticipating the crush of cold metal.

A firm shoulder slammed into her. Arms about her, the man rolled. Together, they escaped death. In the near distance, a crash sounded. Tortured metal shrieked. Glass shattered.

A black object flew toward Lindsey and struck her head. In a flash of pain, darkness closed over her.

~~

End of Excerpt

Books by Anna Zogg

Letters Across Time

Moon Dancing

"Gypsy Gulch" A *Moon Dancing* Mystery
(an e-only short story)

Books in the Intergalaxia Series

The Paradise Protocol

The Xerxes Factor

The Terran Summit